# SHADOWS of SHERWOOD

### A ROBYN HOODLUM ADVENTURE

## KEKLA MAGOON

## BLOOMSBURY

NEW YORK   LONDON   OXFORD   NEW DELHI   SYDNEY

For Kerry
and in memory of E. T.

First published in the United States of America in August 2015
by Bloomsbury Children's Books
Paperback edition published in October 2016
www.bloomsbury.com

Bloomsbury is a registered trademark of Bloomsbury Publishing Plc

For information about permission to reproduce selections from this book, write to
Permissions, Bloomsbury Children's Books, 1385 Broadway, New York, New York 10018
Bloomsbury books may be purchased for business or promotional use. For information on
bulk purchases please contact Macmillan Corporate and Premium Sales Department at
specialmarkets@macmillan.com

The Library of Congress has cataloged the hardcover edition as follows:
Magoon, Kekla.
Shadows of Sherwood: a Robyn Hoodlum adventure / by Kekla Magoon.
pages     cm
Summary: When Nott City is taken over by a harsh governor, Ignomus Crown, and her
parents disappear, twelve-year-old Robyn Loxley flees for her life and joins a group of children
trying to take back what is rightfully theirs in this futuristic retelling of Robin Hood.
ISBN 978-1-61963-634-7 (hardcover)  •  ISBN 978-1-61963-635-4 (e-book)
[1. Robbers and outlaws—Fiction. 2. Adventures and adventurers—Fiction.
3. Government, Resistance to—Fiction. 4. Missing persons—Fiction.] I. Title.
PZ7.M2739Sh 2015          [Fic]—dc23          2014027930

ISBN 978-1-68119-023-5 (paperback)

Book design by Amanda Bartlett
Typeset by Newgen Knowledge Works (P) Ltd., Chennai, India
Printed and bound in the U.S.A. by Berryville Graphics Inc., Berryville, Virginia
4  6  8  10  9  7  5  3

All papers used by Bloomsbury Publishing, Inc., are natural, recyclable products
made from wood grown in well-managed forests. The manufacturing processes
conform to the environmental regulations of the country of origin.

Praise for

# *SHADOWS*
## *of SHERWOOD*

★ "Thrilling. . . . This exciting page-turner will undoubtedly be a hit." —*School Library Journal*, starred review

"An engaging cast of characters. . . . Call[s] to mind the Percy Jackson adventures and will inspire a new generation to connect with Robin Hood's timeless tale." —*Booklist*

"Set in the future and paced with one death-defying escape after another, Magoon's story doesn't end so much as pause." —*Publishers Weekly*

"This colorful adventure does not easily fit into a genre box, as it combines futuristic elements with fantasy and folklore. . . . The adventure and cliffhanging ending will entice readers." —*Kirkus Reviews*

"Magoon cleverly weaves elements of the Robin Hood tale into this futuristic story about social justice, friendship, and identity. The wily kid heroes and thrilling adventures will appeal to young readers." —*The Horn Book*

"A killer female Robin Hood series by the incredible Kekla Magoon." —Bustle

# BOOKS BY KEKLA MAGOON

# SHADOWS of SHERWOOD

# ≪CHAPTER ONE≫

## *Forty-Two Teeth*

The sign on the fence said BEWARE OF DOGS. Robyn scaled it anyway.

*Dogs? As in* plural*?* she thought, as she laced her fingers in the chain link, wedged the toes of her boots into the dia-mond-shaped spaces, and climbed. *That could be a problem.*

There were plenty of problems tonight. For starters, the bare lightbulbs that hung at intervals along the fence had been recently changed to a higher wattage. The coni-cal swaths of light they cast were larger and brighter than Robyn had ever seen. She had also spotted six different guards patrolling the inside perimeter of the enclosed lot. That was three times the usual. And they were packing. Long automatic rifles draped over their shoulders or held loosely at their sides by the necks.

None of it made any sense. The guards at the 410 Compound were usually unarmed, bottom-of-the-barrel in the brains department, and easy to evade. The 410 was a simple refuse depository—a junkyard, basically—with no need for such high security. *Unless something had changed.* Robyn gulped at the thought.

An hour ago, as she slipped out her bedroom window and dashed off into the night, this supply run had seemed like it would be no big deal. Scale the fence, stuff a few new gadgets into her backpack—whatever she could find that appeared useful—and climb back out again. She'd done it dozens of times before.

Normally, staying unseen was easy and fun. Dodging the guards was all part of the adventure. Now, scaling the fence, Robyn felt a hint of trepidation. Things were not as they ought to be. Had she missed something?

Robyn kept on climbing, though her mind ticked around the problems at hand:

Guards.

Guns.

And how many dogs, exactly?

The guys patrolling the fence looked more like soldiers than civilian security guards. Those big guns . . . What could be within the 410 that was worth protecting with so much firepower? Really valuable trash?

Not likely. These changes could mean Governor Crown was up to something new. *As if he hadn't done enough damage in Nott City already*, Dad would say. It was all he could talk about anymore. His government work took up all his time now, leaving no space for any of the things he and Robyn used to do together. He'd entirely stopped bringing home interesting items for them to tinker with, the way he used to, so Robyn was forced to find her own sources of scrap.

Tonight she hoped to end her weeks-long quest for a better voltage adapter for her favorite circuit board. She wanted to improve the elaborate system of intruder alarms in her bedroom suite. She'd been working on it for ages. Next time Dad visited her room, he would see that Robyn didn't need his help to build something awesome. But he hadn't so much as tapped on her door in weeks.

She crept higher. Twelve feet up, she paused to study the coil of barbed wire crowning the fence. Moment of truth. Robyn glanced down at the roof of the parked office trailer inside the fence—her landing surface—and drew a deep breath. She inverted her fingers' grip on the links, sucked in her stomach, and, drawing on years of gymnastics training, kicked off the fence and vaulted her legs over, releasing her hands at what she hoped was the opportune moment.

Almost. The barbed wire slashed her just-bought thrift-store jeans. "Dang it," she murmured, fingering the long, jagged tear as she dropped into a crouch on the trailer top. The thick tail of her single braid coiled over her shoulder and fell against her arm. She flipped it out of the way.

Robyn balanced on the balls of her feet and the tips of her fingers, listening. Had the soft thump of her landing alerted the guards? From this vantage point, the entire lot looked perfectly still. And completely dark, apart from the glow from the bulbs at the fence and the high, pale moon. Still, Robyn could sense she wasn't alone.

The compound occupied a gravel patch the size of a couple of superstore parking lots. Several small tin-walled huts were scattered around. Large tanks of fuel for the garbage trucks filled one section of the compound. There was a recycling station, where trucks deposited cans and bottles all through the day, and an industrial trash compactor, which pressed mounds of refuse into neat, tight bales.

Piles of junk and scrap metal towered over the sloped tin roofs. Mounds of boxes and cases and crates, overflowing with a mix of trash and trinkets. Ropes and gears and batteries and old electronics. Broken things, forgotten things, useful things sometimes. You never knew what you might find.

In a clearing at the far side of the lot, dozens of garbage trucks and box trucks, forklifts and backhoes stood parked in rows, ready for duty. Robyn couldn't see them from here, but she knew—

The pale wash of a flashlight crossed the gravel somewhere in Robyn's peripheral vision. She dropped to her stomach, pressing herself down and hopefully out of sight.

Through her thin black T-shirt, the top of the trailer felt cool against her stomach. She could smell the cigarettes the guards were smoking in the yard. Pungent. And close. She suppressed the need to cough as the wind brought another cloud of the smoke her way. From her flat position, she strained for a glimpse of the guards or to hear the faint crunch of footsteps on gravel. Nothing. She hoped the men weren't as close as they smelled.

Robyn scooted toward the edge of the trailer top and peered down. She could see no movement in the lot, just the cold, hunched shapes of the junk piles. A light had come on in one tin hut, so she hoped that meant some of the guards were taking a break from patrolling the fence.

Robyn slid off the roof and landed silently on the gravel. Well, almost silently. As she dropped into her ready crouch, she heard a rush of fleet footsteps and suddenly found herself staring into the business end of a bulldog. It might have occurred to her that both ends of a bulldog are capable of some pretty serious business, but right then she had other things to worry about. Namely, teeth. Forty-two of them, all sharp and drooly.

# ≪CHAPTER TWO≫

## *Junkyard Jumble*

"Whoa," Robyn whispered.

The dog curled back its lips even further. A low growl started in the back of its throat, and Robyn could tell the dog was working itself up to bark, loud and hard.

But she was a low, dark shape, unmoving. Not tall and long limbed, flailing and running in fear, like a normal human. For a long second the dog growled and grunted in confusion. Its hesitation bought Robyn just enough time.

"Good doggie," she whispered in her most patient voice. She patted the air, then jacked back her elbow, reached into the side pouch of her jacket, and came up with a plastic bag.

The dog barked. Loudly. Robyn cringed.

"I've got something for you, boy." She unzipped the bag and extracted a fat strip of bacon. The dog sniffed and growled. She laid the bacon on the ground between them, a peace offering. She tossed a second strip a few yards to her left, into the pile of gravel casually mounded against the side of the trailer.

The dog froze, turning his nose between the near bacon, the far bacon, and the intruder.

Robyn held her breath, though she needn't have. It worked. The dog slobbered up the near slice of bacon and trotted toward the far one, with part of the first still hanging from his teeth.

Robyn sighed, satisfied. It worked because Robyn was the sort of girl who knew not only how many teeth a bulldog had, but also exactly what to do to get a bulldog on her good side. She folded the remaining bacon into the bag, which she kept clutched in her hand, just in case.

The dog had already barked, and that meant trouble. Keeping low, she crept away from the trailer, away from the pools of light cast by the bulbs at the fence and toward the deeper dark surrounding the junk piles.

Robyn heard the faint scrabbling of boots on gravel. Not her own.

She took off running. Her boots crunched on the gravel. It sounded extra loud, but she hoped the guards might mistake her sounds for theirs. Staying quiet would've been too slow. Sooner or later, probably sooner, someone would come check on the dog to see why he'd started barking. So she ran the width of the lot and pressed her back up against the side of the hut with the lights on, where the people were.

She waited. Sure enough, a few moments later, the door around the corner lurched open.

"Waldo?" A deep voice. "Where are you, boy?"

Across the lot, Waldo barked.

Footsteps. From the sound of them, it was one man, large. The pale wash of a flashlight swept the gravel. Robyn sucked herself skinny and pressed deeper into the shadows. The footsteps receded away from her, toward the dog.

Robyn glanced up at the night sky, at the faint ambient light from the city, hoping that Waldo was the sort of bulldog who ate fast.

She listened to the pace of the large man's footsteps for a few beats, then took up a pace that matched it. He stepped, she stepped. When his foot crunched the stones, hers crunched at the same time. She moved along the tin walls, ducking past the door where the man had come out. She darted across the open lot.

Behind her, the staff-house door clattered open again. "He don't bark for no reason," a second deep voice was saying. "Something's up."

Robyn slipped behind the high piles of rubble as two additional men moved out of the building, silhouetted by the light from inside. Fortunately, they moved away from her.

Robyn wove between the tall junk mountains. She knew her way around this maze, and the height of the piles alone offered some protection from the searchers. She felt safe enough, for now.

*Adapters and circuits* . . . Her thoughts drifted back to the reason she was here. They dumped the most metal and electronics in this section of the compound. She headed toward her favorite pile, to the now-distant sound track of the men calling after the dog.

Waldo, apparently, had other plans. Robyn recognized the rhythm of his paws on the gravel. He bounded around a corner and butted his head against her knee. Robyn laughed—nearly out loud!—at the hopeful, flop-tongued expression on his face. He growled low.

"Shh." Robyn dangled the bacon bag from her hand. "I know what you want."

Waldo nosed the bag, then turned soft puppy eyes on her.

"All right, Bacon Breath." She leaned over to scratch his stubby ears. "Just don't give me away, okay?"

Waldo whimpered in apparent agreement as he scarfed two fresh slices of bacon.

"I hope you got some more where that came from." The words drifted out of the gray air, seemingly from within the nearest mound of sheet metal.

## ≪CHAPTER THREE≫

# *Trouble*

Robyn spun toward the voice, propping her hands on her hips. "Sneaking up on a girl in the dark? That's not very gentlemanly."

A ratchety, rattling laugh filled the darkness. "Got no choice but to sneak," he said. "With all what's going on here tonight."

Robyn peered at the cluster of sheet metal, trying to spot the craggy old face amid the rubble. Even with the near-full moon overhead, she couldn't see him. "Where are you?"

"Hiding," he said. "Like you better do, 'fore they come round again."

Robyn crept closer and knelt on the gravel. A small sheet of metal shifted, and a man's thin, wrinkled face poked through the gap. He still had a bruised-looking gash on his cheek. It had been there for weeks, with no sign of healing, but Robyn made no comment.

"You give that mutt my supper?" he said.

"Only part of it," Robyn said. "Sorry, Barclay." She handed him the bacon bag, empty but for a few crumbs, then unzipped her backpack and took out a foil-wrapped parcel.

Barclay parted the silver wings and sniffed the contents: two thick biscuits, a pile of carrot rounds, and a few strips of cold chicken. The bacon had been an afterthought. *A lucky one*, Robyn thought now.

"I'd hoped not to see you tonight," Barclay said around a mouthful.

"Yeah?" Robyn thought the way he was chowing into the biscuits told a different story. "Why?"

"Shadows on the moon." Barclay tipped back his head and stared up at the high white oval, looming large in the sky. Wisps of darkness drifted over and around it, filtering its light. "It's not normal."

"What do you have for me?" Robyn asked. "Did more of my circuits turn up? Any sign of a voltage adapter yet?"

Barclay pushed a small pouch through the gap. The grubby, folded canvas fit in her cupped hands. It unfolded to reveal a small black box with wires sticking out of it, and several squarish ports along one edge. One thick gray cord wrapped around it.

"What is it?" Robyn asked. It looked like a whole bunch of nothing. But she knew sometimes those were the best finds of all.

"You don't see modems like these so much anymore," Barclay said. "You ask your father, eh?"

Right. "Why don't you tell me?"

Barclay grunted. "Get on home now. Stop coming around here like this."

"You always say that."

"I mean it this time."

Robyn rolled her eyes. "You always mean it. But you don't stop collecting cool things for me." She rewrapped the odd wiry object and stuffed it into her backpack.

"Got nothing better to do," he answered. "You, with all this rummaging and tinkering. It ain't healthy. Ain't you got some friends to play with?" The comment stung. Robyn spent most of her days alone.

"You're my friend."

"*Pfft*. Friends your own age."

"Everyone my age is asleep right now."

"Wonder why that is?"

"No idea," Robyn said. "Everything interesting happens after dark."

As if on cue, dogs started barking. Multiple dogs. Waldo pricked his ears and joined them. He jumped up and dashed away through the junkyard.

"Look what you done," Barclay grumbled. "They'll come a-searching for you and find me."

"I'll go now," Robyn said.

"You get down," Barclay said. "Under that there cardboard. The big sheet."

"*Eww.*" Robyn groaned. It smelled like very dead fish under there.

Barclay chuckled. "Welcome to my world. That'll keep the dogs from scenting you."

Robyn pinched her nose and rolled under the cardboard. Then she let go of her nose immediately—breathing that stench through her mouth was almost worse. Like tasting it.

They waited in silence.

But the men did not come. The dogs' barking died down, and in the wake of it rose the sound of engines idling. Then many tires crunching on gravel.

Robyn rolled out from under cover. She was too curious not to.

"Girl," Barclay protested, but Robyn was already climbing. She scaled the precarious pile of rubble and poked her head over the lip.

Across the lot, the vehicle gate churned open. A row of large trucks drove out through the gate. Not normal trucks or even garbage trucks. These vehicles were dark canvas-covered things. A whole stream of them, more than a dozen perhaps, each with a driver, a passenger, and four dark-dressed men standing on the runners and clinging to the handrails along each side.

Robyn climbed down from her perch and stared through the path in the rubble as they rumbled past the outer fence. Chills coursed over her.

In the distance, the Hightower Clock struck midnight, its deep brass tones echoing out over the city. Black clouds bunched in the sky, obscuring the moon.

"You best get on home, girl." Barclay said. "That's big trouble right there."

# ≪CHAPTER FOUR≫

# *Knives in the Nighttime*

Robyn raced home to Loxley Manor with her heart pounding and her skin sweat-slick. Before tonight, she had never been truly scared while visiting the 410 Compound or venturing around the Castle District alone. But those men—the sheer number of them and the quiet threat they exuded—frightened her. The danger of being caught sneaking around seemed real now.

Robyn had always been the sort of girl who enjoyed breaking the rules. She was almost never where she was supposed to be. One slim, quick person could go just about anywhere unnoticed, even in the daylight. Robyn especially liked climbing walls—simply to see what was behind them—and the Castle District was full of excellent walls. Not to mention gates and hedges and fences. She may have also leaped the occasional moat.

She would have preferred having a friend to join her from time to time, but she found it hard to interest the other girls in even the most harmless sorts of mischief. It stood to reason, since Robyn always, always got into a little bit of trouble when she didn't follow the rules.

Her mother chided her for her impatience.

Her father described her as restless, but he usually smiled with secret pride over it.

Her teachers all thought she was trouble, but her grades were decent and more often than not she did her homework, though she didn't always show up for class.

At night, she loved exploring the woods behind her house, or visiting the 410. She was never the least bit tired at bedtime. The manor house was quite large, with more than a dozen rooms, but as it happened her parents' bedroom was right across the hall. And right next to the closet that housed the alarm system controls. Robyn would tiptoe in and flip the second-floor switch off. Hearing nothing but Dad's soft snores, Robyn would return to her room, close the door, and dash to the half-open window. The night breeze always welcomed her.

The sheer two-story drop never worried her a bit. Scaling down the rough white stones was easy enough. Her feet and fingers naturally found the correct toeholds in the mortar. A thirty-second descent. She'd done it many times and had never been caught. But never before had Robyn's restless, reckless nature actually saved her life.

It would soon become known as the Night of Shadows.

As the Hightower Clock struck midnight in the center of Notting Square, as Robyn raced home seeking the safety of

Loxley Manor, a great evil spread through the streets of Nott City. This evil came in the form of dark-dressed men carrying the sort of sharp knives that are perfect for slicing throats.

The leader of the dark-dressed men was, in fact, not a man at all. An elegant, birdlike woman sat calmly in the passenger side of the first truck in the convoy, studying the small screen resting in her palm. She wouldn't dirty her own hands tonight, of course, but a precision operation like this one required firsthand oversight.

The fourteen trucks steamed through the Castle District, where all the members of Parliament lived, each headed to one of the fourteen addresses on the list they had been given. The task was to take out everyone in those houses, a total of thirty-nine people, including spouses and children. Governor Crown had been clear about that. Tonight was not a night for the squeamish, and the guys in the trucks were not afraid of a little mess.

They parked their trucks and approached on foot, snaking toward Loxley Manor—among others—like tentacles through the pitch-black night.

Few saw them coming. Many would die.

But not Robyn. Because on the night in question, Robyn herself was a shadow.

It took a total of eighteen minutes. At eighteen past midnight, the fourteenth and final truck reported to the leader with a single number, representing the total they had captured or killed.

The leader frowned as she scrolled her PalmTab screen, reconciling the number of bodies in the trucks against the list she had in hand. Things didn't add up. Thirty-nine names, thirty-eight accounted for.

At twenty minutes past, each truck received a blinking message on its dashboard screen: COUNT AGAIN.

By twenty-five minutes past, things still didn't add up, but the leader had figured out who was missing.

Her name was Robyn. A girl. Age twelve.

Things were not in order upon Robyn's return to the manor house. A faint light glowed from the kitchen, where no light had been on when she'd left. She didn't want to get caught. So she climbed the white stones stealthily and pulled herself through her window, holding her breath. The sound of a large vehicle driving off down the street caused her to duck her head low. Instinct.

She crouched beneath her window, feeling the wrongness in the air. She found her bedroom door standing open, which it hadn't been when she'd left. The red lightbulb beside her bed was blinking. Her intruder alarm had been triggered—someone had been in her room.

Her first thought: *Busted!* But there was no sound, no sign of wakeful, worried parents. Just an unnatural, eerie hum in the air, a feeling that something strange had happened. And an unusual scent, a sort of metallic tang mixed with a whiff of sweat, as if from men's skin.

Robyn walked into the hallway. Her parents' bedroom

door stood open, too. The room was empty, their covers mussed and slept in, but all was dark. Her heart pounded. She gripped her backpack straps in tight fists and went downstairs, following the soft glow of the kitchen light. Certainly she would find them there, awake, sipping hot chocolate, waiting to pounce and punish her.

Instead, she found something else.

A white light from within the fridge, door standing open. *Why?*

Smeared handprints on the fridge door. *Smeared in what?*

Robyn flipped on the overhead light. Her body bent toward a scream, but no sound came out. She doubled over and collapsed onto her knees, the scene before her now lit and fully awful. The handprints on the fridge door were bloodred and dripping. The smudges and smears led to the center of the floor, near where she now knelt. A pool of blood. No, a lake of it.

She reached out. First her fingertips caught a bit of it, and it felt strangely warm. So she pressed her whole hand into it, like she was checking the temperature of a bath. Later, it grossed her out, the fact that she had done this. But she never wondered *why*. As if she knew it was the last she'd ever touch of them.

Then she ran straight to the bathroom sink and scrubbed and rinsed until the basin was free of any tinge of pink and the water draining away was as clear as her tears.

⟫⟶

The leader in the truck closed her eyes, thinking it through. Anything less than perfection was unacceptable to Crown. To return one body short meant returning in failure. To retrace steps and continue the search meant returning late, which would require an explanation.

After listening to a round of stammering, unhelpful suggestions, the leader ordered her men into silence. Their opinions didn't matter. It was all her responsibility in the end.

"I'll take care of it," she told the men. "Never speak of this again."

She directed the trucks to proceed to the surrounding counties: Sherwood, Nottingham, Excelsior, Block Six. There were more houses, more dissidents to confront, and no time to waste.

To the driver of her own truck, she ordered, "Take us to Loxley Manor."

# ⪡CHAPTER FIVE⪢

## *Intruder Alert*

Robyn shut off the faucets and dried her hands and face on a small towel. As she brushed away the water and the tears, she became aware of a sound other than the soft sloughing of terry cloth against skin. A sound from beyond the closed bathroom door.

She opened it a crack and listened.

Floorboards creaked in the foyer. A long, wide shadow emerged through the moonlit atrium. A deep, whispered voice said, "Still no sign of the child."

Another man answered: "Look again."

Robyn did not return to the main hallway. She left the bathroom by the opposite door that led to the mudroom behind the kitchen. She ran up the rickety rear stairs and tore down the corridors to her bedroom. She ran toward the canopy bed, planning to slide under it into the deep shadows behind the dusty zoo of outgrown stuffed animals.

Halfway across the room, she froze.

Her covers had been mussed in an unusual way, the sheets torn back and the comforter strewn across the wooden chest below the footboard. Her childhood toys disturbed.

Who was in the house? Why were they looking for her?

It didn't matter—she had to get out of there. Robyn ran toward the small ballerina painting on her wall and lifted it aside. She pressed her fingertips against the four indentations in the tiny wall safe. The latch clicked open. The slim space contained a pair of fingerless black gloves, a silver sphere the size of a golf ball, and a single pale-brown envelope. Nothing more?

Heavy treads on the staircase. Robyn whipped her head around. The bedroom door was still wide open.

Robyn didn't have time to wonder further. She scooped the items into one hand and tried to jam them into the side pouch of her backpack as she ran to the window. She thrust her legs out and—oops! The silver sphere popped out of her grip and bounced down the stones.

Trembling fingers made it harder to scale the wall. Fragmented instructions flitted through her mind, things her father had told her. *If anything ever happens to me or your mother . . .*

But these dire warnings were the sort of thing Robyn usually tuned out. Her father worried too much. He was always afraid of the day the government would come for them. But the fears were just carryovers from the old days of the Crescent Rebellion, her mother insisted. The rebels had won, and formed a Parliament. Her parents were *part* of the government now. Who would try to hurt them?

But blood on the kitchen floor told a different story. Strange men in the house . . .

Robyn's sweating fingers lost their grip on the stones. She slid the last few feet to the ground. She scooped up the silver sphere, which lay in two pieces on the ground. Ignoring the fresh scrapes on her wrists and knees, she pushed off the wall and started running.

"It's done, sir." The leader stood in the Loxley Manor driveway and reported the news to the governor through the PalmTab screen. She held her hand up in front of her. The screen remained gray-black, which was Crown's choice, but she knew he could still see her. "All dissident High Office personnel accounted for."

"Excellent." The merest quiver in the responding voice revealed profound excitement. Months of planning, and now, perfect execution. "You know where to take them?"

"Yes, Governor."

The voice in the radio cleared its throat. A sinister little scratching sound. "I thought you said you'd achieved your objective."

The leader experienced a flutter of panic. Crown couldn't know about the missing girl, could he? "Yes. We did, sir."

"Then, I'm no longer simply the governor, am I?"

"Oh no, of course not," stammered the leader, relieved to discover the simplicity of her mistake. "Congratulations, Your Highness."

"Thank you." Crown paused. "There is a position open in my administration."

"I would imagine there are several," said the leader.

Over the thin airwaves, Crown's laughter sounded like the squeal of distant tires. "Indeed." Pause. "How does 'deputy commissioner of the Nott City Military Police Department' sound to you?"

The leader smiled in the darkness. *Deputy Commissioner Marissa Mallet.* "That has a nice ring to it. I'm at your service, Your Highness."

"Of course, I'll need you to take care of Sherwood a while longer, Sheriff Mallet. Just until the dust settles."

"Yes, sir."

"Keep up the good work, and the job will be yours."

The screen flipped to a deeper black. Mallet clicked off the PalmTab and lowered her hand. She glanced around at the group of dark-dressed men from her truck. When she spoke, her voice resonated with the fresh authority that had just been bestowed upon her. "Every man here will hold a high rank in the new world order," she said. "You are my inner circle."

She strode around the arc, looked into each of their faces one by one. Loyalty could be bought, she knew, for she had sold her own to Crown many years ago. Now she would reap the benefits. She made a second round, hardening her face as she locked eyes with each of them in turn. To be sure they understood.

One little girl, one little white lie, would never be her downfall.

# ⋘CHAPTER SIX⋙

## *Into the Untamed Woods*

Robyn dashed across the manor's wide lawn for the second time that night. Unlike the first time, her heart was racing with terror, not delight. Unlike the first time, she stopped at the edge of the grass, and glanced back at the manor house. Tears filled her eyes, and she fought the urge to cry out loud.

*Be quick, and be quiet*, her father had said, each and every time they'd practiced this flight. He had always been beside her, holding her hand. Now she was alone.

Robyn spun away, forcing herself out of sight. The pitch-dark woods became her refuge. But for once, Robyn found no solace in the swaying of even the most familiar branches. She sprinted toward her favorite tree, a massive live oak with low, thick arms, and knobs in the trunk at just the right spacing to climb. Robyn's toes could feel their way up that tree on even the pitch-blackest moonless night. She longed to climb it now, but . . .

*Get as far from the danger as you can.*

Robyn dashed past the huge live oak, vaulting its exposed, sprawling roots. The woods' black air gave way to a slight clearing, and Robyn tumbled to her knees on the leaf-strewn floor. She cupped the pieces of the silver sphere—what was it? And was it ruined? There was not quite enough light to tell.

The moon's white glow drifted through the dappled leaves overhead. Robyn lifted her tear-streaked face and gazed at the white circle in the sky. Not a full moon, but full enough to receive the brunt of her anguish.

"What happened?" She begged of the moon. "Where are they?" Her desperate whispers echoed loudly in the cavern of the wood.

The elders said that the moon knew all. If you learned well enough to read its face, you could find any answer. Robyn stared upward, gripping the sphere with a careful fist. *Shadows on the moon*, Barclay had said.

Leaves danced across the moon's face, obscuring its particular pattern of shadows. It didn't matter. Robyn had never learned to read the moon. Her parents believed in the moon lore, but she had always been too impatient for lessons about tricks of shadows and light. If only she'd paid more attention . . .

Leaves began to rustle behind her. Not a breeze, but a thrashing. As if someone was coming. Robyn's heart pounded. She scrambled to her feet and spun around. Unnatural, pointed lights shone through the tree trunks, like dots in the distance, but growing larger.

*You will not know whom you can trust.*

Robyn did not wait any longer to see who was coming. A rescue? A threat? She thought of the blood on the kitchen floor and instantly she knew what her father would want her to do.

She ran.

Robyn left the moonlit clearing behind. She bounded toward the darkest space she could find. She did not look back again.

*Go to our place in the woods and hide. I will come for you.*

But she had already passed all the places where her father used to take her when she was small. The ring of live oaks edged the Loxley property, creating a boundary between the landscaped region, with its manicured shrubbery and art-fully mulched trails, and the untamed woods beyond.

Within moments, Robyn could no longer see more than a few feet around her. She moved as quickly as she could, not knowing what lay ahead. She tucked the sphere securely in the side pocket of her backpack and took out the gloves. The fabric was thin, but it held snugly, comfortably. There was a bit of structure to the gloves, in fact. She could feel the slight frame of spidering wires across the back of her hands. It was similar to the fit of the PalmTab devices her parents owned, except sized for Robyn and not a grown adult. It reminded her, too, of the sort of BioNet sleeve she had to wear in the doctor's office sometimes. The sleeve monitored vital signs and blood levels and organ function through the skin.

Robyn held her hands out in front of her and raised her feet high with each step to stay atop the maze of brambles and uneven roots. The woods quieted around her. The midsummer air grew cool.

She brushed away strings of web from her mouth, kept her eyes closed so they wouldn't get poked by reckless branches. When she peeked now and again, the view was mostly dark. She could barely even see the light-brown backs of her own hands stretched merely arm's length in front of her. In places where the trees were thin, moonlight streamed down in patches.

Owls hooted and other night birds wailed. Robyn, who had never been scared among these dark trees for a moment in her life, felt a terror so deep it seemed to pass right through her, sharp and unending, like a very long knife. The sort that might draw a very large pool of blood.

She stifled a sob and kept walking. The moon held no answers. The darkness only reminded her of the questions. She clung to the hope that her parents would return, somehow, and find her. She hummed to herself for comfort, an old lullaby her parents used to sing, though she couldn't recall the correct words.

Robyn pressed slowly on, through the darkest hours of the night, easing her way among the damp, brushing leaves and scratchy sticks. When the sun began to rise, she sensed it. The foliage remained thick, but there was a lightening of the air and the chirping of new birds and insects awakening with the dawn. The trees seemed to thin, finally, as shafts of light peeked through.

Robyn blinked her eyes to ward off sudden sleepiness. She had walked all through the night. Her stomach growled. She began to think seriously about what would happen when she reached the other side of the woods.

The Castle District was edged by Notting Wood on the east side and Notting Lake on the other. Most homes in the Castle District had property that bordered one or the other. "Are you lakeside or wood shear?" people would ask each other at parties. The outlying counties were scattered around the outskirts of the central loop, like wedges of pie.

*Mmm* . . . pie. Robyn's stomach growled again. She struggled to remember things her father had said about Sherwood County. How much farther could it be? She had to eat soon, and surely there would be stores over there.

*Do not use your Tag. Do not even show it to anyone.*

As her father's voice drifted back to her, Robyn remembered how she had giggled when he said this. Not use her Tag? Ridiculous! Points were the only form of currency; the only way to buy anything in a store was to scan your Tag and have the payment drawn from your account.

*They will track you,* he'd told her. *Just do what you have to do until I find you.*

There were fruit trees somewhere in the Notting Wood, she remembered. A few years ago, her class had taken a tour of the natural orchards. The students had been allowed to pick apples and pears from the trees, and there had been people from the other districts there, too, gathering fruit into baskets. If she could find those trees, she could eat without using her number.

As soon as the light came up, Robyn reached for the envelope in her pocket. The front was plain, which she already knew. She turned it over and opened it swiftly, heedless of the scratches and cuts on her fingers after the plunge through the woods. Scrawled across the flap in Dad's handwriting:

The gloves will protect you—always wear them.
The map will guide you—keep it close.
The cash may come in handy, when the time is right.

The envelope contained a folded piece of old parchment and a collection of thin, rectangular colorful papers, with various symbols in the corners of each. The papers were uniform, and just the right size to fit in the letter envelope. The parchment unfolded into a ragged-edged map the size of a dinner plate. It was hard to hold the edges of the map up with the rest of the things in hand, so Robyn stuffed the envelope of colored papers into her backpack and focused on the map. She didn't know what "cash" was, but it must

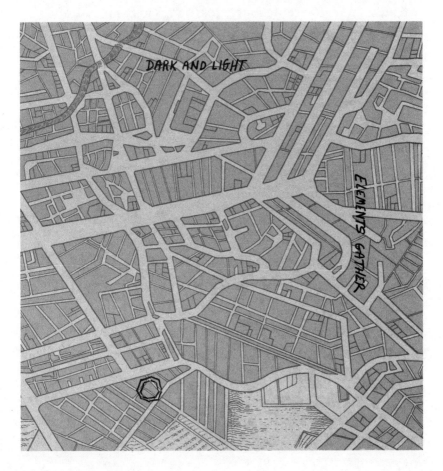

be important if it was all Dad had left for her in the event of an emergency.

Robyn didn't know what to make of the symbols. It wasn't a map of Nott City, as far as she could tell. Nothing looked familiar on it, except for a green blotch that could possibly be the Notting Wood. But she wasn't even sure which end of the map was up, or if she was anywhere on it right now.

She folded the map and brought out the sphere again to examine it in the daylight. It was not entirely broken. The two pieces were unevenly split across seams in the metal, and sinewy wires snaked between the sections. Robyn pushed the halves together until they fit. The words *Breath, Blood, Bone* were etched into the metal in tiny script.

Robyn turned the strange sphere over in her palm. What was it? With her scratched-up fingers, she wiped off some smudges of dirt from the sphere, then she blew away a few leaf fragments from its surface.

The sphere vibrated in her hand. Robyn gasped, holding her arm outstretched. The thin silver surface began to glow. Up from the glow stretched a tiny figure. It looked like— Dad! The hologram grew to life size. Robyn tipped her head back, dizzy from the illusion. She set the sphere carefully on the bed of brown needles at her feet and stepped back.

"Robyn, honey, if you're receiving this message, I fear the worst has happened. Listen closely, love, for there is much I will need you to do now."

The lifelike image brought tears to Robyn's eyes. Dad. He seemed so real that she reached out to touch him, but there was only light and air.

"I'm sorry you will be alone to deal with the challenges ahead. There are many others who can help you, but you will have to—"

The hologram blipped and blurred.

"Dad?" Robyn cried into the cavern of trees.

"You must visit the shrines. Gather the Elements. They . . ."

His voice came through clearly one moment, then faded the next.

". . . moon lore has promised us there is one who can save us. One who will lead us through darkness and light, and Robyn . . ."

"Dad," she whispered, stretching out her hand as the image dissipated once more.

". . . for you and you alone . . . ancient map of Sherwood holds many secrets . . . every arrow . . ."

The sphere's light dimmed, but Dad's voice carried through in static fragments.

". . . conceal your Tag . . . the gloves . . . are strong and brave . . . love you . . . believe in you alwa——"

The hologram blinked and faded. Robyn tucked away the sphere pieces, blinked back her tears, and kept walking. If only she hadn't dropped it. Dad's message might have been complete.

If Robyn had had any tools with her, she could probably have fixed it. She could have at least made sure all the wires were tightened and properly rebound the pieces to one another. She would have to find the right tools somehow and try. She had to hear the whole message and understand what Dad needed her to do. She couldn't let him down.

After a short while the terrain of the woods began to change. The trees thinned, the branches raised and straightened, and their leaves gave way to needles. The viny ground morphed into a carpet of brown needles. Robyn gazed around in wonder. She remembered coming into this part of the Notting Wood once, on the same class trip. The area was known as Sherwood Forest because the trees were evergreen and it bordered Sherwood County.

For the first time in a while, Robyn felt the slightest bit hopeful. She kept walking. It wasn't long before she heard voices among the pines.

# ≪CHAPTER SEVEN≫

## *Voices in the Forest*

Robyn quickly tucked the map into her jeans pocket. She whirled this way and that, seeking the source of the voices. She saw nothing.

She stood stock-still and cocked her head to one side, listening. She heard nothing more. Perhaps the wind was playing games. If she could only—

Someone grabbed her from behind.

Robyn screamed. She fought the strong hands that gripped her upper arm. She wrenched herself around to see who was holding her. All she caught was a glimpse of a crisp brown sleeve.

A second man appeared in front of her, wearing the same uniform. A tall, hefty guy. "What have we here?" he said.

"Let me go," Robyn cried.

The man smiled, but not to be nice. The smile revealed deep-set wrinkles. His skin was burnished gold from sun exposure, such that his thin blond mustache almost blended into his lip. His shirt was not simple brown, it turned out. It was camouflage-swirled and emblazoned with a large purple shield that read, Nott City Military Police.

*Police!* Robyn thought, flooded with relief. Someone who could help her. "Please," she cried. "You have to help me. My parents—"

"Please," the military policeman whimpered, in a mocking echo of Robyn's plea. "Please help me," he mimicked. Then in his own rough voice declared, "What do you think, I was born yesterday?"

The other still held her fast by the arms. "Let's go," he said. "Haven't you heard? The woods are off-limits."

"Since when?" Robyn demanded, outraged that they dared hold her so roughly. "Let me go this instant," she insisted. But the grip on her did not lessen. Robyn's outrage dissolved into fear. Were these the same men who had come after her parents? Nott City had a military, and it had police, but the two were supposed to be separate.

They tugged her backpack off her shoulders. *No,* Robyn thought. *The gadget from Barclay. The envelope from Dad. The hologram!*

The MP in front of Robyn hefted the bag in his hand, testing the weight. It must have felt close to empty; he didn't unzip it. "Planning to fill this with contraband, eh?"

"I—I haven't done anything wrong," Robyn stammered. "Please—"

"Trespassing," he responded. "Resisting arrest."

The PalmTabs the MPs wore pinged in unison. A voice through the speakers mumbled something Robyn could not make out.

The MP in front of her raised his hand to his mouth. "Negative. It's just some girl from Sherwood."

Robyn struggled. "No!" she blurted. "I'm from Castle."

The two men laughed. "Sure," said the one holding her. "You were just out for a twenty-five mile stroll." Had she really walked that far?

Robyn tried to fight off his grip. "Let me go. My father will—" She clamped her mouth shut. Best not to reveal who she was until she knew what was happening.

Both MPs had their hands on her now. One at each arm, they carried her between them. Her feet barely touched the ground. They hustled her to a clearing where a small jeep sat waiting.

The jeep burst out of the forest and snaked through the grid-like streets of Sherwood. The two MPs rode up front. Robyn finally got a glimpse of the one who had been holding her. He was much younger than the other, with dusty-brown hair and strong, chiseled features.

In the backseat, Robyn's hands were bound with a thin elastic rope, secured to the jeep bar above her head. Through the gap between her elbows, she studied the unfamiliar scenery. Tall buildings with many windows, built close together. The buildings did not have front lawns but were right up against the sidewalks, which were right up against the street. Small shops and many nondescript doorways flitted by, separated only by the occasional alley. In the distance she recognized the iconic twin steeples of the Nottingham Cathedral, standing tall above the city.

Robyn had seen pictures of Sherwood, of course, but she hadn't ever seen it in person. She concentrated hard on the buildings and the people to counteract the looming question in her mind: Where were they taking her?

Along the sidewalks, people walked and talked and gathered. People everywhere. Some of them looked quite ragged, Robyn thought, but Sherwood was a poor district, so maybe that was to be expected. She noticed hunched elder women pushing small, loaded carts along the sidewalk. Men in ill-fitting suits standing in line beside the padlocked door of a building tagged Employment Office. Barefoot children jumping rope and chasing one another through a blacktopped empty lot.

Many of the people were dark skinned, some light, and some in between, like Robyn herself. A whole range of colors, whereas most people in Castle were either quite dark or quite light. The dark-skinned men reminded Robyn of her father. He never spoke much about growing up in Sherwood, but she knew he had gone into politics to try to help the people back home.

The jeep bounced to a stop alongside a wide, low concrete building. The young MP exited the jeep and when he reached in to untie her, Robyn renewed her struggle to get free.

He grabbed her wrists tightly and yanked her toward him. She fell halfway out of the jeep.

"Don't fight it," the young MP whispered. "If you value your life." He had striking green eyes. Their gaze upon her seemed incongruously kind. The words seemed less like a threat and more like a warning. He lifted her out and set her on her feet, then led her inside.

Robyn followed calmly.

The larger MP opened the metal door, carrying Robyn's backpack. The young MP ushered Robyn into the cool, dry lobby of Sherwood District Jail.

The room was very plain and very intense. No windows. Three doors, including the metal one that led outside. The other doors were glass, studded with vertical steel bars and fitted with computerized keypad locks. One led to a room with a row of glowing blue computer screens on one side and a rack of cubbyholes filling the opposite wall. The next led to a long row of old-fashioned, metal-barred cell blocks. Robyn swallowed hard.

Behind a tall desk sat a heavyset woman in a wider version of the MPs' brown uniform. The desk surface held a computer monitor, a hefty ring of metal keys, a placard that read WARDEN, and an open magazine. Next to the warden stood another short, thin guard.

A large portrait hung on the wall behind the warden's desk, but the woman in the photograph was not the warden. A plaque on the gilded frame read, Marissa Mallet, Sherwood County Sheriff. Her still, dark eyes pierced the room. Pale-brown hair hung straight at the sides of a light-brown face similar in shade to Robyn's own.

"This is the girl?" The warden turned a page in her magazine without even glancing up. Robyn forced her attention down from the portrait above.

The guard came forward and took Robyn's rope from the young MP. He yanked her toward the desk by her wrists. Robyn stumbled, her hip slamming painfully into the edge of the desk. She lurched forward and found herself staring down at a double-page spread of stylish stiletto heels. The warden was reading a fashion magazine. Robyn wondered if that kind of shoe came in camo print.

"Hands on the desk," the warden said. Robyn complied. She pulled a wand from a drawer and waved it over Robyn's gloved hands, then sighed. "No Tag. Why am I not surprised?"

Robyn was confused. Of course she had a Tag. The ID chip was right there in her hand, like it was in everyone else's. You just couldn't see it, under the gloves, but the scanner should be able to read through the cloth just fine.

"Would you like me to input her?" the larger MP offered. "The prisoner database looks like it's up and running." He moved toward the door of the computer room, Robyn's backpack in hand. The warden punched a button on the edge of her desk and the door buzzed, allowing him to enter. Robyn watched as he stuck her bag in one of the cubbyholes and tagged it with a paper on a string.

"I'll process her later." The warden flipped to a page full of purses. "Burle, put her in the end. With the street rats," she said.

The thin guard laughed. "She smells like one of them."

"Hey," Robyn blurted, automatically offended. It wasn't like there'd been a shower in the jeep. And she'd been running through the woods all night. Her clothes had been shredded by unseen sticks and branches. Not to mention that she'd been lying under fishy-smelling cardboard before that. No wonder they thought she was from Sherwood.

There was no chance to protest her arrest. The guard was already dragging Robyn toward the other glass door, which buzzed open to allow them access to the cell block. He led her down a dim corridor, lined with bars on one side and a solid concrete wall on the other.

The cells were crammed with people. Dozens. Hundreds maybe. Sitting, lying, standing. Heads in their hands, reaching their arms through the bars, as if there was some help to be had there.

Their evident despair sliced at Robyn's heart. The walk seemed to grow longer and longer as the strange new reality settled over her. She was a prisoner now, just like them. The thought left her cold, afraid.

The final cell in the row was empty, except for a small pile of rags in one far corner. The guard slid open the gate and pushed Robyn inside, harshly enough that she stumbled. She landed on her knees, thrusting her still-bound hands down to help break the fall.

The bars clanged shut behind her.

# ≪CHAPTER EIGHT≫
## *The Rags Come to Life*

"My hands," Robyn said, holding them up to the guard. "You didn't untie them."

"Tough luck." He barely glanced down before he strode away, his boot heels clicking down the concrete hallway.

Robyn sat alone in the cool, dank cell as the echoing sound of his steps receded to silence. She blinked into the gray air. The surreal sensation of being under arrest quickly settled into actual fear. She was locked up. Behind bars. In jail. A prisoner. It was the sort of thing that happened in the movies, not in real life.

The cell was cold, with solid cement on all sides. Except, of course, for the bars that formed the door. Beyond them, the dim concrete corridor was lit only by the occasional bare bulb.

"I'll untie you," whispered a small voice.

Robyn scrambled around to look behind her. The cell remained dark and empty. But she was sure she'd heard something.

The pile of rags in the corner began to move. Robyn edged away, until her back pressed against the corner where the bars met the cool concrete that separated this cell from the next one.

The pile of rags unfolded into a shabbily dressed, stick-thin girl. She emerged through the shadows, ghostlike and small, scooting toward Robyn on hands and knees until she reached Robyn's place at the front of the cell.

"Oh no," Robyn gasped upon seeing her in the light. The girl had a bleeding gash along the right side of her face from temple to ear. "What happened?"

The girl gazed back at her. Curious brown eyes, wide open and unblinking. Her hair might once have been something akin to blond, but for now it hung in matted locks around her face, almost blackened with dirt and blood.

"What happened? To your head," Robyn added.

"Oh." The girl's fingers flitted absently to her temple. "Burle."

"What?"

"The guard."

"He hit you?"

The girl tipped her head, offering Robyn that curious gaze again. "I'll untie you," the girl said finally. "Then you can do me." She put out her hands, revealing slim, bound wrists like Robyn's own.

"Deal," Robyn said. She extended the knot toward the girl. In a matter of seconds, Robyn felt the cord loosening. "Ahh." She shook free. "Okay, give me yours."

The girl tipped her wrists upward. Even in the dim light, Robyn could make out the thin traces of blue veins beneath her pale skin. The girl was bone thin. Starving.

"When was the last time you ate?" Robyn said softly, as she worked the knots. "Don't they feed you in here?"

"I just got here," the girl said. "But, yeah, they do. That's the only good part." She blinked and her eyes began to sparkle with excitement. "Three meals a day."

Robyn's heart cracked a little. "You're happy to be here?"

The girl frowned. "Of course not. I'd be eating right now if they hadn't caught me." She tossed her matted hair proudly. "I've never been caught before."

"You steal food?" Robyn said. She knew people in Sherwood couldn't afford fancy things, but surely they could eat.

"Not exactly. But all of my food comes from the forest," the girl said. "I have nothing to eat now."

"You mean you don't have grocery stores in Sherwood?" Robyn asked.

The girl gazed at her with the same wide, liquid brown eyes. "Of course we do," she said. "That's how I ended up here."

"Oh." Robyn ducked her head, embarrassed.

"I couldn't go into the forest, so I took things from the store."

"And you couldn't use your Tag?"

The little jail cell fell silent. Silent except for the faint reverberations of the clanging bars. The smattering of low voices from the enclosures beyond. The noiseless yet deafening aura of fear.

"Who are you?" the girl said quietly.

"I'm . . . Robyn."

"Laurel."

"That's a pretty name."

Laurel smiled, showing small, surprisingly clean teeth. She reached up and tucked a knot of hair behind her left ear. Her bare hand caught Robyn's attention. She reached out as if to touch the blank spot, but Laurel flinched.

"Where's your Tag?" Robyn asked.

"I don't have one," Laurel said.

Robyn frowned. "Everyone has one."

"Maybe where *you* live."

Robyn was dumbfounded. She'd never seen anyone without an ID chip. Never even known it was possible. "How do you buy things?"

Laurel's liquid brown gaze remained steady. Robyn dropped hers to the floor, embarrassed once again. She knew better. The girl had just admitted having to steal food to survive. And Robyn's father had told her about growing up in Sherwood. About how there are people who struggle, who are poor, who live without. But as usual, she hadn't wanted to listen or believe.

"That's how I got caught," Laurel said. "There's a new scanner thing at the grocery. Two sliding glass doors." She held her hands parallel to each other.

*New?* Robyn thought. *How else would people buy groceries?* All the shops in Castle District had InstaScan doors.

"I went in like usual. No one saw me take anything, I'm sure of it," the girl said, with a mix of pride and confusion. "But when I came out, the doors closed on both sides and locked me in."

"Probably because you don't have a Tag," Robyn said. "When you step through the door, it scans your Tag and your purchases all at once." The system made purchases very convenient if you had plenty of credit, but if your account was too low to afford what you tried to leave the store with, the system locked down. When this occasionally happened to people in Castle District, it was always embarrassing.

"Oh," said Laurel. "Well, that explains it."

"When we get out," Robyn murmured. "I'll help you." She didn't know what she would do, or how, but it just didn't seem right for someone to be so desperate, or so thin. Never mind that Robyn herself was hungry now, too. And she couldn't use her own Tag, which was tantamount to not having one.

"Why don't you understand how it is?" asked Laurel.

"What do you mean?"

"Everything's different now." Laurel hugged her twig-like knees to her chest. "We're not going to get out. We're going to disappear."

## ≪CHAPTER NINE≫

# *A Plot to Take Over the World*

"Disappear?" Robyn repeated. The concrete walls of the jail cell seemed to contract around her.

Laurel nodded. "They don't let you back out anymore."

"Anymore?"

"Ever since Crown appointed the new sheriff," Laurel said, "they've had Sherwood on lockdown. I guess it was only a matter of time before they started another Purge."

"Another Purge?" Robyn echoed. She knew about the Purge—from history class. It occurred almost fifty years ago, when the Crescent rebels began plotting to overthrow King Simeon. The king tried to shut down the Crescent Rebellion by murdering, capturing, or "disappearing" the known leaders. The hunt lasted days, if not weeks, and when it was over, the rebellion was decimated.

But the rebellion did not die. Over the next ten years, a new crop of leaders emerged. Full-scale war broke out, and the rebels triumphed. Nott City formed a democracy, led by the governor and Parliament—an elected body of leaders.

"Why would there be another Purge?" Robyn wondered. "There's no rebellion."

Laurel's eyes widened. "There's always a rebellion," she said. "But especially now."

"Now?"

Laurel's curious gaze turned puzzled. "You've heard the announcements. Everyone has."

Robyn shook her head. "Announcements?"

"Where have you been? You must have heard them."

"I've been in the woods," Robyn mumbled, puzzling over the new information. Crown, purging rebels? That made some amount of sense to Robyn—Dad always said Crown could not be trusted. That he'd stop at nothing if he ever had a chance to consolidate power, despite Nott City Parliament's efforts to keep democracy alive. But what did it have to do with her parents?

Robyn had seen Crown in person a few times, at important gatherings she'd had to go to with her parents, but at the moment she couldn't exactly picture his face. There were always lots of official people at those kinds of parties; she found them all pretty boring.

"Well, you'll be hearing them soon," Laurel said. Her voice sounded ominous.

"What?" Robyn asked.

"Crown's announcements. They've been happening more than usual today. Ever since the disappearances."

"How do you know about that?" Robyn snapped. How could this girl know her parents had gone missing?

Laurel's gaze grew more troubled. "How do you *not* know? They've been showing it all day."

"Showing what?" Robyn asked.

"All the leaders who have been taken. Crown came for them last night."

*All* the leaders? Not just her parents?

And had it really only been one day? It felt like a lifetime. Her canopy bed in Loxley Manor seemed like part of a dream life. Out of nowhere Robyn was overcome by tiredness. She leaned against the wall and closed her eyes.

A high electronic whine screamed from somewhere overhead. Robyn's eyes flew open. Had she slept? How much time had passed?

Laurel and Robyn plugged their ears. "See?" Laurel shouted. "I knew it was almost time."

"ATTENTION, CITIZENS OF NOTT CITY. A word from Royal Governor Ignomus Crown."

The rear wall of their cell lit up, with a four-by-two-foot box, like an instant television set. Robyn hadn't noticed the screen corners at first—four tiny round projectors mounted on the wall at each corner of the image.

A man's face appeared. Robyn recognized him as Governor Crown.

"Good morning, my dear citizens," he said. "And it is indeed a beautiful morning."

Across the cell, Laurel moaned, holding her fingers in her ears.

"In recent days, a minority of unhappy citizens have chosen to make trouble for you all. Fear not, the situation is well in hand. I am your governor," he emphasized. "From this day forward, I—and I alone—am the leader of this city."

He spoke in a firm, slow voice. "Parliament has approved my resolution to restructure. All dissenting members of the lower house have abdicated their posts."

Robyn leaned toward the flickering image. Abdicated? What did that mean? Her father was a representative in the lower house of Parliament. Her mother was fourth chair in the upper house, because of her ancient noble lineage. After the Crescent Rebellion, the last king's cruel dictatorship had ended, but the royal bloodlines still counted for something.

"Some went voluntarily," Crown continued. "Others had to be . . . encouraged." Static rolled as the video feed cut to the image of a man handcuffed to a post. Robyn recognized him from her parents' cocktail parties. A lower house representative: Connor? Collins? Something like that. "Democracy forever!" he cried out. Then a strange sound erupted from somewhere offscreen. As Robyn watched, the man slumped down to the base of the pole, lying limp.

"Is he dead?" she said aloud. "Did they kill him?"

"Citizens would do well to respect the new regime," Crown said, his face coming into focus again. "Dissent will not be tolerated. But law-abiding citizens have nothing to fear. This is a glorious day for all of us. Nott City will be great again. I will see to it."

The makeshift screen went dark.

"Stay tuned for further developments in this exciting time. All hail, Nott City!" concluded the first voice. The overhead static hum died and the jail cell became quiet again.

Robyn blinked, as if to shake off the images she had seen, and the things she had heard. But they could not be shaken.

Parliament . . . restructured? The lower house at least—but what about the upper?

Governor Crown . . . no longer simply governor, but royal dictator?

Robyn understood little about the politics in Nott City, but she had sat at the dinner table night after night while her parents rambled on about it. Her father had called Crown ruthless and power hungry. He had been worried that something was going to happen.

The truth began to sink in. If the governor was responsible for her parents' disappearance, for the blood on the kitchen floor, then they really might be . . . but she didn't want to even think the word. *Dead.* She thought it anyway. It was out of her control.

Robyn huddled against the cell wall. Tears filled her eyes again. *Mommy. Daddy,* she thought.

She was trying so hard to be strong, but it was getting harder. She had always liked going off on her own, but now . . . she was alone. Really and truly alone. And very afraid. The world as she had known it no longer existed.

# ≪CHAPTER TEN≫

## *Jailbreak*

"Last night it became official. But it really started months ago," Laurel said. "Here and there. New uniforms. New rules."

Robyn wrapped her hands around the bars. "We have to get out of here." She jammed her shoulder against the space in the bars. It wedged itself immediately. No room to maneuver.

"I tried that. And the lock is too thick," Laurel said. "I couldn't pick it."

Robyn raised her eyebrows. "You know how to pick locks?" Unlike the hallway door, the cell door was latched with an old-style key lock. They were fairly rare; nowadays almost everything locked electronically. At least in Castle District. Here in Sherwood, many buildings seemed much older, like the jail.

Laurel reached into her grimy hair and extracted a small bobby pin. "I do it all the time. Regular-size ones."

Robyn smoothed a hand over the crown of her thick and intricate braid. Her fingers poked at the seams. Somewhere in there . . . aha! She withdrew a longer hairpin.

"With hair like mine, you need something heavy duty," she said. The extra-large bobby pin was twice as long and twice as thick as Laurel's.

Laurel's eyes lit up. She stretched out one small hand and took the pin. She scraped off the rounded plastic tip, exposing the metal corner underneath. "That should work."

"Great. Let's do it," Robyn said, rising to a crouch.

But Laurel simply sat there, toying with the pin. Finally she said, "Maybe after lunch?"

Robyn's stomach growled in response. "I'm hungry, too," she said. "But there has to be another way to get food." She didn't want to stay in jail a minute longer than absolutely necessary. Right now, they thought she was just a street rat from Sherwood, but that thing the warden had said about processing her later might involve scanning her Tag into the computer system. If so, they would learn who she was, and whose daughter she was. Based on the attack on her house last night, and Crown's video clip, Robyn feared her life would be in even more danger once she was processed. "We should go now," she insisted, "and find food later."

"Please?" Laurel asked. "I mean, they bring it right to the cell. We could wait until nighttime. It's always better to escape in the dark."

Robyn licked her dry lips. "How do you know? I thought you said you'd never been caught before."

"I know about things," the little girl declared haughtily. She crossed her arms. "I can handle all kinds of trouble. And I'm the one who can get us out of the cage."

Robyn held back a smile. Tiny but fierce. She liked this girl. Robyn sat down and crossed her arms, too. "Fine. We'll wait."

They waited for hours. Robyn leaned against the cold concrete and tried to sleep. It didn't work, though, because what she was really doing was trying to wake up. Hoping it was all still a dream, and any minute she would open her eyes, safe and sound in her canopy bed, with her parents alive and well across the hallway.

Robyn in jail? Crown taking over? Military police who were not here to protect the people in the community but instead to suppress them? It was all too surreal.

Robyn pulled out Dad's map and studied it. The cryptic markings seemed no less mysterious on closer inspection. The map contained more than streets and landscape. Small symbols arose in places. A strand of DNA in what looked like the forest. An image of flames. The cryptic words at the edge . . . Elements Gather . . . echoed something Dad had said in the hologram. "Gather the Elements." What did that mean?

The only things Robyn knew called Elements came from a painting Mom had in the manor. It was four separate canvases, arranged together: squares for earth, air, and water. And beneath them was a strip to represent fire. But what would it mean to gather those things? Or was it a different kind of Elements altogether?

Finally the thin guard, the one Laurel called Burle, came down the line and clattered a plastic tray through a narrow slot at the base of the cell doors. The tray contained two tough rolls, two soupy piles of vegetables adorned with some stringy meat, and two flimsy plastic paddles for spoons. Hardly a meal worth waiting for.

Laurel dived right in as if she hadn't eaten in days. Maybe she hadn't. The so-called meal seemed pretty disgusting to Robyn, but a moment later she had to admit that, like Laurel, she was too hungry to push it aside.

"Okay." Laurel stood up and began fiddling with the hairpin in the lock. The soft, steady clicking in the otherwise quiet space reminded Robyn that getting out of the cell was only the first part of the problem. There were other doors and hallways, not to mention guards who liked to hit people.

"Wait," Robyn said. "How are we going to get out of the building?"

Laurel didn't look up from the lock. "Oh, that's the easy part," she said. "Bring the ropes."

Robyn gathered the cords that had once bound their hands. Together, the length measured perhaps five or six feet. By the time she had the ropes' full length wrapped around one palm, Laurel was sliding the cage door open.

Robyn was impressed. The small girl had mastered the cell-door padlock in under sixty seconds. Laurel held out the bent bobby pin for Robyn to take back.

"Keep it," she whispered, and the pin disappeared into Laurel's nest of hair. The small girl edged out into the concrete corridor, keeping her back against the bars. To Robyn's surprise, Laurel didn't head toward the door. Instead, she moved farther down the corridor, away from the other cells, into a deep black stretch of hallway that sent chills up Robyn's spine.

There were more hallways in the building than Robyn had anticipated, and very little light. Every few feet the walls were punctuated by narrow recessed doorways. The doors were all metal and appeared quite thick. These old doors had been fitted with new computer locks. Individual cells, Robyn figured. Very small.

The girls discovered a single metal door in the outside wall, at the end of a dark hall, but it was locked. Impenetrable. The push bar was adorned with all manner of wires and alarms, plus an electronic keypad full of blinking red lights. The alarm wouldn't matter if they could get the door open, but it would matter a whole lot if they couldn't. They hurried on.

Laurel stopped in the middle of one corridor, seemingly for no reason. When she looked up, Robyn's eyes traced the same path. They were standing underneath an air vent at ceiling height.

"Boost me up," Laurel said. Robyn cupped her hands. Laurel's small bare foot landed at the intersection of her palms. Small fingers balanced on Robyn's shoulders, then released, stretching upward.

Laurel used her fingernail to unscrew the vent's slotted cover. Her knees knocked against Robyn's cheek, until she tipped her face away. Laurel's ragged clothes stank from days of wear.

"Higher," Laurel whispered. Robyn pushed her upward. It wasn't much worse than lifting a packed book bag; Laurel weighed next to nothing. The small girl's torso disappeared into the wall. Then her hips. Then her thighs.

Book bag . . . Robyn's backpack! The guards had confiscated it, and Barclay's strange tech treasure box along with it. Robyn's heart sank. There was no way to retrieve the bag from the front of the jail. It was lost. Dad's hologram . . . Everything Robyn had in the world now. Gone.

"Come on," Laurel's urgent voice jarred Robyn out of her distress. Laurel stuck an arm back. "Throw me the rope."

Robyn unwound the cords from her palm and tied their ends together. By stretching her arm up and jumping a little, she could almost reach Laurel's outstretched fingers. She tossed one end of the cord to the girl and held onto the other.

Laurel progressed farther into the vent shaft. Robyn wrapped her end of the rope around her palm and waited for it to grow taut. Somewhere in one of the corridors, a door slammed. Robyn flinched in the direction of the sound. A man's voice shouted something garbled. It included the words "rats" and "out."

*Thump-thump.* Boots on concrete. Moving fast.

# ≪CHAPTER ELEVEN≫

## *Getting the Shaft*

Robyn tugged at the rope. It felt firm. Would Laurel's weight be enough to hold her?

"Hurry," Laurel whispered, her voice echoing oddly from the narrow metallic cavern.

Robyn was accustomed to climbing walls. Though this one was smooth and quite slick compared to the walls of Loxley Manor, it didn't matter. In gymnastics, she had always been the best at climbing: walls, poles, ropes, piles of mats. If it was tall, Robyn could scale it. No problem.

Robyn let the rope support her as she moved foot over foot up the slick wall. She stuck her head in the opening and saw Laurel spread-eagled against the four sides of the vent, bracing herself and gripping the rope. The girl was surprisingly strong for her size.

"Go," Robyn said, once her elbows were hooked in the vent.

Laurel relaxed and rolled onto her belly. Robyn followed. They wriggled on their stomachs into the cobwebby metal shaft.

"This is the easy part?" Robyn grunted, half out of breath. She wedged her knees against the angles and nudged herself forward enough to drag her feet up out of the corridor.

Laurel giggled. "It's not so bad. Relatively speaking."

Robyn pushed forward again, but this time she couldn't gain traction off the wall. Her foot slipped and jutted back out of the opening. Her shoe nudged the vent cover, knocking the last screw loose.

"Oh no!"

Laurel whipped her head around, eyes widened.

The vent cover made a clattering sound as it tumbled into the concrete hall.

"Oh!" Laurel echoed, realizing what had happened.

From the corridor, the guards' call rose. "Did you hear that? This way." From below, the sound of heavy footsteps grew closer.

"Faster," Robyn urged. "Keep going."

Laurel scrambled forward with fresh urgency, Robyn right on her heels.

When they reached the outer wall, they knew it immediately. Slivers of sunlight illuminated the tunnel through the vent slats. They had misjudged the time—it wasn't remotely dark. The bigger problem was, the vent cover was screwed on from the outside. There was no way to unhook it from inside.

Laurel contorted herself until her feet were facing forward. She kicked at the vent cover with all her strength, mindless of the slight echo it made. It didn't budge.

"Come on," Robyn urged her. "They're going to hear. Kick harder. You can do it."

Laurel clenched her fists and ground her teeth and pounded with her bare heels as hard as she could. She threw her head back, and Robyn saw tears streaming from the corners of her eyes.

"You can do it," Robyn repeated. The close quarters made it impossible for her to help further. She bent her neck and nudged Laurel's shoulder with her forehead. "I know you can do it."

Laurel kicked. The slats began to give. Finally one screw broke loose, and a corner of the vent cover sprang free. Laurel kicked until a second one popped. The vent eased open sideways, swinging from its remaining screws.

The instant it was wide enough, Laurel dropped out of the hole. They didn't use the rope. Robyn moved forward, took the girl's hands, and held her, easing her down toward the ground. Their hands remained clasped until Robyn's waist was bent over the open vent, and Laurel's legs dangled a few feet from the ground. Robyn then took the sheer one-story drop easily. No worse than sticking a landing after a vault, she figured.

Well, it was a little worse, landing on pavement instead of floor pads. She felt the impact in her knees, but not too badly.

As soon as her feet touched down, she started running. Laurel had a dozen yards' head start. Robyn followed her path, marked by tiny bloody heel prints.

The jail had no fence, on account of being basically an exitless concrete box. They crossed a large patch of gravelly pavement, making for the nearest wall they could hide behind.

Within moments, the building was out of sight, though not out of mind. Guards could still be coming after. The girls zigzagged around two corners and into a narrow alley. Robyn, with her long-legged stride, caught up to Laurel and touched her shoulder.

"Stop, stop," she said. "You're bleeding."

"We can't stop," Laurel said, stopping anyway. She tucked into the gap between a Dumpster and a drainpipe. The space smelled like rotting trash and wet cardboard.

"But—"

"It doesn't hurt that bad," the small girl insisted.

Robyn still had their cords bound around her hand. She cast them aside among other refuse in the alley. "It's leaving a trail," she said. She knelt and touched the girl's ankle. Laurel obediently bent her knee, raising her foot like a horse getting her hooves checked.

Robyn used her tattered shirt hem to blot at the lines of blood. The slats had left thin slashes across Laurel's calloused feet.

"How'd you know about those vents?" Robyn asked, still breathless.

"I didn't," Laurel said. "But there's always a way out if you're small. We have to go now."

Robyn shook her head, amazed. "You didn't have a plan?"

"I guess I just expect things to work out. And they usually do."

"Things don't always work out." Robyn reminded her. "I mean, you were just in jail."

Laurel grinned, displaying her pretty teeth. "And now I'm not. Let's get out of here."

"Stay on your toes."

Laurel shot her an amused look. "Like you have to tell me." She skittered down the alley. Robyn laughed and followed Laurel's lead, assuming the girl had a destination in mind. It was her neighborhood, after all.

Following was nice, actually. It let Robyn push away the nagging truth. She didn't have anywhere to go. At least not until she figured out which way was up on Dad's map. Without Laurel, Robyn wouldn't have the first clue where to run. And Robyn was used to being sure of things.

*I just expect things to work out. And they usually do*, Laurel had said. Maybe Robyn could try Laurel's way of thinking. *I expect that my parents are still alive, somehow*, she thought. *I expect to find out what happened to them. I expect that we'll all get to go home again. Together.*

# ≪CHAPTER TWELVE≫
## *Escape through Sherwood*

After running what felt like a mile, Laurel slowed to a walk. The wide, grid-like streets turned narrower and more twisty. The apartment buildings they passed stood short and square with concrete walls and plain windows. There were also some houses, small and built of wood, and mostly fallen into disrepair. Looking around, Robyn wondered if the worn-looking old brick homes she'd passed on the way to the jail represented the nicer section of Sherwood. She now realized there was a difference between old and worn, and truly dilapidated.

A parade of tiny schoolchildren passed them. Kindergartners, maybe, carrying backpacks and lunch boxes. Laurel waved at them. The children waved back. They laughed and leaped around, as if the whole world wasn't spiraling toward awful. Robyn would be coming home from school right now, like usual, if she hadn't been forced to run away.

The thought made her laugh out loud. Yesterday, Robyn would have said that school was the worst imaginable thing to have to endure. School didn't seem like such a bad deal anymore.

"What's funny?" Laurel asked.

"Cute kids," Robyn answered, though she knew the laughter had come up from someplace deeper—a part of herself that hurt too much to think about. "What is this place?" she asked.

"It's called Getty," Laurel said.

"Never heard of it," Robyn said. Getty wasn't one of the six outlying counties. "Are we still in Sherwood?" She followed Laurel into the backyard of one of the wooden homes. This one seemed well kept compared to some of the others. It appeared freshly painted, and the lawn was decorated with pretty plants and trimmed shrubbery.

"Yes. Getty's just what we call this part of the neighborhood. There's also Sherwood Plaza, the Brownstones, Sherwood Park . . ." Laurel rattled off a long list of names as she went to the back of the house and began unwinding a long garden hose with a spray nozzle. She handed it to Robyn and turned the spigot on. Nothing happened.

"Squeeze the nozzle," Laurel said. "It's like a shower." She overturned a large rock and dug up a plastic bag containing a toothbrush, toothpaste, and a bar of soap.

Robyn stood, staring at her. "What?"

"Hold the hose over my head," Laurel said. "Like a shower." The small girl stepped out of sight between two big bushes and stripped her stained T-shirt off. It landed in the grass beside Robyn's feet. Then came the ragged shorts.

"Won't someone see us?" Robyn glanced around.

"The people who live here work all day," Laurel said. "Everyone's away. They won't even notice."

Robyn raised the nozzle over the bush and aimed it down at Laurel's head. "Everyone? How many people live here?" The entire footprint of the house was about the size of Robyn's bedroom suite in Loxley Manor.

"Two families," Laurel answered. "Seven people that I know of. I might not have seen everyone."

Robyn stared at the small house. Seven people? Where did they all sleep?

"That's good," Laurel said, much sooner than Robyn expected. One sticklike arm snaked out and retrieved her clothing. She popped out of hiding, looking clean and damp, her hair wet and finger combed. Without the caked-on blood and dirt, the cut along the side of her face looked thin and fresh but not as bad. Even the gross clothes didn't look quite as gross against soap-scrubbed skin. "Your turn."

"Um . . . that's okay," Robyn said.

"You have to wash up before we get new clothes," Laurel said. "You can't go to the market looking like that. You have leaves in your hair."

"I—I can't wash my hair under a garden hose," Robyn said. Bound up in its intricate braid, her thick, curly black hair tapered neatly to the middle of her back. Unbound, it became a beautiful but unruly cascade that took hours to tame. "There's just no way."

Laurel came around and picked the leaves and twigs out of Robyn's hair. "Neat braid," she said. "This looks way more complicated than a French braid."

"It's similar," Robyn said. Except her braid started with six strands instead of three. Weaving and lifting and smoothing all the pieces at once was quite challenging. Robyn had only recently mastered it without her father's help. *Your grandmother would be so proud*, he'd whispered, hugging her close.

"Just get the mud off, at least," Laurel said, placing the slick bar of soap in Robyn's hand. "We'll get you a toothbrush later. And floss." She frowned. "I'm completely out of floss." She said this like it was her biggest problem.

Laurel held up the hose and Robyn stepped behind the bush. She took off her clothes and piled them beside her. The gloves, she left on. Dad had said wear them *always*. The fabric was so thin, it would wash and dry quickly. They would protect her, he had said. The spidering threads that felt like metal inside—maybe there was something about them that made her chip unreadable. That would explain what had happened with the warden's wand.

The water was cold, but it felt good to scrub away the dirt. If she could scrub away the whole past day, she would.

Her heart was heavy with the knowledge that Laurel had toiletries ready and waiting to shower in someone's backyard. This day was a crisis for Robyn—a temporary one, she was sure—but for Laurel, apparently this was everyday life. She fought down the choking feeling that came, knowing that. *There are people who struggle*, her father had told her. *There are many who are forced to live without.* Robyn had never before understood what that really meant.

As she shivered under the garden hose, her heart cried out for Mom and Dad. For Mom to swoop in with a warm, plush towel and hug her dry. For Dad, to talk to him about what was happening. He would have answers, she was certain. She begged the sky, *Let me find them. Let me see them just one more time.*

"It's market day," Laurel said. "The market is the best place to shop. And there's always a good crowd around closing time, when the best sales go on."

"We don't have any money," Robyn reminded her.

Laurel sighed. "I know. 'Shop' just sounds nicer," she admitted. "We need to grab some new clothes. If we don't look different in a hurry, they're going to catch us."

"You mean . . . steal?"

"I don't like that word," Laurel said.

"But that's what you mean? You're just going to steal new clothes and some shoes—"

"I don't need shoes," Laurel said, indignant. "I only take things I really need."

"And that makes it okay?" Robyn asked, meanwhile thinking, *Who doesn't need shoes?*

"You don't have to come," Laurel snapped. "You can take your fancy Tag and go to the stores. I bet they have nice stores where you come from."

*They do*, Robyn thought. But using her Tag was still too dangerous.

"All right," Robyn said. "You'll have to show me how."

It was surprisingly easy. They found a row of clothing stalls and made their way down the line, picking up items they needed. When the vendors looked the other way, the girls blended into the crowd. Robyn ended up with a black T-shirt and a pair of gray stretchy exercise pants with a green elastic waistband. They even had one small pocket at the hip for her map. Laurel opted for calf-length jeans and a blue tank top.

They changed in the bathroom at the public library. Laurel explained that it was one of the best places to use because it was normal for kids to be in there alone, so no one bothered you, and you didn't have to buy anything.

Robyn felt bad about the thefts. It was just a few small items, and she really needed them, but Robyn knew it wasn't right. She vowed that when she and her parents were reunited, and she could use her Tag again, she'd come back and pay the vendors double for what she had taken. *What if her parents were gone forever?* whispered the nagging voice in her mind. But Robyn wouldn't allow herself to answer.

# ≪CHAPTER THIRTEEN≫

## WANTED!

Robyn emerged from the bathroom stall to find Laurel bent over a sink, flossing her teeth. Laurel must have read the question in Robyn's eyes. "A lady had it in her purse," she explained. "She had TWO packs. I only took one."

"Uh-huh," Robyn said.

Laurel rinsed and spat. "I'm ready now," she said.

They took a last glance at themselves in the mirror. "The hats are a good touch," Laurel declared. She wore a plain blue baseball cap, while Robyn had coiled her braid up under a knit beret in a deep green that complimented her skin and dark eyes.

"Your hair is so unusual," Laurel added. "It would be easy to recognize."

"Yeah." Robyn chose not to say anything further.

As they headed out of the library, Laurel stopped to study the bulletin board near the entrance. The large digital screen was full of flyers and posters and pamphlets, scrolling in and out of different-size spaces. Anyone could upload a flyer to the board using ports along the edge of it. The board automatically rotated them all through the display. There were ads for babysitters, renters looking for roommates, guitar lessons, community events, and anything else that might be happening. "Sometimes the library has parties with free food," Laurel said. "I always look." Robyn perused the items along with her.

"Uh-oh," Laurel said.

"What?"

Laurel took Robyn by the arm and turned her around. She led her across the entryway to a second, much less friendly, display of flat-screen tablets positioned edge to edge and bolted to the wall. Each tablet contained a Wanted poster, courtesy of the Nott City Military Police Department. Every ten seconds or so, at random, each screen would dissolve into pixels and a new poster would pop up.

Robyn stared in awe at the display, but the shock had only begun. There was no picture, but the written description was eerily accurate.

## STREET URCHINS, FEMALE

Escaped from Sherwood Jail. Presumed to be traveling together.

**One:** 5'7". Black hair, last seen braided. Thin. Athletic. Light-brown skin. Wanted for Trespassing and Resisting Arrest.

**Two:** 5'2". Dirty-blond hair. Very thin. White skin. Wanted for Theft and Resisting Arrest.

"It's official." Robyn spoke softly. "We're fugitives for real now."

The girls rushed out onto the street. "How did they get a Wanted poster up so fast?" Robyn asked. She was doubly relieved now that the warden hadn't processed them when they arrived. The MPs could only post a rough description; they didn't really know who she was. "Why do they even care that we escaped?"

Laurel affected her voice like a TV advertisement. "Welcome to the new, more punitive Sherwood. Courtesy of Sheriff Marissa Mallet and the Nott City Military Police Department."

They joined a line of pedestrians headed back toward the market. In her normal voice, Laurel said, "Now that we look okay, we can go for some food."

Robyn's stomach growled in response. The tray of mystery meat had barely put a dent in her hunger. "All right," she said. "With that poster out, we'll have to be careful."

"Getting food is harder than clothes. Most of the food vendors know how to look out."

"Just show me what to do," Robyn said nervously.

"Oh no. Let me do it," Laurel added. "I have a lot of experience. You'll probably get us caught."

"I'll distract them," Robyn said. "While you . . . shop."

Laurel grinned and clapped her hands. "Maybe it won't be so hard with two of us."

They walked along a row of real shops, amid a gathering crowd of people who all seemed to be headed toward the market. They passed a large grocery store–pharmacy, and Robyn glanced through the InstaScan sliding doors that automatically opened as they went by. Perhaps because of the pleasant weather, or because it was market day, all the shops had things outside. Tables and chairs in front of the cafés, racks of discount T-shirts outside the fashion boutique, and large metal animal statues standing guard outside a home-decor store that appeared to contain nothing anyone would ever want to buy.

In front of a small produce stand, a spindly woman in an apron stood arguing with a thick-chested MP with a digital clipboard in hand.

"The edge of these crates is too close to the edge of the sidewalk," the MP said. "It's a violation."

"I've never had a problem," the shopkeeper protested. "There's plenty of room."

"You have a problem today," the MP said. "These will be confiscated."

The woman's dark face slackened. "But that's half of my produce for the week! I—I can move them closer—"

"Too late." The MP lifted the front row of boxes and placed them on a rolling dolly by the curb. He turned away to grab the next crate.

Robyn didn't plan it. It just happened. Her arm snaked out, as if of its own accord. When it returned to her side, a bag of small oranges came along with it, lifted right off the top crate on the dolly.

# ≪CHAPTER FOURTEEN≫

## *A Proper Thief*

"Whoa," Laurel said. "What did you do?"

"I—I don't know," Robyn said. She hunched her shoulders around the sack and clutched it to her chest. The girls hurried down the sidewalk.

"The MP was RIGHT THERE," Laurel cried. "That is exactly how you get caught."

"He wasn't looking," Robyn said. There was really no defense for what she had done, but she'd done it.

"Well, gimme some." Laurel held out her hand. "We have to get rid of the evidence. NOW!"

Robyn tore at the mesh and poured three baby oranges into Laurel's cupped palms. The bag contained over a dozen—more than the two of them could eat quickly.

"Here you go." Robyn tossed two oranges each to a pair of barefooted boys scampering through the crowds. They rewarded her with matching grins.

"Oranges," she whispered, placing a few on the lap of a blind woman sitting on a blanket on the street corner.

It didn't feel so bad, taking food that had already been taken by an MP. It felt even better to share it with other hungry people. Robyn discarded the mesh bag in a corner trash can.

Laurel watched with dismay as the fresh haul dwindled to nothing. "Leave the rest up to me, would you?" she mumbled around a mouthful of citrus sections. "You are *not* a proper thief."

"Sure," Robyn said, peeling and scarfing down the last few oranges herself.

The sidewalk was seriously crowded at this point, full of objects and people browsing and strolling. Around the corner, they passed a bookstore, a coffee shop, a shoe store, and a hair salon that appeared to specialize in braiding. The bottom half of the window was plastered with pictures of various braided styles. The sidewalk was lined with loudly chatting ladies braiding one another's hair.

One old woman among them had a gray braid as long as her body, woven in a similar manner to Robyn's own hair, which Robyn had never seen on anyone else. Her own hair was currently tucked up in her hat, in disguise, so the woman would have no way of knowing she wore it. And anyway, the old woman sat with her eyes closed, gently flicking the tail of her braid across her palm.

Robyn wanted to stop and talk to her but found that she couldn't stop. When she slowed her steps, the people behind bumped into her. And there were many people behind, all of a sudden.

"What . . . ?" Robyn started.

"I don't know . . . ," Laurel said.

It felt like they were leaving a place after a parade or fireworks display, or on the exit ramp from a stadium after the final buzzer: hundreds of people in a narrow space, everyone moving in the same direction.

Robyn and Laurel were being carried along with the surging crowd. "Ack!" Laurel cried as a large man stepped on her foot.

"Sorry, kid," he murmured.

The crowd pushed and jostled. The girls became separated. Robyn snaked her hand through a gap between the people and grasped Laurel's hand. Her small fingers clutched Robyn's in return. Where were they going?

The large man who had stepped on Laurel used his arms to ease people aside so the girls could come back together. He put a hand on each of their shoulders, keeping them inside his wingspan. He had a big backpack on his shoulders, so altogether he commanded a fair amount of space in the crowd.

Robyn looked up at him and saw a kind, worried face. He had a Y-shaped, rough-looking scar along one side of his jaw. "What's happening?" she asked him. "I can't see anything."

"It's the MPs," he said, "rounding people into the square for some kind of announcement."

At one edge of the square a line of MPs gathered on a raised wooden platform. It reminded Robyn of the bandstand in Notting Square in Castle District, where her family often went with a picnic blanket to hear an orchestra or watch a summer-stage production. Robyn imagined this space often filled with crowds to watch bands and performers, though there was little grass beneath her feet here, just a stretch of rough concrete.

The big man scratched his cheek along the scar, then shrugged out of his backpack. "Here, stand on this," he said, laying it at his feet. The girls climbed up and he rested his hands on their waists to steady them.

*The kindness of strangers*, Robyn thought. Her father had always talked about the kindness of strangers, but in a fairy tale kind of way. Most people in Castle District would not randomly help each other that way.

No sooner had Robyn thought this than Sheriff Marissa Mallet herself took the stage. She stood center stage, hawk-like eyes piercing the crowd. Standing on the backpack, Robyn's head poked above the crowd. She studied the sheriff. In person Mallet was actually tall and slim. She was dressed in a gray pantsuit with her badge pinned to her blazer pocket. She would have been pretty if not for the severe expression and tense line of her mouth.

Mallet flicked her wrist and the MPs behind her jumped to action. They stuck up screen corners on the wall behind the stage and images jumped to life. A larger-than-life Wanted poster appeared over the sheriff's shoulder. The grainy, old-style photo showed a dark-skinned man her father's age. One MP handed her a long wooden arrow, with a rock arrowhead and a feather tail.

"Those who wish to dissent," Mallet called, holding the arrow aloft. "We know who you are. You cannot hide from our eyes any longer." Her voice was strangely amplified above the circle of the crowd, a microphone taped at her temple like an actor onstage. She reached up with her other hand, gripped the shaft of the arrow in both fists, and snapped it in two. She tossed the pieces to the ground and stomped on them.

From the Wanted poster, Mallet read: "Charles Lorian. Wanted for theft of government property, arson, and political agitation."

Another, more modern, picture of a young woman flicked into place. "Nessa Croft. Wanted for political agitation and illegal broadcasting."

Mallet called up additional Wanted posters, one by one. Unlike the smaller versions that had scrolled by in the library, these seemed starker and more permanent. At some, the crowd murmured in recognition.

"Thieves. Trespassers. Agitators. Resisters," Mallet declared. Robyn began to fear that the sheriff's review of blown-up posters would include the one that was most painfully familiar, of two young girls who escaped from Sherwood Jail this afternoon.

Robyn surveyed the fringes of the crowd and realized the MPs were standing in a ring around the gathered people. There would be no easy way out of the square. They were blocking every exit!

"It is only a matter of time," Mallet said. "Surrender and there will be leniency. Fail to surrender, and . . ."

A scuffle began at the edge of the stage. The crowd surged and leaned, all trying to get a better view. MPs dragged a woman onstage. She wore a feathery green dress over brown tights.

"Nyna Campbell," the sheriff shouted. The woman's Wanted poster flashed up, with a red stripe across the bottom of her picture: "Apprehended."

Nyna Campbell stretched and strained against the MPs' grip. "My blood, my breath, my bone," she cried, all manner of pain in the hollows of her voice. "Forever yours, Sherwood. The rebellion lives on—"

Mallet sidestepped toward the woman and slashed out with an elbow to her throat, cutting off her call. Nyna Campbell's head dropped forward and she fell still and silent. A low trill rose up from the crowd, from all corners. People rolling their voices together, wordlessly.

"Silence." The sheriff motioned with her hand and the MPs bound and gagged the woman more tightly, then carried her back out of sight.

"Fugitives, beware! We will find you." Mallet continued, "Maybe even right here today." She made a threatening, stalking journey across the front of the stage, pointing into the crowd. "All citizens of Sherwood will abide by the law." She spread her arms to indicate her corps of military police. "We are here to ensure cooperation and a smooth transition to our new way of life." The sinister edge to her voice was less than comforting.

"We should go," Laurel said. She made a snaking motion with her hand, as if to indicate sneaking through the crowd.

*There's always a way out if you're small*, she'd told Robyn. Well, Robyn wasn't quite as small.

"The MPs are everywhere," Robyn whispered back.

Mallet barked an order, Robyn caught the word "fugitive"— and the MPs around her leaped into action.

"Uh-oh," Laurel said. She gripped Robyn's hand tighter as two MPs began charging through the crowd, headed straight toward them.

# CHAPTER FIFTEEN

# The Sheriff of Sherwood

Robyn was sure the MPs were about to carry her and Laurel away. Many people stood in the way—at first. As MPs smacked more and more people aside, the crowd naturally parted to let the officers storm through. Robyn knew: they were goners for sure.

The big man froze behind them. Robyn felt his breath through the back of her T-shirt as he ducked his head behind her. His hand disappeared from her waist. Robyn and Laurel wobbled, stumbling off the large pack as the MPs swirled a vortex around them.

"No," Laurel wailed.

But the MPs converged behind them and grabbed the large man instead. His eyes displayed a mix of fear and resignation as they yanked him forward. Twisting backward, he stared directly at Robyn, catching her eye. Then he dropped his gaze meaningfully to the backpack, and looked back at her. When he repeated the glance a second time, Robyn felt herself nod. Yes, she would keep it for him.

The MPs carried the scared man toward the stage. The gap in the crowd eased shut, but Robyn had to see what was happening. At the risk of exposing herself, she pushed through after him. "Watch the bag," she called to Laurel over her shoulder.

Onstage, Mallet called up yet another Wanted poster. "Fugitive Floyd Bridger!" she declared. "Fugitive no more."

The MPs held him in front of the stage. *What had he done for the rebellion?* Robyn wondered.

"You should be ashamed," Mallet told Bridger. "Using children as a shield."

The MPs prepared to chain the large man's hands and feet together with a collection of restraints shaped like the letter *I*. They held him by the shoulders and kicked him in the back of the knees until they bent. He refused to bow his head. Robyn felt like he was looking directly at her, still.

Robyn burst forward. "What are you doing to him?" she blurted out, much to her own surprise.

"Run, girl," Bridger cried, as the MPs tightened their grip on him.

But Robyn could not run. The fear and resignation in his face called out to her.

Robyn raced toward the MPs. She grabbed two of them by the arms and threw her weight against them. Startled, they released Bridger. The other two still held him, but Robyn's disruption proved enough to weaken their grip. Bridger seized the moment and broke free. He stumbled forward, plunging headlong into the crowd.

Mallet spoke in that eerie, low-but-projected tone. "Stop him! The safety and security of Sherwood depends on all of us working together."

The people did not stop him. Instead, a low hiss rose up from somewhere in the crowd, from different corners, like an echo.

It must have come from multiple people, because it was loud enough to hear across the park. But it wasn't everyone. Someone somewhere was trying to rile up the crowd.

"Grab the girl. Find the others," Mallet ordered. "Break it up." Then she marched offstage. Robyn sprinted off in the opposite direction. She bent, dodging people, trying to find her way back to Laurel.

The MPs moved in from the edge of the crowd. As the people began to disperse, Robyn watched closely as everyone threaded out through the surrounding streets. Could they ever get out unnoticed?

"Robyn," Laurel breathed, appearing through a gap in the jostling bodies.

In a surprising show of strength, the small girl hefted the enormous bag over her shoulders, clutching the much-too-wide straps against her chest. Laurel valiantly struggled beneath the weight of the pack, but her pace slowed with each step.

"Robyn," her small voice echoed, uncertain.

"Here," Robyn cried, racing to catch up. The huge backpack appeared to be darting along on its own. Robyn caught occasional glimpses of a bare heel, but that was it. "I'm here."

Robyn jammed herself up against Laurel's shoulder and slipped her arm through the outside strap, lifting part of the weight.

Laurel dropped her arm and locked it around Robyn's waist so they wore the backpack as if they were one person. They hurried onward with matching stride: middle feet forward in unison, then the two outside.

"Three-legged race," Robyn muttered, having a flashback to Field Day at her school each spring.

"What's that?" Laurel asked. The girl seemed barely out of breath from the exertion. For not knowing what a three-legged race was, Laurel was doing a pretty perfect job of running one. The two of them had no trouble staying on rhythm together.

Laurel took Robyn's arm. "This way," she said, pulling Robyn toward the stage. "No running."

"Um . . . ," Robyn protested. The thickest cordon of MPs remained in the vicinity of the stage. Maybe Laurel was too short to see them.

But the girls walked right past that line of MPs, who looked over their heads, searching the crowd attentively. *Hidden in plain sight*, Robyn thought, as they ducked behind the stage and took off running down a virtually empty street. Laurel was brilliant.

Bridger's massive pack weighed them down with each step. "Let's rest," Robyn said, when she didn't think she could run anymore. "Is it safe?"

Laurel's skeptical expression told the truth: there was no such thing as safe. Not in Sherwood. Not today . . . or any day soon, it now seemed.

Laurel sighed. "That was close."

"It could just as easily have been us they dragged up there," Robyn agreed. They unshouldered the backpack, with relief.

Laurel studied it like an adversary; the thing stood almost as tall as she was. "What should we do about his stuff?"

"We have to keep it," Robyn said. "I promised." The look she had exchanged with Bridger meant something. But who knew if they could ever find him again? Or how long it might take? "Do you think Bridger is part of the rebellion?" she said.

Robyn felt a strange tug deep in her gut, a strong desire to find Bridger, as if following him could actually lead her home. She remembered the woman, Nyna Campbell, and the words she had shouted out. *Breath, blood, bone.* The same words etched on Dad's hologram sphere.

"Earlier, you said we would disappear if we didn't escape," Robyn said. "Where did you think we would disappear to?"

"Rumor is, there are many jails and facilities around the city. Different security levels. Sherwood Jail is a temporary holding cell. Low security." She grinned. "Obviously."

"So, they must be taking Nyna Campbell to one of these places." To be disappeared, perhaps. Disappeared, like Robyn's parents? The tugging feeling grew deeper—the sense these things must all be connected. Were her parents a part of this new rebellion?

Laurel shrugged. "Possibly."

The afternoon light was waning quickly. Robyn worried about what might happen when the sun went down. "It's getting late. We should get . . ." the word that came to mind again was *home*. Suddenly the crowds and the MPs and even jail seemed less scary than the great unknown.

"Where can we go? Where do you live?" she asked Laurel, although it seemed like the girl might be homeless.

"Oh, there's tons of places to sleep when the weather is nice," Laurel said.

"We can't stay in Sherwood," Robyn said.

"There's nowhere else to go," Laurel said.

"We're wanted in Sherwood. Maybe our best bet is to go back to Castle District. Maybe"—she put all of her hope into her voice—"my parents have returned, and they can help us. Maybe it's all a misunderstanding." Laurel looked skeptical, but Robyn couldn't think what else to do, except try to get home.

"Go through the woods?" Laurel asked. "Are you serious? You know they're patrolling all the paths, right?"

"I'm going home," Robyn said, in a burst of desperation. "You can come, or not." Robyn liked having Laurel with her. She didn't want to make the long journey alone again. She added, "Either my parents will be back and everything will be fine, or . . . or the house will be empty. There's food and clothes and beds and everything. We can just stay there."

Laurel's eyes brightened over Robyn's offer, but she chewed her lip. "The woods are too dangerous."

A pair of MPs strolled past the mouth of the alley. The girls froze, hoping to go unnoticed. As they passed, Robyn said, "It's looking pretty dangerous here, too."

# ≪CHAPTER SIXTEEN≫

## *Hope*

Nyna Campbell dragged herself to a sitting position on the bandstand. "Why don't you just kill me now?" the prisoner managed to say. Her teeth stayed clenched in pain.

Sheriff Mallet smiled. A smile so slick it almost passed for friendly. "I'm not going to kill you, Nyna."

The prisoner shivered at the sound of her name on the enemy's lips. "I don't believe you."

"Death is quick. And finite," Mallet said. "After all you've done, how can I let you go so easily?"

The prisoner's eyes narrowed. Each breath, a valiant struggle. She radiated a despicable sort of courage. Defiant, in and through her suffering. *How noble.*

"You're going to live, Nyna," Mallet promised. "And every few months we'll bring you out and show you to people. They'll never move on. They'll never forget." She paused for a slow breath. "Your friends will waste time searching for you. Waste energy worrying about what has become of you."

The prisoner's gaze flickered out over the crowd. Missing someone, perhaps. Or imagining being missed.

"Preserving hope where there is no hope is draining," Mallet informed her. "The rebellion will wither and die. Unlike you."

The young woman's attention snapped upward.

"You see?" Mallet smiled again. "It's in your eyes. The weight of the knowledge that you might survive." She grabbed hold of Nyna's bruised forearm and squeezed.

The prisoner cringed.

"Ah. The pain is worse now, isn't it? Now that the end is not in sight."

"I gave myself and gladly," Nyna insisted. She raised her bound hands to her heart. "You cannot kill this fire."

Mallet called the MPs forward. The prisoner's faith in her people would have been admirable, if it wasn't so misguided. Mallet knew she had spoken the truth. Every captured rebel, imprisoned alive, was a drain on the rebellion. Mallet intended to pluck their hopes bare, one by one.

Once you let go of hope, you could let go of anything.

# ≪CHAPTER SEVENTEEN≫

## *The Stair in the Woods*

"We have to get going," Robyn said. But when she tried to lift Bridger's pack again, she groaned with effort. The bag definitely was not designed for someone of her size. "It's a long walk back to Castle District. I don't think I can carry this all the way."

The girls moved farther into the alley. "Let's see what's in it," Laurel said. Robyn unzipped the pack. Smelly, preworn clothing spilled out. Robyn wrinkled her nose at the stench, but Laurel took it in stride. She tweezed things out of the pack with dainty fingers.

"Clothes. Clothes. Soap. Fork. Wow. Nice cooking pan." She turned the small saucepan over in her hands. Something rattled beneath the lid. A small brown box, like a jewelry box that might contain a ring or a necklace. It was round, with a hinge and a clasp, but neither Robyn nor Laurel was able to wrench it open. Beneath it in the pan was a strange ragged piece of folded silver cloth. A bandanna maybe, or just some loose fabric to protect the box thing. It was thick and gloriously silky to the touch; Robyn wanted to hold and rub it longer, except that would be too weird. She dropped it back into place.

Among the clothes were other items, a small hatchet, plastic bags in various sizes, a ball of brown twine, duct tape, a short length of real rope, a plastic tarp, matches in a plastic canister, a battery flashlight, four granola bars, a worn paperback novel, and a leather journal full of what must be Bridger's notes and writings.

"Toothbrush!" Laurel exclaimed, waving it in the air victoriously. But the bristles were all frayed and whitened. "Too bad it's used." She dropped it back in. "It's just his regular stuff," she said. "Nothing good enough to sell." She reached for the jewelry box again and tried one more time to pry it open. "Weird."

Robyn grabbed the box and tucked it back away in the pan, with the silver cloth. "Stop. We're not going to sell his things out from under him anyway." She jammed his things back into his pack as best she could. Except for the granola bars. She figured they constituted a reasonable fee for protecting his belongings. They would go stale eventually anyway. Robyn handed two to Laurel and zipped up the pack.

"Hey." Laurel scarfed one granola and pocketed the second. "We can use some of that other stuff, too."

"It's not ours," Robyn said. Laurel stared blankly at her. Robyn considered how to explain her thinking to Laurel. Yes, they had stolen clothes earlier. Yes, she had taken the granolas just now. But Bridger clearly had nothing; Robyn didn't want to make it worse. "Is there someplace we can hide this backpack?" she asked.

"Yeah, but we need the *stuff*," Laurel said. "Get out the rope. And the biggest plastic bag."

Robyn did, as Laurel proceeded to unveil an ingenious hiding spot. Along the curb in the alley was a sewer grate, which Laurel pried up using a piece of metal pipe someone had discarded near a Dumpster. She fit the garbage bag over the backpack like a sleeve and poked a hole in the top just big enough to squeeze the handle loop through. She tied the rope to the backpack loop, and the other end to one of the bars on the sewer grate. Robyn gasped as Laurel pushed the backpack into the sewer hole. It tumbled out of sight, but its weight yanked the sewer grate back into place, leaving the pack dangling inside the sewer drain. All that was visible was the rope knot on the sewer grate, and who would notice something like that, in a deserted alley near a Dumpster?

"Brilliant," Robyn told Laurel, who smiled.

"Oh, I have things hidden all over Sherwood," she said cheerfully. "It's not that hard to live here once you learn a few tricks."

But Robyn wanted to go home. So Laurel led the way through the neighborhood, favoring alleys and more deserted streets. They tiptoed calmly through the streets as if they weren't on the run.

When they reached the woods, the girls traded places, with Robyn taking the lead. They skirted along the edge of the forest until they were far from the main trails and hopefully out of sight of any guards, entering the woods in an unmarked place. Robyn knew the general direction of home, but the sun was setting, and the shadows in the forest changed with each step.

"Faster now," Laurel whispered, as Robyn eased her way beneath the pine canopy, looking for human shapes among the tree trunks. "They'll be patrolling."

The two girls raced among the trees. Robyn's eyes and ears remained alert for any sound or sign of other motion in the forest. She glanced back occasionally, and each time Laurel was right on her heels, looking barely winded. The girl could run.

"Wait," Laurel said suddenly. Robyn turned to find her rummaging in the brush. "Oh, never mind. I thought I saw some bitterstalk," Laurel said, sounding disappointed.

"*Eww*," Robyn said. "You like that stuff?" The grasslike weed tasted worse than licorice, but some people loved it. Her dad did.

"It's not it anyway," Laurel said. "We can go."

Robyn looked to the sky. There was no way they'd make it before dark. As she lowered her gaze toward the path again, Robyn spotted an arrow-shaped carving in the bark of a tree. Her footsteps faltered. The arrow pointed up and to the right. She followed the line of the point and on another tree there was another arrow!

"Look," she pointed out the pattern to Laurel, and the girls began to follow the path of the arrows. It led into deeper shadows, a section of woods draped thickly in vines.

"I can't see anymore," Laurel complained. "Let's go back."

Robyn was inclined to agree. Even if there were more arrows, how could they see them?

Retreating from the dense copse of trees, the girls almost missed seeing the staircase. It was artfully disguised behind a draping of woven leaves and vines. When Robyn first caught sight of it, she thought she was seeing a mirage. She turned and grasped Laurel's arm to stop her. The circle of vines concealing the staircase rippled slightly in the faint evening breeze.

Robyn parted the draped greenery with her arms. Laurel, too, stared at the strange sight. The narrow, deep wooden planks appeared to be hand cut. They were not uniform, like the planks in each of the perfectly carved staircases in Loxley Manor. These stairs twisted and rose into the canopy of leaves. They spiraled in such a way that at first glance they would appear to be the trunk of a very wide tree, like many of the very wide trees in the Notting Wood.

Robyn knew nothing of what a strange staircase might be doing in a wood or where the stairs might lead. They had been running full speed for at least twenty minutes—what kind of place would be found so deep in the woods?

The arrows that led her here looked the same as the arrows on Dad's canvas map. The same type of arrow that Sheriff Mallet had broken. Could this place have anything to do with Dad's message to Robyn? If so, she'd have a starting point for figuring out the rest of the map!

Robyn slipped behind the vine curtain and peered up from the lower steps. She couldn't see where the stairs led. Too many leaves and branches jutted into the column. Should they climb? It might be nice to sit here awhile, just to rest, to hide beneath the careful draping of vines. She was so tired, nearly breathless, and the whole weight of the day had only strengthened her heartache. Yes, to sit for a minute, somewhat hidden, would feel good.

Robyn touched the pocket where Dad's canvas map rested. She remembered seeing something on it that looked like a DNA strand among the trees. What if it wasn't DNA; what if it was this spiral staircase?

"What do you think is up there?" Laurel breathed.

Nothing good, Robyn feared, the way the day had been going. But her curious, restless nature got the better of her. If Dad had wanted her to find this place, there must be some meaning behind it. "Let's find out."

# ≪CHAPTER EIGHTEEN≫

## *The Radio in the Corner*

The arduous climb carried Robyn and Laurel high into the treetops. Robyn clutched a thin, carved railing and pulled herself upward. Looking down, she could see the ground for only a short while before the view gave way to a carpet of leaves.

The strange stairs led to a tiny, delightful one-room cabin, high up and hidden. A few days ago Robyn would have been ecstatic to find such a place—she'd have immediately turned it into her own private tree house.

The door was but a notch in one wall, with a flap of plastic that Robyn pushed aside as she crawled in. She held the flap aside and motioned to Laurel to look inside. The small girl's eyes rounded.

There was no furniture, but a wall of shelves on the far side held a few cans, jars, and boxes of food. Laurel beelined for the rations. The remaining two walls held small, round portal-like windows, though all you could see through them were leaves and leaves and more leaves. A larger window on the ceiling opened up to the dimming sky, letting in just enough light to see around the space. There was an old-fashioned battery-powered lantern, a black plastic radio with antenna outstretched, and a pile of soft folded blankets atop an ancient wooden crate. The crate contained a muddle of miscellaneous clothing items. Screen corners were mounted in a small square on one wall. In the center of the floor lay a braided-rag rug.

The cabin was an amazing find, but Robyn was far too exhausted and pained to feel much joy over the discovery. She felt relief, though.

It was warm, and it was quiet. Robyn flipped on the lantern. The batteries worked. The bulb cast a soft yellow light. This would be as good a place as any to hide out and wait. It crossed her mind that maybe her father had even built this place, exactly for this purpose, knowing she would go to the woods in a crisis and what she would need to find there in order to survive.

"Can we stay here?" Laurel cracked open a can of beans and steadily sucked them out.

Robyn wasn't sure. She wanted to believe Dad had built the place, but there was nothing to indicate his presence. No note, no clue. Just the few stockpiled provisions. Dad would have left something more, she was sure.

"We can stay long enough to eat, anyway," Robyn agreed.

Robyn joined Laurel at the shelves of food and selected a can of peaches. She drank the syrup and ate the slippery fruit. She pulled a blanket off the pile and wrapped it around her shoulders to ward off the evening chill. She picked up the old radio—it was so old it had a crank handle to power it!—and fiddled with it.

Robyn knew what it was only because Dad had a radio similar to this one. He and Robyn took it apart and rebuilt it once, on a Saturday, just for fun. She knew how it worked. When you turned it on, there was supposed to be static, unless someone was broadcasting. But when she flipped the power switch on this one, nothing happened.

Robyn took the fork she'd used to eat the peaches and unscrewed the back of the radio, tinkering to see what might be wrong. Not that it would do any good. No one used radio waves to broadcast anymore. But it felt nice to do something with her hands. Something familiar. Something of home. She fiddled with the radio for a while as Laurel sat across the room quietly scarfing canned goods.

Out the windows, the trees had grown quite dark. Robyn was about to tell Laurel they could stay the night, when the space between the screen corners began to glow.

"See," Laurel said glumly, "it's everywhere. The message plays on all the screens in Sherwood." "ATTENTION, CITIZENS OF NOTT CITY. A word from Royal Governor Ignomus Crown."

Then Crown's face came on. "The glorious dawn of our new regime continues. From this day forward, I—and I alone—am the leader of this city. The events of the last twenty-four hours may seem shocking to some of you."

Robyn grunted. "You think?"

"My fellow citizens, I urge you to place your trust in me. You will soon see that with the restructuring of Parliament, I have all of our best interests at heart."

"Restructuring of Parliament?" Robyn echoed. *That's still what we're calling it?*

"The Nott City Police Department and the Nott City Armed Forces have been joined into one unified military police force. As your former police commissioner, I can assure you that this union will best serve the people."

The background noise changed to the sound of many boots marching and many voices chanting. Robyn wondered if right about now the people in the jail were also seeing this video clip of the military police marching in formation. Robyn herself had seen enough of the MPs up close and personal.

"Thanks to our new military police force, Nott City will be safe and secure." A ratcheting round of gunfire, probably meant as emphasis, belied this claim. Laurel flinched as if the tree house was under attack.

"Our borders will be closely monitored. The Notting Wood, once a haven to thieves and bandits—those who have attempted to live off the land rather than participate in our booming economy—remains closed to the public. These changes are for your security and well-being. As ever, I remain your faithful governor."

"Stay tuned for further developments in this exciting time. All hail, Nott City!" Crown's announcer concluded.

The screen glowed for a few moments longer, then sputtered to silence. The small cabin grew ominously quiet.

"Things are going to get bad," Laurel whispered. "Very, very bad."

Robyn shivered, feeling exactly the same. All the more reason she wanted to get back home as soon as possible. "Look, let's sleep here tonight, so we don't have to walk in the dark, and then as soon as it's light again—"

". . . most recent announcement is no surprise to anyone . . ." Speech fragments, in a woman's voice, drifted out of the radio. Robyn had been absentmindedly fiddling with the tuning dial but not expecting anything to happen. She tuned back to the voice.

". . . remind them, Sherwood, we won't give up without a fight. This is Nessa Croft. Signing off. Zero six thirty."

"Cool." Laurel beamed. "I've never actually heard her. Is that a radio? Can I turn the handle, too?"

Robyn nodded, handing it over. "Who uses radio anymore?" she mused.

"No one, I think." Laurel cranked the radio enthusiastically. "Except Nessa Croft. She—"

*Thump.*

*Thump.*

*Thump.*

Laurel's explanation was interrupted by a soft, steady tread of footsteps on the stairs. Someone was coming.

Robyn and Laurel glanced at each other in alarm. They were trapped!

## ≪CHAPTER NINETEEN≫

# *The Boy in the Tree House*

The boy who entered the tree house jumped about a mile when he saw Robyn and Laurel standing there. His eyes popped open wide. He looked at least as startled to see them as they were frightened to see him.

"Um, hi," he said. Robyn thought that quite a weak opening on his part, which added to her optimism.

Laurel, on the other hand, spooked like a prodded animal. She emitted a tiny shriek, then darted past the boy in a daring escape attempt that went a little too well. She threw her arms out to push him out of her way, but he willingly stepped aside, so all her momentum carried her out the door and—based on the thumping—sent her tumbling down the spiral stairs.

Robyn cringed.

"No, don't go," the boy called. "Please."

Robyn stayed. Laurel's fleet footsteps sounded like miniature thunder, fading in the distance.

"Who are you?" Robyn demanded, indignant. As if the cabin had actually become hers the moment she discovered it, and thus the boy had been caught trespassing.

The boy was well dressed, in a pair of fitted jeans and a slim suede vest over a dark green shirt. The boots on his feet were mud caked, but quality. He was short and lanky. Sandy blond and smiling. Perhaps a year or so older than Robyn. Draped over his arm was a very odd-looking cloth that appeared to be woven of sticks and branches.

"I'm just a guy in a tree house," he answered. "Who are you?"

Robyn didn't know quite what to make of that. She stood tall and replied, "We thought it was abandoned. We—it's been a while since we ate."

The boy dumped the sticks in a pile and went to the shelves and took down two new cans. He handed them to Robyn. She took one in each hand. Something was better than nothing. If she could even catch up with Laurel at this point.

"Eat all you want," the boy said.

"Well, thanks." Robyn moved toward the door.

"You don't have to go," he said. He was still smiling. Friendly green eyes twinkled beneath the wavy, flopping locks of hair on his forehead. "I wouldn't mind the company."

For the first time, Robyn felt wary. "Who are you?" she repeated.

"Call me Key," he said.

Key was clearly older, but Robyn was nearly as tall.

"Robyn."

"Go get your friend, Robyn. It's safe here."

Key seemed nice enough. Nonthreatening. Robyn ducked back through the flap, wondering where to begin looking for Laurel . . . but she was right there. Crouched behind the door flap, fists clenched around a long, broken stick that was thicker than any one of her limbs. She had it raised up like a bat, a fierce expression on her face.

"Hi," Robyn said. Her lips spun into a smile.

"Hi," Laurel whispered. "Are you okay?"

"Yeah." Robyn showed her the cans of food. "I thought you left."

Laurel lowered the stick. She shook her head. "I never had a friend before," she said. "I like it."

Robyn motioned the girl close and hugged her. It was a bit awkward, their arms wrapping amid the cans Robyn held and Laurel's unwieldy bat branch. But the little girl rested her forehead on Robyn's shoulder and sighed softly. "So let's stick together," Robyn said. She was pleased that Laurel hadn't wanted to leave her behind.

"Are we staying?" Laurel asked, still leaning into Robyn.

"Yeah," she answered. "I don't think he's going to hurt us. Two against one, okay?"

Laurel nodded. Robyn released her and stepped back inside the tree house flap. "Key, this is Laurel. Laurel, Key."

"Hi," Key said.

Laurel, seeming suddenly very comfortable, strolled across the room and selected another can of food off the shelf. She snapped it open by the tab and began eating with her fingers.

From a small box behind him, Key extracted a metal fork and handed it to the girl. "Here."

Laurel folded the fork in her hand and, without missing a beat, continued shoveling food into her mouth.

Robyn smiled slightly. At least she'd done one thing right so far today. "We're just going to eat, and then we'll be on our way."

"No trouble," Key said. He moved closer to Robyn, offering her a fork as well.

She cracked one of the cans in her hand. More peaches. Her fingers brushed against Key's as she took the utensil. Was it her imagination, or was he moving closer still?

"How did you find this place?" she asked.

"Probably same as you. Followed the signs."

"What do the arrows mean?" Robyn asked.

"They point the way," Key said simply. He paused. "This is the kind of place you don't find unless you're supposed to."

He was definitely closer. She concentrated on the fruit, but she could feel him near. He brushed hair out of his eyes and blew out a small breath.

"What's the deal with the radio thing?" Robyn commented. "That's weird."

Key frowned. "I know. It's totally busted. I'm trying to find another one. I need to know what's happening."

"I fixed it," Robyn said. "I meant, what's the deal with Nessa Croft?"

Key leaned forward. "What? You heard her broadcast? What did she say?"

"Didn't really hear much." Robyn related the small snippet they'd caught.

"Yeah. That's great. Perfect." He seemed really excited, like those few words meant something to him. "Zero six thirty. I can't believe it. Thank you."

"I can't believe any of this is happening," Robyn admitted. "I don't know what we're going to do." For a second, she thought that Key was going to reach out and hug her. So close he seemed. But when she raised her head, he stepped back again.

"You can eat here," Key said. "You can even stay here."

"How do we know we can trust you?" Robyn said. An impulsive comment. Perhaps reckless.

Key's green eyes sparkled. "You don't. That's half the fun."

But strangely, Robyn wanted to trust him; she considered his kindness to Laurel, the look in his eye. In the last day and a half she'd seen plenty of things that had made her fearful. Key was not one of them.

"We'll stay," she said. "For now."

# ≪CHAPTER TWENTY≫

## *A Ragtag Band of Outlaws*

It had been an eventful twenty-four hours. Two missing parents, two narrow escapes, two shoplifting excursions, a Wanted poster, more time in the woods than she'd ever thought possible, a mysterious tree house, and a semipublic shower. Robyn was beyond exhausted, yet she huddled under the blanket for hours, unable to sleep.

Robyn lay on Key's sleeping pallet with Laurel curled beside her, tucked safe between Robyn and the tree house wall. The smaller girl's face looked calm and innocent in sleep. Robyn wished her good dreams, a respite from the quiet storm that rumbled behind her waking eyes.

Key sat leaning against the tree house wall across from them, arms folded over his chest and legs crossed at the ankles. Robyn stared up at the stocked shelves above him. The snacks and provisions in the cabin might last another day or two, but no longer. Robyn hoped they wouldn't need to.

Late into the night, like clockwork, the screen corners lit up from time to time, and Crown's stern voice shared another bulletin with the citizens of Nott City. Each time he revisited the new strange horrors, it all felt a little deeper. More real.

Concrete walls were being built between the districts, with monitored checkpoints for crossing in between.

The Notting Wood, once public land, had been declared private government property. Citizens from most counties—all but the Castle District, it seemed—were not to enter the woods anymore without permission.

Crown's desire to crush all rebellion was taking a hard toll on Sherwood.

Everything—*everything*—was going to change.

Robyn was too numb to feel any additional fear. She couldn't even comprehend what all of these changes meant for Nott City.

Robyn stared at the shelves. She stared at the annoying screen space. Her mind clicked around the problems at hand. Her parents had not come for her, despite her deepest hope. She now knew they might never come, though she still didn't want to believe it.

Across the room, Key sat wakeful, gazing through the small window at the leaves, the sky, the moon. She could tell by the soft, studious expression on his face that he was trying to read the moon. Her father used to get that very same look on his face, late in the night, from the moon porch on the roof of Loxley Manor.

"What does it say?" she whispered.

Key's attention shifted to her. "Nothing," he answered. "At least, I don't know."

"Oh." Key was older, and seemed to know about things. Robyn had hoped he might understand more than she did.

"It's okay to fall asleep," he says.

Robyn sat up in the darkness. "I can't."

"I was kidding before," Key admitted. "You can trust me."

"How do we know you won't sneak out the second we're asleep and turn us in?"

"The woods are off-limits to everyone," he says. "In case you hadn't noticed, I'm an outlaw, too."

Robyn had noticed. She'd wondered, in fact, how Key could seem so calm in the face of everything. He moved around the tree house with familiarity. Whatever had sent him running to live in the woods must not have happened recently. "I—"

The screen snapped on again. Key groaned and covered his ears. Laurel's tiny frame twitched under the blanket, but she didn't wake.

"If we put on a movie or a show, would it block these messages?" Robyn asked.

Key shook his head. "No, I've tried. Crown's signal overrides whatever you're watching."

"Why is he doing this?" Robyn asked. The segments now played on a loop, repeating themselves. The same information, hour after hour. Though it had all seemed new at first, apparently there were only six original reports. Now everything was a rerun.

"Intimidation. He wants to remind everyone that he's in charge. Everything happens on his terms now." Key sounded sure, and it made enough sense that Robyn believed him.

"He must be a horrible person," she said.

"Understatement," Key agreed.

Robyn remembered Crown a bit better now. He had offered her candy once, at a party a long time ago, before he was elected governor. A chewy caramel-nut bar that didn't happen to be among Robyn's favorites. If she had liked the candy, things might have gone differently. As it was, Robyn remembered, she merely glanced at the slender bar in his hand, then looked him square in the eye and said, "I don't take candy from strangers."

"I'm not a stranger," he answered.

"How can I be sure of that?" she told him. "You seem strange enough to me."

Crown laughed. "I'm a colleague of your father's."

"How do you know who my father is?" Robyn asked him.

She didn't like the cold smile she received in return. "He stands out in a room like this, don't you think?" Crown said.

*Dad stands out in every room*, Robyn thought. He's handsome and smart, not to mention a well-liked member of Parliament. But she knew enough to know that Crown didn't mean those things. He was referring to Dad's dark skin.

"Yes, he's very well-known," Robyn answered, to avoid being impolite. She couldn't help adding, "Which is why some people who are strangers to me think they are not."

Robyn especially remembered Crown's incisive stare following that comment. "Very well," Crown said. He ripped the candy wrapper off and bit into it himself, right in front of her. "See? Perfectly safe."

But Crown had not made Robyn feel perfectly safe. Then or now.

"Yes, he's horrible," she whispered. She tried to push his leering grin out of her mind. Tried to picture Dad, instead. His wide brown face and big smile that lit up the room. He would have loved Key's tree house. Dad was always looking for an adventure—Robyn got her restless bug from him, Mom liked to say. Lately Parliament had been enough of an adventure, though, and Dad had been concerned about all manner of things.

Dad had known something was brewing, Robyn now realized, but Dad acting weird hadn't seemed like such a big deal a few days ago. Everything with Dad was either very serious or very silly. If Dad was laughing, everyone was laughing. His laugh was loud, bursting and deep.

Mom, on the other hand, rarely laughed out loud, but she constantly smiled. She had a soft, strong way about her that made her good at caring for people and for plants. Mom loved working in the garden, which was good because in other ways she was very proper and prim. Gardening meant Mom didn't mind dirt, and Robyn was almost always getting herself dirty. Somehow Mom could get elbow-deep in her garden and be able to just brush herself off afterward, whereas Robyn could take a simple walk through the lawn and come back looking like she'd been through a tornado. They used to smile about it together.

Robyn's heart welled up. Would she ever hear Mom say, *There's my smudged-up kiddo*, again? Or hug her and feel the warmth of the white stone pendant she always wore around her neck? When Robyn was very small, sitting on Mom's lap, she would play with the pendant. If you closed it in your hand, it would grow warm. When Robyn asked why, Mom always said, *Because it's special.*

It had been so easy to think that things would always just be fine. Robyn and Mom had always teased Dad for his paranoid ways. Now Robyn wished she'd paid more attention to Dad's lessons and drills, even if they seemed a little overboard. A simple alarm system wasn't enough for her dad; he put in the security cameras because he wanted to be able to see if anyone came in and out of the house. He was more afraid of spies than of burglars . . .

Robyn sat bolt upright again.

"What?" Key said, startled. "What is it?"

Cameras! The security cameras in Loxley Manor must have captured Crown's men breaking in. The video would show what happened to her parents, too. Robyn had to get back to the house and view them. Then she would know for sure—did they somehow get away, like she did?

"Nothing, sorry," Robyn told Key. He didn't need to know what she was thinking about. Robyn lay back down, though her heart threatened to pound its way out of her chest. She closed her eyes and tried to sleep. She felt herself drifting almost immediately this time. It helped, knowing what she had to do tomorrow. No matter what, she was determined to make it back to Loxley Manor and find out what had happened to her parents. They could still be alive—no, they had to be! Robyn would find them, and as soon as she did, things could go back to the way they should be.

## ≪CHAPTER TWENTY-ONE≫

# *Home, Sweet . . . Barracks?*

In the morning, while Key slept, Robyn quietly shared her plan with Laurel. "I'm going home," she told her. "Like I planned. I don't know how long I'll be gone, but—"

"I'm coming with you," Laurel said, frowning as if this was obvious.

"What?" Robyn said. It hadn't occurred to her that the girl would still want to come. Robyn didn't think the idea of going to Castle District would appeal to Laurel as much, now that they had found this excellent tree house.

"You think I'm going to stay here?" Laurel whispered, hitching her chin toward Key. "With HIM?"

"Well, I didn't think—"

"And," Laurel said, tapping a small foot indignantly. "Do you really think I'm going to let you do something crazy like that all alone?"

Robyn smiled, unexpectedly happy and relieved. "It's a long walk," she said. "We'd better get going."

≫⟶

The walk home didn't take nearly as long in the daylight—largely because Robyn didn't have to feel her way along. Instead the girls jogged easily through the woods, leaping stumps and dodging vines and finally relying on a tried-and-true trail.

When they emerged onto the grass, Robyn said, "There it is. We made it."

"Whoa." Laurel's eyes popped open wide at the sight of the enormous home. "You live here?"

Running across the lawn toward Loxley Manor, Robyn's heart leaped into her throat. She couldn't contain the blossom of hope that had bloomed inside her. The hope that her parents might be inside . . .

But the house was dark. The back door, locked. Robyn wasn't surprised at that. Her parents usually kept it locked unless one of them was out in the yard or the garden. What surprised her was that the locked door failed to open, even when she touched the coded pad beside the door. It should've recognized her prints and let her into the house.

"That's strange," she murmured. So instead Robyn led Laurel to the familiar spot beneath her window.

Laurel glanced up at the sheer white wall. "You think we can climb that?" she whispered.

"I do it all the time," Robyn said, shimmying up a few feet. She glanced back. Laurel's nimble toes curled around the corner of a stone, ready to go.

They climbed inside. With one glance at the state of her bedroom, the excited flutter in Robyn's throat became a lump too hard to swallow. Robyn's canopy bed had been pulled down. Not just the ruffled canopy—the whole bed was gone. In its place stood four metal bunk beds, space enough to sleep eight men. All her old toys and belongings were piled in a corner.

"Which bed is yours?" Laurel asked. "And where are all the other kids?"

Robyn shook her head, disgusted. "This is *my* room. Someone took away my things." She marched into the other half of her bedroom suite, her playroom.

Additional bunks lined the room. Her circuit board still sat atop the bookcase, but all the wires she'd spent hours carefully arranging around the room now coiled haphazardly on top of it.

Laurel pointed to a cardboard box on the foot of one bunk. The open box flaps revealed a pile of mottled brown uniforms, brand new and wrapped in plastic. Nott City Military Police–issue camouflage.

The MPs had taken over her house!

Robyn's pulse surged in outrage. She ran into the hallway, heedless of the fact that she should take care not to be noticed.

In her parents' bedroom, she found the same. Twelve bunks, for the room was much larger.

Robyn couldn't help herself. She dashed into the adjoined master bathrooms. They were full of towels, some neatly folded, some draped and damp. The counters were piled with massive shampoo bottles, aerosol shaving cream canisters, and wrapped stacks of soap. Nothing familiar remained. Not even a whiff of her mother's perfume.

Robyn dropped to her knees on the rug—even the rug was new, a locker-room-style rubber mat, with hair tangled beneath its woven rings. Gross.

Robyn lunged toward the toilet and heaved.

"*Shh*," Laurel whispered from the doorway. "Someone could be here."

Robyn shot her a wry glance. "I'll try to keep it down next time." She wiped her mouth with a piece of industrial toilet paper and reached for the flush lever.

"No!" Laurel blurted, grasping Robyn's wrist. She was right. Better to take the chance of someone seeing the vomit later than someone downstairs hearing the flush right now.

"Good call," Robyn said. She shook her head as she stood up. She used to think she was all kinds of stealthy, running away and sneaking around. Doing stuff her parents didn't know about. The worst thing that could've happened back then, if she got caught, was some length of grounding or maybe extra chores. Real sneaking around, with deadly consequences, well, that was still pretty new.

Robyn and Laurel tiptoed down the hall to the second-floor security room. The room had no windows, but Robyn had never seen it this dark. The entire system was shut off. Every screen was blank. Maybe if you had a house full of the baddest bad guys, you didn't worry about other bad guys breaking in.

Her father had worried about it. In fact, Robyn wondered what had happened the other night, why her father hadn't been able to hear the alarm and stop the intruders. Then a new thought slipped in, cold as ice against her skin. Robyn herself had shut off the second-floor alarm system that night, so she could get outside. What if . . . what if that was how the intruders got in undetected?

Robyn powered the system on. The lights flicked on in sequence. Now it looked familiar. Laurel nervously kept watch from the doorway as the machines buzzed and hummed to life. If anyone came down the hall right now, they'd be trapped.

"Close the door," Robyn suggested. She sat in the large chair and fiddled with the controls. "Obviously they're not using this room."

Laurel did as asked, then came and perched on the arm of Robyn's chair. They stared at the monitors. The live image came up immediately. "You can see all the entrances," Laurel observed. "That's a lot of doors."

There were eight monitors altogether, each with a split screen. Each showed two views of the same entrance: an inside angle and an outside one. Outside the driveway gate and inside the driveway gate. The front door, the back door that led to the porch, the back door from the kitchen to the garden, both garage doors, the side door, and even the door to the moon porch on the roof.

Robyn knew which buttons to push. She had watched her father do this before. She got caught sneaking out through the kitchen one night, and Dad had shown her the footage to prove that he would know if she ever sneaked out of the house again. That was when she had started using her window.

Robyn cued up the recordings to midnight, two nights ago. She took a deep breath and pressed Play. Then she used the little roller ball on the keyboard to advance the frames faster than real-time.

"There," Laurel said, pointing at a flash of movement at the front gate. Robyn released the ball and let the video play normally. Her heart raced and the queasiness returned. She knew she had to see, but here and now, she didn't want to.

A truck drove up to the gate. It was a small mover's or delivery truck. Something like that. It parked outside. Four darkly dressed men leaped off the runners and two more came out of the cab, leaving the doors ajar. They scaled the high gate—just jumped right over it with moves that would have impressed Robyn if she wasn't occupied with hating them for what they were coming to do. They breached the front door and disappeared into the house.

"They came in the first floor," Robyn commented, relieved. She was positive she hadn't shut off the first-floor alarm. Maybe it had gone off. These cameras did not capture sound. Maybe Dad heard it and tried to respond. Maybe that was why her parents ended up in the kitchen.

Long tense seconds passed.

"There he is!" Robyn slammed her hand against the side of the monitor. Dad was making a run for the kitchen door.

# ◄CHAPTER TWENTY-TWO►

## *A Message in Blood*

Robyn watched in horror as Dad, clad only in boxers and his second-favorite robe, plunged toward the kitchen door. His fingers snapped the door lock open, but before he could reach for the knob one of the men grabbed him. He threw his arms around Dad and pointed a blade at his throat. Dad fought anyway. He elbowed the man and tried to duck loose. The pair grappled their way backward into the kitchen, out of sight.

Robyn stifled a scream, along with the urge to run downstairs and try to save him.

The camera angle allowed only a partial view of the kitchen floor. Her father's feet thrashed into view two more times.

Then his arm lolled into view. It smacked against the tile, bloodied fingers twitching. Robyn slammed her eyes shut. She couldn't bear to watch it.

"No, look. He's drawing something," Laurel said, nudging her.

Robyn squinted at the screen again. Dad's hand moved in a deliberate pattern. "*L-I-V-E*," she read. "*Live.*"

"He wants to live?" Laurel said.

The fingers twitched again, then fell still. "Is that a *C*?" Robyn couldn't tell.

Laurel shrugged, looking nervous.

"*C* . . . or *O* . . . or *G*," Robyn said. "*Q* maybe?"

A large booted foot stepped onto the letters, smearing them beyond recognition. Then it disappeared and that screen remained blank, except for the blood smear, and the seeping edge of the puddle Robyn would find upon her return.

Motion shifted to the front-door cameras. The men lugged Dad outside. One carried him under the shoulders, the other held his ankles. Dad's body arced between them, completely limp, head lolled against his chest. The pale blue bathrobe wound around him awkwardly, soaked with blood.

Robyn let out a strangled, choking cry.

"Are you going to throw up again?" Laurel asked. She glanced around, as if looking for a receptacle.

"No," Robyn said, although she wasn't too sure.

A third man followed shortly, carrying Robyn's mother.

"She's moving," Laurel exclaimed. "Doesn't it look like she's moving?"

Robyn scrolled back. Sure enough. The man had her mother draped over his shoulder like a sack of potatoes, but her arms did not hang limp at his back. She was reaching, stirring . . . and then they passed out of sight.

Robyn had seen enough. She hit a button, ending the playback.

The cameras blinked and displayed a large van pulling into the driveway. At the same time, a line of men in MP uniforms entered through the front door. "This is when they came back in the morning?" Laurel asked, puzzled. The footage had clearly been shot in daylight.

"No," Robyn said, her voice rising. "That's the live feed."

# ≪CHAPTER TWENTY-THREE≫

## *The Mystery of the Live Oak*

There was no way of knowing how many men had already come inside. Laurel cracked open the door, and the sounds of the MPs' laughter and chatter wafted up the stairwell.

The girls looked at each other. So much for their hopes of food and rest.

"Run for it," Robyn suggested. After seeing that footage, she felt certain the men downstairs would stop at nothing to subdue and detain them, if not kill them outright.

Laurel didn't need to be told twice. She sprinted to Robyn's room and in one smooth move, vaulted over the dresser and drove herself feetfirst out the window.

Robyn raced into her playroom and grabbed her circuit board. She hugged it to her chest—it was coming with her this time. But there was no bag to put it in. How could she get it down the wall? The board was practically indestructible, but she couldn't just throw it out the window. Not after what had happened to the hologram.

Robyn responded to a sudden impulse and lunged for the box of MP uniforms on the bed. There were somewhere around a dozen plastic packages in the box. She tore a slit in one with her fingernail, then shoved the circuit board inside, slipping it between the folded shirt and pants. It barely fit, but it would do. She grabbed two more uniforms and stacked them as padding above and beneath it, then wrapped the wires around to somewhat hold things together. She lobbed the parcel gently out the window, startling Laurel amid her descent. It landed in the grass with a soft thump.

Robyn lowered herself out the window, and by the time she reached the ground, Laurel had taken her cue and scooped up the unwieldy package. Robyn gathered stray wires from around Laurel's knees as they darted for safety.

Robyn breathed a sigh of relief once they reached the cover of trees. It didn't seem they had been noticed. Looking back at the manor house, all seemed calm and still. It looked . . . normal. Robyn's heart panged with sorrow. Deep inside, she had thought by coming home, everything that had happened might be erased. That they would have walked in the kitchen door and Mom would be there, worried and angry and relieved.

Robyn grabbed the package with the circuit board and took a moment to properly tuck in the wires. She gave Laurel the other two uniforms to carry. They might come in handy later.

"Let's get out of here," Laurel said, tugging Robyn's arm. She dashed along the path. They raced across the ring of live oaks, into the untamed woods.

*Wait!*

Robyn stopped running.

Her father's message in blood had to mean something. It had to be a message to her, something he hoped she would see. A clue.

Yards ahead, Laurel stopped, too. "What is it?" she called, in what amounted to a loud whisper.

"We have to go back," Robyn said.

"No way," Laurel answered.

"He wasn't writing *live*, as in *I want to live*," Robyn said. She understood the message now. The note was much more important. "He was writing *live*, as in *live oak*."

Her father had told her time and again: *Go to the live oak. I will find you.*

Robyn and Laurel crept back through the woods to the edge of the Loxley property. "Are these all live oaks?" Laurel asked, when they reached the ring of ancient trees.

"Yes, but there's one in particular," Robyn said. "Our favorite."

She led Laurel to the largest, oldest tree. They climbed on the live oak's sprawling roots. Robyn hugged the trunk. When Laurel did the same on the opposite side, their hands did not touch.

Robyn pressed her ear to the bark. *Can you guess how old the live oak is? A tree like this holds many secrets.*

*What secrets did the tree hold?* Robyn now wondered. "Why did he want me to come here?" she said aloud. This was where he was to meet her if anything bad happened.

Maybe the message was just a reminder. But he must have known the men in the house were ruthless. He must have known that he . . . Robyn swallowed hard . . . might not survive to meet her. But he wrote *"LIVE O"* anyway.

"There must be something to find," Laurel said. "It was a clue to something."

Robyn agreed. She grasped the lowest branch, about a foot thick, and the height of her shoulders.

"Maybe he carved a message into the trunk?" Laurel suggested. "Like the arrows?"

"I don't think he would do that," Robyn said. "He wouldn't hurt this tree." She swung up and began to climb. If Dad had left a message in the tree, it would be someplace only she was likely to look.

She climbed to her favorite seat, four levels up, in the small upward curve of a branch. She didn't see anything out of the ordinary. The leaves hid her, like always. This tree didn't even lose its leaves in the autumn, like a normal oak. All the live oaks stayed green through the winter. It was part of their beauty.

*What are you doing all the way up there?* Robyn climbed down and around, to the place where Dad sat when they climbed together. *Ah, no, this is the spot,* he'd say. *I'm lucky that you leave it for me.*

It was a lower, wider, flatter branch, more comfortable to sit on if you were very big. If you were smaller, there was a tuft of leaves sticking out of the bark that tended to hit you in the face. Robyn got a mouthful of chlorophyll now, like usual. She blew and spat, then pushed the thin branch aside with her fist. Beneath the tiny rogue branch was a knot the size of Robyn's head, caked with years of dirt, leaves, and mud. The knot had always been filled in this way, as long as Robyn could remember.

*This is the spot.* She could see Dad in her mind's eye, patting the knot as he said it.

"Get me a stick or something," she called to Laurel. Laurel picked up a handful of sticks and bark from the ground and climbed it up to Robyn. Robyn selected a thick, short stick and began gouging at the layers of caked-in, sun-dried mud. When that stick snapped, she used a piece of bark to scoop.

The excavation revealed a small cavity within the knot-hole. In the cavity rested a plastic sandwich bag, muddied brown, but obvious because all the dirt in the world couldn't mask that colorful zipper.

"Whoa," said Laurel. "Buried treasure?"

A gift from Dad. Robyn popped open the bag with a quick tug. Three things fell out into her hands: a Sherwood College key ring with two keys, a folded note, and a heavy black stone on a chain.

Laurel plucked the keys right out of her hand and studied them, but the stone grabbed Robyn's attention first. It was shaped like a crescent moon and black as night, with not a blemish or streak apparent anywhere. The polished surface reflected the silhouette of her face. Robyn didn't know much about jewelry, but she knew most stones have streaks or blemishes or flaws of some kind if you look closely, and this

stone didn't appear to. It fit comfortably in her palm, just a
little bit longer and thicker than the curve of her thumb. On
the inside curve, a wide, shallow groove ran down the center
of the stone. If you held it up like a smile, from the top it
looked like a thin-walled bowl. The attached chain was simple silver, weighty enough to handle the heft of the stone
and attached with what looked like a little silver crown.

Robyn slipped the chain around her neck. It was long
enough to fit over her head without a clasp. The black moon
dangled low on her chest.

She opened the small folded note. Robyn's chest tightened at the sight of Dad's handwriting.

Dearest Robyn,

Keep these things very close and very safe.
I intend to give them to you when you are of
age. But if you find them early . . . if something
has happened to me, or your mother . . . I'm so
sorry, my love. You are strong and brave and you
will get through anything. Do what you have to.
These things may help. I'm sorry I can't say more.

Follow your head. Follow your heart. Follow the
Moon.

Love,
Dad

Robyn hugged the small note, but nothing changed. Her father did not burst from the page to hug her in return.

"They're very regular," Laurel said, examining the keys. "One electronic door key and another that looks like the key to an old padlock or something smaller."

Robyn recognized the electronic key. "This opens the garden shed in the backyard." It had a green plastic cover on its head. Her mom had color coded all the keys in the house so that the Loxleys would always know what they unlocked, but if one was lost or stolen, no one else would be sure. The whole family had stopped carrying keys when Dad installed the biosecurity touch pads all over the property. So he must have planted these items for Robyn a while ago. Why hadn't he just given them to her? Or told her what was going on? A small surge of anger rose up in her throat. She swallowed it.

"What about the little one?" Laurel asked.

"I don't know." Robyn stared through the leaves as if she could see the open yard they'd have to cross to get to the shed. "We have to check it out," she said.

"Back toward the house?" Laurel seemed skeptical. "Are you sure?"

The key was a gift from her father. He hadn't just been paranoid about someday, someone being out to get him. He had planned ahead. Robyn tucked the black pendant inside her T-shirt.

"Come on." She climbed down the tree. Laurel followed, dropping from branch to branch like a monkey.

The girls crept along the tree line until they were directly behind the shed. The closer they got to it, the more the shed would hide them from the sight line of the house. But it was a big lawn. If even one MP was looking out the windows . . .

Robyn took a deep breath and stepped into the open.

# ≪CHAPTER TWENTY-FOUR≫

## Useful Gifts from Dad

Robyn raced out of the woods at top speed. She ran straight toward the shed and pressed herself against the back wall, the way people always did in the movies. The flattened position with hands splayed had always looked silly and overdramatic to Robyn on-screen. Here and now, she understood it. She desperately wanted to make herself as small as possible. Laurel smashed herself right up beside Robyn as they inched around the building.

The shed was about the size of a one-car garage. It had no windows, just an extra-wide set of creaky wooden doors big enough to drive a riding mower through. Unfortunately that entrance faced the house. Robyn used the key. Maybe her fingerprints would still work on the shed, but she didn't want to waste time finding out. She opened the groaning door just far enough to slide inside with Laurel.

"If they saw us, we're trapped," the smaller girl sighed.

Robyn felt trapped already. It was very black inside the shed, with no windows. *Why were there no windows?* Robyn wondered for the first time ever. There was the tiniest bit of light sneaking in through the cracks around the door, but it was barely enough to see two feet of concrete floor in front of her.

It had been a while since she came out to the shed. Months, in fact. Since Dad stopped having time for her, she had rarely come to the place where they used to tinker. She wasn't allowed to use the power tools alone, so she mostly played in her room, with her own small tool kit and her circuits. Lately the shed was mostly used by the landscapers who took care of the grounds. And it was usually daytime, so they left the doors thrown open and sunlight lit the room. *Was there even a light?*

*Yes,* Robyn remembered. One bulb, with a pull chain overhead. She felt her way forward, touching the large wheels and smooth seat of the riding mower parked in the center of things. She eased her way around it, batting her hand in the air through the middle of the room. Finally she hit the string.

The single bulb was bright. Now they could see everything. Dad's workbench and tools and the wall of trowels, spades, rakes, clippers, shovels, and brooms Mom used in the garden.

Robyn fingered the smaller key. She glanced around the room. Her eye fell on the rear wall, which had a smaller, single door in it. A door that was always locked. That must be it!

Robyn had noticed the rear padlock ages ago. *What's back there?* she'd asked Dad.

He never gave a proper answer, and he'd never let her peek inside. *Just some of my old things,* he'd said, then kissed her on the top of her head and added, *I'm hoping we'll never need them.*

Now, Robyn used the smaller key to pop open the padlock. The back room was small, only a few feet deep, but as wide as the shed. The air smelled musty and cobwebs crisscrossed the rafters.

The secret space was dominated by a green-and-black moped, balanced by a metal kickstand that looked like a pair of insect feet. The bike's body was a rich forest green, with splashes of bright green-and-black flames and lettering. The long leather seat was black, as were the wide-set handlebars.

"Whoa," Laurel said.

Robyn was thinking the same thing.

The solar panel on the console had a small yellow note taped to it, with an *F* scrawled on it. The bike was charged and ready. Dad had thought of everything.

A small cardboard box beside the bike contained a large wood-handled pocketknife and two old battery-powered cellular TexTers.

"Whoa," Laurel said again. "Do you think those things still work?"

"I don't know," Robyn turned the TexTers over in her hands. Each was small enough to close one fist around. They were thick black rectangles, with gray screens in a little banner across the top edge. They had thin metal bars on the back, for clipping the device over the edge of your belt. On the front, a tiny keyboard of raised letters and numbers.

They were funny old things; very clunky looking, compared to the small earpiece satellite phones that most people used now. Even more people used satellite-linked tablets to message each other or video call. People rarely bothered with cellular phones or TexTers at all. They had been popular back when Dad was Robyn's age.

The pocketknife looked pretty ancient as well. It wasn't even automated. You had to pull each utensil out by grabbing a groove in the edge of the metal. It had plenty of gadgets though. Screwdrivers, can opener, knives, hooks, and more. The wood handle had designs seared into it—the now-familiar arrow on one side and a design of lines and circles on the other. Robyn slid it into her pocket. Between the knife tools and the circuit-board wires, maybe now she could fix Dad's hologram . . . if she could get her hands on it again.

The bike was too great a find to leave behind. And it was a gift from her father, too. Robyn ran her hands over it, thinking. She put the TexTers in the seat cavity, along with the circuit board and the wrapped MP uniforms.

"Do you think you can drive that thing?" Laurel asked. Robyn saw in her eyes a spark of hope that they might not have to spend the rest of the afternoon and evening walking all the way back through the woods.

"Yeah," Robyn said. "My dad taught me." Not on this bike, but once, on vacation, he'd secretly taught her to drive.

She'd driven a golf cart, a moped, and a speedboat on that trip. "You need to know these things. Just don't tell your mother," he'd whispered.

Laurel ran her hand over the black bike seat. "This is so awesome," she said, and let out a breath. "We could go anywhere!"

*But where would they actually go?* Robyn wondered. The front gate would surely be locked. *Could they get to the road?* It would be best to return to Sherwood via the woods. She hoped they could find their way back to the tree house. She'd watched for landmarks along the way, but on wheels they'd have to take a slightly different route than on foot.

She pulled out Dad's map. Two paths marked there wound through the woods from Castle District to Sherwood. One of them must be the trail the girls had found to get here. Laurel looked over Robyn's shoulder as she put her finger on it and traced it to the end. Robyn thought it might be smooth enough to ride the bike on—but the girls had stumbled onto that path by accident—where did it really start and where did it end?

"What does it mean?" Laurel asked, cocking her head curiously.

"I don't really know," Robyn said. "I'm trying to figure it out." She pointed at the various symbols. "Any of this mean anything to you?"

It felt strange, sharing Dad's map with someone else, but Laurel was a friend now, after everything they'd been through in the last day and a half.

"It looks old. Like something you'd see at the museum. Why did you write on it with marker?"

"I didn't," Robyn said. "What are you talking about?"

Laurel pointed at a tiny spot on the map. "See? You can tell the difference."

She was right. Robyn slanted the map to better receive the light. Some of the markings shone differently than others. Fresher ink. A clue from Dad?

"Is that a house?" Laurel asked, pointing at a drawn-on symbol that to Robyn had looked like a fat arrow.

"Maybe," she answered. "If so, it's probably my house, don't you think?"

"Sure, why not?" Laurel mused.

Robyn grinned. If the spiral in the woods was the treehouse, and the marker-inked house was Loxley Manor, then she'd solved the map!

"Let's try this path," Robyn said, tracing the line that appeared to start closest to the house. At least they knew where to find the start of it—it dumped out just down the tree line from the Loxley property. "What do you think?"

"Yeah," Laurel said.

Together the girls pushed the moped to the front of the shed. Robyn took a deep breath. She eased the door open and poked her head out. She could see the MPs moving around inside the kitchen.

## ≪CHAPTER TWENTY-FIVE≫

# *A Daredevil Ride*

The girls stood inside the shed considering their options. If they got on the bike here and rode it right out through the door, the MPs would definitely see and hear them making their getaway. If Robyn couldn't get the thing started in time, they'd be sitting ducks.

"We could push it all the way to the woods," Laurel suggested. "It would be quieter."

"But it'll take forever." Robyn made the decision. "If we can wait to start it until we get behind the shed at least, they might not even know we took it from here. Maybe they'll think we're just joyriding, passing through."

"Okay," Laurel said. They opened the door and rolled the bike out as quickly and quietly as they could. Robyn looked over her shoulder at the house. The MPs' outlines moved about. Cooking dinner, maybe. Robyn felt a surge of anger. In *her* house.

The girls pushed the bike around the shed. Robyn straddled the seat and eased it off the kickstand. Laurel climbed on behind her. The long seat was plenty big enough for the two of them, with room to spare.

Robyn squeezed the hand brake and pushed the ignition. The bike coughed to life beneath her. Laurel's arms tightened around her waist as the jouncy engine rumble intensified. Robyn twisted the throttle again and the bike shot forward. Laurel shrieked.

"Sorry!" Robyn cried. "I learned this a while ago." She tried again, more gently. There. Now they were rolling along nicely. They plunged into the gap in the trees where the trail they had followed to get here began.

Laurel hugged Robyn's back and ducked low as they zoomed through the undergrowth. The motor buzzed and thrummed beneath them, but Robyn thought it made relatively little noise for a moped.

Robyn kept the bike on the trail. Riding on a cleared path was difficult enough; it was much too hard to go off-road over even bigger roots and brambles. According to the map, the trail dumped out in Sherwood. When they broke through the trees, the bike zoomed onto a blacktopped lot strewn with a strange maze of cardboard boxes, canvas tents, and various draperies Robyn couldn't identify. Robyn braked to avoid a collision with a pair of rainbow-striped beach chairs. She steered the bike back to the edge of the woods.

Laurel poked her head up. "Oh," she exclaimed. "Here we are."

"Where's *here?*" Robyn asked. Her father's map only detailed the wood trail. It didn't show anything beyond the marker in the clearing. It looked like a tongue of flames.

"T.C.," Laurel said matter-of-factly. Then she sighed. "But I like our tree house much better."

Robyn stared out over the sea of recyclables and realized she was looking at a collection of makeshift shelters. Heads popped up here and there, people walking among the construction.

"I stay here sometimes," Laurel continued. "Some people call it the *un*fairground, and everyone always laughs, but I don't know what that really means. We mostly just call it T.C."

An older dark-skinned man staggered out from between two refrigerator boxes and tossed himself into one of the rainbow chairs. He carried a paper bag in one hand. A thicket of coarse salt-and-pepper hair obscured most of his face.

Robyn gripped the throttle and prepared to jet off, but Laurel waved cheerfully and slid off the bike. "Hi, Chazz!"

"Who's that?" The old guy squinted. "Laurel? That you, girl?"

Laurel dashed over and plopped herself down into the other rainbow chair as if she was lying out for a day at the beach. Robyn wheeled the bike around and pushed it closer. She kicked the bike stand and went to stand by Laurel. Robyn rapidly grew uncomfortable under Chazz's intense stare.

"Chazz, this is Robyn," Laurel said. "Robyn, this is Chazz. He's the mayor of T.C."

Chazz waved a hand and severed the piercing stare. "No, no. I wish they would stop saying that. I'm retired." From the brown sack he brought out a tin of tuna and cracked it open.

"You hungry, honeys?" he asked. "I got six tins. Name your price."

"No, we're okay," Laurel chirped. "We found a whole tree—"

"Laurel," Robyn butted in. She didn't know Chazz from a hole in the wall. She wasn't about to let Laurel give away her dad's secrets to some random guy.

"Take off that beret, Robyn," Chazz said. "Make yourself comfortable." There was something about his voice that made her nervous. Take off her beret? That was a strange request. She straightened the hat instead. The tail of her braid had popped out at the neck. Robyn tucked it back inside.

"That's a good-looking bike," Chazz said. "You could get the heck outta Dodge with wheels like that. Maybe that's what you should do." His voice was edged with something, almost threatening.

He returned his attention to his sack of tuna cans. He looped his finger through the pull tab on the first one. It snapped off without opening the can. "Aw, nuts."

"Here." Robyn took Dad's knife out of her pocket. Chazz eyed the symbols on the knife's handle. Robyn could feel him watching her. She worked the opener quickly and handed him the can, then hurried the knife back into her pocket. The air now smelled faintly of fish.

With work-roughened fingers, Chazz bent the thin lid into a scoop shaped like a taco shell. "Take my advice, girl," he said quietly. "Get on that bike and just keep riding."

"Actually, we do have to be going," Robyn said. She laid a hand on Laurel's shoulder and squeezed. "Nice to meet you, Mr. Chazz."

Chazz laughed. A rich throaty howl that was ten times friendlier than his gaze. "Hoo! Just Chazz, baby girl. I ain't mister anybody," he hooted, pinching the bridge of his nose. "Heh. That's the best laugh I've had in a minute."

"Bye," Laurel said.

"You stay beautiful, sweetheart," Chazz said, patting Laurel's cheek. He seemed kind and friendly when addressing her. "Robyn," he said, in a heavier voice. "You watch your back."

## ≪CHAPTER TWENTY-SIX≫

## *All Manner of Camouflage*

Robyn couldn't decide if Chazz's words were a threat or a warning. But Laurel seemed to trust him, Laurel, who claimed to never have had a friend. Robyn knew something about going it alone, but Laurel seemed to know even more.

The girls climbed back on the bike and zipped around the cardboard city. It was quite the elaborate arrangement, really. At the other side of the lot, Robyn steered the bike between two large stone pillars bearing signs that read City Fairgrounds. Suddenly the "*un*fairground" joke made sense. She'd have to remember to explain it to Laurel later.

Riding on the road was much easier than riding in the woods. They tooled along the streets quickly and smoothly. Robyn decided she could get used to traveling this way. They passed through a deserted street, all boarded up with sheet metal. Robyn glanced up at the abandoned structure—a massive brick church that filled the entire block—the famed Nottingham Cathedral, now gone to ruin.

Robyn stopped the bike along the side of the road. Something was nagging at her. She pulled Dad's map from her pocket and looked at the marked insignia. These rectangles could be the two towers of the church! The location would be about right.

"Look, Laurel," she said. "If the spiral in the woods is the staircase, maybe this is the cathedral!"

They circled the block, looking for the door. But there was no way to get inside. The structure was boarded up tight on all sides.

"The map is too old," Robyn said. The sudden rush of hope and excitement drained away in a flash. With the hologram message incomplete, all of Dad's clues were turning out to be dead ends. Maybe none of the points on the map were what she'd guessed, after all. She needed more clues.

"Gather the Elements," Robyn mused aloud. "What are the Elements?"

"Earth, air, water," Laurel chimed in. "I know that one." She raised her pointed chin to the sky and recited:

*Gather the Elements as you will:*
*Earth to ground you, Water to fill,*
*Air to sustain, a Fire to ignite;*
*Elements gather, all to fight."*

The smaller girl smiled proudly. Robyn stared openmouthed. "Where did you hear that?"

"It's an old song," said Laurel. "Do you want me to sing it?" She paused, and frowned. "Well, I don't exactly remember how the music part goes. It's from the old moon lore."

Robyn felt a trill of certainty in her chest. So, that had to be it. "Earth, air, water, and fire."

"Earth, air, water," Laurel corrected. "I'm not sure about fire."

"It's right there in the song." *And it was in Mom's Elements painting . . .*

"Yeah, but . . . ," Laurel said, and shook her head. "I don't know. Anyway, I'm hungry. Aren't you hungry?"

They drove back beneath the trees. Riding the bike in the pine forest was not as treacherous as riding it in the woods; the ground was a soft bed of needles with few exposed roots. But Robyn had been caught here before, so she knew danger could be just around the corner. When they reached the hardwoods near the tree house, Robyn said, "Where are we going to park this thing?"

"Do you think Key's camouflage trick would work?" Laurel suggested, referring to the cape of sticks and branches he wore to move through the woods unnoticed.

"Let's give it a try," Robyn agreed. The girls parked the bike between two bushes. They plucked foliage from the forest floor and carefully built a natural tarp. Robyn's fingers braided leaf stems together easily, and Laurel turned out to be an expert weaver of bark. The bike's green-and-black coloring helped—it only needed to be disguised, not completely concealed. Before long, they had a decent shroud over the moped. When they stepped back ten feet the spot didn't attract any particular attention.

They stood beside the tree house entrance longer than they should have.

"What are you doing?" Key asked. He shed his own camouflage cloak and popped up near them.

"I don't know," Laurel said, with a big, cheesy wink at Robyn. "What do you think we're doing?" She spread her hands out, inviting Key to look around. He glanced left and right.

"I think you're giving away the hideout, standing here," he said in a tight voice.

The girls giggled. "Don't worry. We just got back," Robyn said. She clapped Key on the shoulder. "We'll tell you all about it upstairs." They climbed into the tree house.

"We forgot the camo suits," Laurel reminded Robyn.

"Oh, right," Robyn said. And her circuit board, and the TeXers. They'd left them stuffed inside the bike seat. Robyn jogged down to retrieve them. She returned to find Laurel regaling Key with a dramatized tale of their bike ride through Sherwood.

Robyn freed the circuit board and tossed down the plastic packages. "We swiped a couple of MP uniforms. Thought they might come in handy for getting in and out of the woods."

Key smiled. "You want to masquerade as MPs?"

"Better than wearing sticks on our heads," Laurel quipped.

Key's grin broadened. "That's debatable. Where'd you get all this stuff, anyway?"

"Oh," Laurel started. "That's the best part. Robyn's got this great big—"

"My parents left a few things for me," Robyn said, interrupting before Laurel gave away too much about her past.

"They . . . they were taken on the Night of Shadows," she told Key. A lot of people had been taken. Robyn figured it was okay for him to know that much.

Key's eyes widened. "Oh. I figured you were an orphan, or something. Like me." He lowered his gaze. "Sorry."

"I kind of am right now, I guess," she admitted. *At least, temporarily.*

"Me, too." Laurel chimed in. The three looked at each other. Well, they had that much in common.

Robyn set the circuit board carefully on the floor. It wouldn't take long to rig the wires up around the tree house. That way, if anyone came snooping around, Robyn would know. She could also use the connections to test the batteries in the TexTers and see if they worked.

But it could wait. She and Laurel hadn't eaten since the morning. They went straight to the food stores on the wall. The shelves above seemed all too empty; just a few boxes of juice and cans of fruit and beans remained.

"Is this all we have?" Robyn asked. "It's definitely time for a shopping run."

"There's a new wrinkle," Key said, turning serious again. "Big mess down at the market, didn't you see?"

The girls shook their heads. Neither mentioned that they hadn't been in Sherwood most of the day.

"By tomorrow, there won't even be a market," Key said. "MPs are shutting the whole thing down."

# ≪CHAPTER TWENTY-SEVEN≫

## *A Food Problem, Compounded*

"Nooooo. How can they close the market?" Laurel moaned. She lay flat on her back, her spaghetti limbs sprawling.

"They have their ways," Key explained. "Intimidation, buying people out. Arresting vendors for so-called infractions to threaten others into backing off."

"Yeah, we saw some of that the other day," Robyn said.

Key nodded. "It's been going on forever. But it's official now. No market."

Laurel threw an arm over her eyes, despondent. "It's so much harder to shop in the real stores. Hello, even I got caught doing it last week. Me!"

Key and Robyn exchanged a glance. Laurel's melodrama would have been amusing if the situation hadn't been so serious. "How are we going to eat?" Robyn asked. She wondered if Key now regretted sharing his stockpile with them. His brow furrowed, but he didn't seem upset. He was just working on the problem.

"We'll figure something out," Key said.

"Everyone in Sherwood shops at that market, at least for some things," Robyn protested. "There's probably a hundred vendors. How can they just close it?"

"You need a street vendor license to sell goods in public," Key explained. "Nott City just revoked them."

"The only way to get food now is through the groceries, if you have a Tag, or else the new food depots the MPs are setting up," Key said. "And everything is protected with security cameras and InstaScan checkout. People without Tags are going to get some kind of card, or something. No more bartering."

"That's just stupid," Laurel wailed. "How are we supposed to SHOP when there's SECURITY?"

Robyn circled the girl's thin wrist and squeezed lightly. "It's okay," she said, although it sounded to her, right now, like it wasn't. "Where are these food depots?"

"There's going to be one right down on the Cannonway," Key said. "I saw them confiscating goods at the market and trucking them over there."

"Crown wants to control everything in the city," Key said. "And the quickest way to get control of people is to get control of the food supply. He has that now." He ticked off the items on his fingers. "One: block public access to the woods, so no one can pick fruit or forage. Two: stop the market, so independent farmers and producers can't sell their goods direct to the public anymore. Three: take control of the grocery stores so everyone has to buy everything from you."

"People still need food," Robyn said. "Where is it all going to come from?"

"Crown is going to buy from food suppliers, at a lower wholesale cost, then store the goods in big compounds around the city."

"*Eww*," said Laurel, wrinkling her nose. "That's just creepy."

"It'll be all profit for Crown and no profit for anyone else."

"How do you know all this?" Robyn asked.

Key shrugged. "It's basic economics."

"Eco-what?" Laurel repeated.

Key leaned over and tousled her blond hair. "That's what you get for not staying in school," he told her.

"Bo-ring," Laurel droned. She rolled back and forth over the wooden floor slats.

"Let's get a look at these new food depots," Robyn suggested.

Laurel perked up immediately. "Just a look?" she asked.

"We have to know what we're dealing with," Robyn said.

"Not a good idea," Key said. "What are you going to do, walk up to the MPs and see what they're doing? Your Wanted poster could be right outside. The description is pretty accurate."

Robyn grinned. "Are you volunteering?"

Key shrugged. "I already saw them. It's safe for me to get a little closer than you can, sure."

"Aren't you wanted?" Laurel asked him.

Key's voice tightened. "I don't think they've made any posters for me, if that's what you mean."

"Oh," Laurel said cheerfully. "You're lucky." But Robyn found herself wondering once again about Key's fugitive status.

They left the bike in the woods. Robyn was concerned about the amount of power in the battery and having to recharge it if it got low. Plus, riding around on a bike was a lot more conspicuous. Better to save the wheels for later, when they might really need a quick getaway.

When they got to the market, the girls' eyes widened in shock. MPs swarmed the large lot, one by one stripping vendors of their goods. They loaded boxes and crates and piles of wares onto trucks lined up along the edge of the market square. A separate group of guards had cordoned off the area with police tape.

"See?" Key said. "I told you it wasn't safe for you here."

They moved along the edges of the crowd. The familiar stalls looked desolate without their occupants. The streets were cluttered with refuse from fallen products and collapsing stands. Vendors clamored around the boundaries of the scene, shouting and shoving in effort to have their wares returned to them.

"Oh," Laurel cried, "this is terrible!"

"It'll be okay," Robyn said. She put her hands on her hips. "So, no more easy pickings. It'll be Crown's food depots or bust."

Robyn felt strangely pleased about this development, despite Laurel's agonized moans. She felt like a burden of guilt had been lifted off her. Stealing to survive was necessary, but it didn't make it right. Robyn still felt the need to pay back the vendors from whom she had taken food and clothing. If she could ever find them now.

The only good news was, no more market meant no more taking things from regular vendors. Robyn wouldn't feel guilty at all about stealing from Crown. *In fact*, she thought, *it would serve him right.*

# ≪CHAPTER TWENTY-EIGHT≫

# *Smells Like Team Spirit*

Down on the Cannonway, the food depot was nothing fancier than a warehouse. The small building had tin walls and a black tar roof that barely sloped at all. The front doors were tall glass sliding doors, currently locked, but with business hours posted. The building filled half a block and stretched back to a wide alley, where a small group of workers unloaded crates off a parked truck.

Robyn watched as they piled crates onto the truck's tailgate and then lowered it like an elevator. Using dollies and hand trucks, the workers began rolling stacks of crates.

But in the middle of each load, the remaining crates sat unattended on the tailgate.

"This doesn't look that hard," Robyn said. "Am I missing something?"

Laurel shook her head. "Easy as pie. No, cake. Cake is easier than pie. It doesn't drip around. And from a box, you can bake it on a steam grate. Pie just turns out soggy. Do you think they have cake in there?"

Key lightly tugged on the ends of Laurel's hair to stop her rambling. She fell quiet, but Robyn was left with the powerful feeling that she could do with a piece of apple pie. "I bet they do," Robyn said. "Let's try and get some."

The two girls darted out of the hiding place, leaving Key whisper-calling after them. "Wait, what are you doing?"

Robyn and Laurel knew what they were doing. They hadn't been friends long, but they had spent most of it sneaking about and stealing together. Long enough to know that quick and light was all you had to be.

Robyn scooped up a couple of cabbages and a fistful of carrot greens from a box of loose produce. Laurel, apparently unable to secure an actual pie, grabbed two bags of apples and a long loaf of bread. Rather than doubling back, they ran the rest of the length of the alley, around the block, and rejoined Key in the corner hiding spot.

"Geez," Key said. "A little warning next time?"

"Warning is how you get caught," Laurel said, echoing Robyn's own thought.

Robyn exchanged a look with Laurel, a question in her eyes. *One more pass?* It seemed likely that once the workers got all the food into the building, it would be a lot harder to steal anything at all. As for now, the crates were just sitting there, ripe for the taking. The MPs were acting far too confident that their presence was enough to ward off any attempts.

"No, I don't think . . ."

The girls ran out again, leaving Key sputtering in confusion. This time they were bolder. Laurel grabbed a giant sack of rice. Robyn picked up one entire crate—it wasn't very heavy, full of smaller pouches of dried fruit. Again they made it around the corner unseen.

Robyn and Laurel circled the buildings, but this time Key met them on the back of the block. "Stop it. We gotta go," he said, leading their dash away from the scene of the crime. Instead of taking the streets, they kept to the alleys, then cut across Sherwood Park. "I can't believe you guys did that. What were you thinking?"

The girls knew better than to answer. They hurried in silence through the park, keeping an eye out for strange shadows that could be hiding MPs. Finally Laurel said, "We were thinking we needed food, obviously." She struggled under the weight of the ten-pound sack of rice; it was the size of her torso.

Key said to Laurel, "Here, give me that." He dumped the bread and apples he was clutching on a park bench and relieved her of the rice. He stuck the carrots and cabbage on Robyn's crate, glancing around nervously. "We shouldn't be out in the open with this stuff."

"It's fine," Robyn said. "No one needs to know where it came from." She glanced around. No MPs in sight. No one in sight at all, except a woman with two children about Laurel's size, huddled together beneath a tree alongside the gazebo. The children lay with their heads in her lap, apparently asleep. "It's fine," she said again.

"But . . . but . . . ," Key sputtered, hefting the bag of rice. "We didn't have a plan."

"Yeah, we did," Robyn argued. "The plan was to get some food. We got some." She set down the crate of dried fruit and began riffling through it.

Laurel nodded in agreement.

"No," Key groaned. "We were just supposed to get the lay of the land. So we could come back and actually steal stuff."

Robyn waved a pouch of apricots in his face. "Check and check."

"No, we need a plan," he insisted. "Maybe I create a distraction, so you can go in and pick up things we can actually use." He pointed at the sack of rice. "I mean, what good is this? We can't even cook it—"

"Easy," Laurel answered. "Steam grate—"

"And how are we supposed to get this all back to the tree house?"

Robyn knew how to solve that one. "Hang on." She grabbed one sack of apples, a cabbage, some carrots, and a few dried fruit packs and headed across the lawn toward the family. The mother cupped her hands protectively around the children's shoulders as Robyn approached.

"It's okay," Robyn said, laying the food in front of her. "We have plenty to share."

"Th-thank you," the woman gushed, clearly startled. Her fingers closed around a corner of the apple sack and dragged it closer. "How can I—what can I . . . ?"

Robyn shook her head. "Have a good night," she whispered, and ran back to her friends. Laurel stood with her hands on her hips, head cocked to one side as if to inform Robyn that she was nuts for continually giving their food away.

"We can *hide* the rest," Laurel said. "I have places." She led the way across the park. The large cannon sculpture at the edge of the field had a loose panel in the metal base. They stashed the crate in the cobwebbed gap, alongside a scuffed-looking pouch that Robyn assumed was one of Laurel's hidden hygiene packs.

"Fine," Key said, acknowledging the wisdom of hiding the food. "But it would be better to aim for more dry food. Canned goods. That sort of thing."

Again Robyn waved the apricots. "Relax, okay?" she said, tearing open the pouch. "We got it."

"We should have done it together," Key grumbled. "You can't just . . ." he waved his hands. "We're a team now."

"Are we?" Laurel said, around a mouthful of cabbage leaves. The soft, hopeful question sliced across the air, gentle as a breeze. The three knelt there silently for a moment, looking at one another. Long enough that Robyn's heartbeat slowly steadied as she relaxed after the adrenaline-pumping run.

Robyn didn't need a team. She knew she would be fine on her own. She always had been fine alone. It was just that, at the moment, she wasn't. Laurel looked comfortable and was clearly excited to have made friends. She felt safe when they were together. Robyn did, too. And despite Key's crossed arms and glower, the atmosphere among them certainly had an all-for-one feel about it.

Robyn crossed her arms and stared back at him. She wasn't going to be the one to admit it.

"Yeah," Laurel said finally. "I think we are."

# ≪CHAPTER TWENTY-NINE≫
## *A Robyn by Any Other Name*

The three friends sat in the grass and ate dried apricots and fresh apples as the afternoon sun sank lower over the trees of Sherwood Park. Laurel scooped handfuls of rice into the now-empty apricot bag. "I have a place I can cook this," she said. "But it's better if I go by myself. Meet you back at the tree house?"

"You sure?" Robyn said. "I thought we were a team."

The small girl nodded and flashed a sly grin. "I don't think you can fit in this place."

Robyn and Key headed back toward the tree house. Robyn kept her eyes peeled for other things that might remind her of the markings on Dad's map. She knew it would lead her somewhere eventually. It had to.

But she stayed quiet about it as Key led the way through the neighborhood, winding through the sinewy streets with comfort and ease.

"You really know your way around Sherwood," Robyn commented.

"I grew up here," Key said.

That was a surprise. He looked and acted more like a Castle District boy than any that she'd seen in Sherwood. "Really?" Should she show the map to him? Could he help?

They were a team now, but somehow it wasn't quite the same with Key as with Laurel. She didn't know enough about him.

Robyn gathered her courage. "Do you have a last name?" she asked.

"Yeah." Key's gaze cut to her. "Do you?"

Fair enough. Robyn tugged on the cuff of her fingerless gloves. She glanced at Key's hand. He had taken a more permanent solution to the Tag problem. The back of his hand bore a rectangular black scar, where his Tag had evidently been removed.

"You shouldn't tell people your real first name, either" Key said.

Robyn thought back to the day they met. "Call me Key," he'd said, which made Robyn want to kick herself. She hadn't been thinking like a fugitive. Maybe she shouldn't be introducing herself all over town as "Robyn." Although it was a little too late now.

"Exactly what makes you think Robyn is my real name?" she teased, to cover up the feeling of making such a blunder. Jokingly, Robyn nudged Key with her shoulder. Key nudged back.

"Oh, please." Key hooked his elbow around her neck and noogied the top of her head, through the beret. "You're such a rookie."

"Don't mess up my hair," Robyn's voice rang out with urgency, though it shouldn't matter at all. She felt herself sounding like her classmates from Castle, forever worried about how their hair looked. Robyn hadn't become close friends with any of those girls for a reason.

"Are you kidding?" he joked. "That braid is so tight you could bounce a quarter off it. How do you even make that thing?"

Robyn's joking mood slipped right off her shoulders. "My father taught me," she said softly. "There's really nothing else to do with so much hair. Apparently all the women on Dad's side of the family have . . ." Robyn's throat tightened.

Key kept his arm around her. But gently now. "Sorry," he said. "I didn't know."

They walked in silence for a minute. "I don't know why I got so upset," Robyn said. "It's just a silly hairdo," she finished. But as she said it, she realized it wasn't. It was something more.

*Follow your head. Follow your heart. Follow the moon,* her father had written. *I'm sorry I can't say more.*

*Follow your head.* Suddenly Robyn suspected the braid wasn't silly at all.

## ≪CHAPTER THIRTY≫

# Wisdom of the Ancients, Party of One

Robyn grasped Key's arm. "We have to get back to the market," she said. "There's someone I need to talk to."

"The former market," Key said. "Remember?"

"But the regular shops along the street should still be open, right?"

They ambled down the Cannonway, keeping a casual pace. Arm in arm like this, they probably resembled a young couple out for a stroll, so Robyn fought the urge to race along the sidewalk. It was better to remain calm. With her hair hidden under the beret, she blended into the neighborhood quite well.

Robyn approached the braiding salon with trepidation.

"Are you sure about this?" Key asked, noting her hesitation.

"I think so," she answered. "I think I'm supposed to follow the braid."

"Follow the braid?" Key echoed. "What does that mean?"

"We're about to find out." Robyn spoke confidently, despite her nervousness, as she pushed through the door of the salon.

The shop was full of energetic women, chatting and braiding and shampooing and blow drying. Key took one look around and said, "Maybe I should wait outside."

"That's fine," Robyn said, and he retreated gratefully.

Robyn stood alone in the entryway, unsure how to proceed. She'd been in a hair salon exactly twice before, both times with Mom. She recognized the cutting stations, and the mirrors, and the reclined chairs for hair washing, and the big domed dryers. Everyone seemed busy.

She approached the desk near the door and stood patiently. A young stylist stepped away from her station and came up behind the desk. Her head was covered by an expansive crown of twisted locks. "How can we help you?" she said. "Braids, twists, a little bit of color, maybe?" She tilted her head as if the new angle would allow her to see beneath Robyn's beret.

Robyn took another quick scan of the room. The old woman with the braid didn't seem to be there. "Um, actually I'm looking for someone. I don't know her name, but she's very old with very long hair, and she wears it like this." Robyn tugged off her beret.

The young stylist's face flashed with recognition. "Yes. I'm afraid she's not here."

"Do you know where I can find her? It's very important."

The young stylist frowned. "Mom," she called, addressing one of the older stylists, who left her station and approached them. "Do you want to come talk to this girl? She's . . . ," but her voice trailed off as the elder woman Robyn was looking for emerged from a doorway at the back of the store.

She wore a long, thin dress of white that covered her so that as she moved, she seemed to glide.

"Nana, you're supposed to be resting," said the young stylist.

"I sensed something," the elder woman said as she approached Robyn and clasped the girl's face between gentle hands. "I have been expecting a girl to visit," she murmured. "But you cannot possibly be the child of my vision."

"I—" Robyn started to explain, but the woman referred to as Nana held up a hand.

"This is not the place. Come with me." The old woman lifted her massive braid and wrapped it around her waist like a belt. Robyn followed. Key perked up as they exited the shop. He glanced from her to the elder woman and back. Robyn shrugged and motioned for him to wait.

The old woman led Robyn through a nondescript doorway between the salon and the shoe store next door. A narrow hallway led to a flight of stairs. As they climbed, Robyn stared at the thick gray braid and refrained from asking the very rude questions that came to mind—such as, how did she manage to wash all that hair, let alone comb and braid it? It was truly gorgeous, but Robyn couldn't imagine actually dealing with it.

The braid woman let them into a second-floor apartment. The single room was very clean and only sparsely decorated.

A narrow bed draped in white linen, two armchairs, a lamp stand, and two chairs around a small dining table made up all the furniture. The room was extremely ordinary, except for a massive skylight in the ceiling, positioned directly over the bed. Late afternoon light poured in, showering the sheets in a warm golden glow.

The woman closed the door behind them and motioned for Robyn to turn. Her tone became sharp: "Who did your hair like this?"

"I did it myself."

"You lie."

Robyn faced the woman, remaining silent.

The woman perused her with a clear-eyed gaze. "It cannot be. You're much too young."

"Too young for what?" Robyn said.

"Why have you come to me? Why now, when the pressure on all of us is so great?"

Robyn tried to conceal her confusion. "It's—I had to-well, I'm in a bit of trouble, to be honest."

"Tell me your name, child."

Robyn thought about taking Key's advice, but it didn't feel right. "I'm Robyn."

The old woman's entire face softened and widened. "My name is Eveline," she said, in a tone that was suddenly very pleasant. "What does this mean to you?"

Robyn bounced the name around her brain, then shook her head. "Nothing. I'm sorry. Does my name mean something to you?"

Eveline smiled. Her eyes appeared to dance. With a flat hand, she invited Robyn to sit in the armchairs. They sat across from each other.

"Show me your pendant, child."

"Pendant?" Robyn asked, nervous again. How did the woman know?

"We are each of us nothing but blood, breath, and bone," Eveline said.

"Um . . ." The refrain, though confusing, was growing quite familiar. "What does that mean?"

"One cannot exist without the others. One cannot survive without others."

*Well that was helpful*, Robyn thought.

Eveline smiled as though Robyn had spoken her thought aloud. "If a small flame is burning, how do you put it out?" Eveline asked.

"Why do you want to put it out?" Robyn asked in return.

The old woman's gaze sharpened. "Fire is quite dangerous, don't you think?"

Mom loved campfires. They used to light them in the backyard all summer long. "Not necessarily. You can use fire for light. For warmth. For cooking. For fuel."

"Remarkable," Eveline murmured.

"What is?" Robyn asked.

"Ask your friends the same question. They will help you understand." Eveline extended one wrinkled palm. "You touch your chest too often. I know the pendant is there. Take it off your neck and hand it to me."

Robyn was not about to part from her father's precious gift. She pulled it out of her shirt and moved to the edge of her seat, leaning the necklace forward in her palm. "Can't you see it from there?"

"My eyes are not so good anymore."

Robyn hesitated.

"If you are to succeed in this journey, you will be required to trust." Eveline held out her hand. "It will be back where it belongs in a moment."

"You mean, you'll give it back to me in a minute?" Robyn clarified.

The old woman laughed—a light bursting tinkle of sound that filled Robyn with unexpected hope. "You are clever enough, indeed. You may end up doing just fine."

Robyn laid the pendant in Eveline's palm. The old woman turned it over and examined it closely. "Black moonstone," she said. "Blessed by the ancients. Incredibly precious."

"Okay," Robyn said.

"If you are to be the one of my vision," Eveline said. "You will need to know two things: this stone was once part of a very special key. But the door it opens . . . common wisdom suggests it no longer exists."

*Great. That sound helpful.*

"The lessons of the moon lore will guide you, if you let them."

Robyn gulped. She didn't remember the moon lore. It had always seemed like old, boring riddles and stories. "What's the second thing?" Robyn asked.

"There is a storeroom directly below us. Something to be found there will help you. Take whatever you need."

*Now we're talking,* Robyn thought. "Thanks." Feeling bold, she added, "Um, so, the whole moon lore thing . . . can you remind me how that goes?"

"For a moon child, you know so little," the old woman lamented. "There is much to be learned." She picked up a pen and scrap of paper from the lamp table and scrawled something on it.

"Moon child?" Robyn asked. "What does that mean?"

Eveline sighed. "The nature of such a destiny is for it to be uncovered," she said, folding the note and handing it to Robyn. "I cannot give you the answers, any more than I can tell you what has happened to your parents."

"How—how did you know about them?" Robyn was sure she had said nothing related to her parents' disappearance.

The old woman tipped her head back, raising her face toward the skylight glow. She closed her eyes and drew two slow, deep breaths. "The hope of the ancients is still alive," she told Robyn. "With every breath, I feel them. Your search is not in vain."

## ≪CHAPTER THIRTY-ONE≫
# Library Books: 398.26 ML

Robyn darted down the stairs and stuck her head out the door. "Key," she called, motioning him inside. He pushed off the side of the building and came toward her. Robyn glanced at the old woman's note. All she had written was a strange series of numbers:

*398.26 ML*

"What happened?" Key asked. "Who's the old lady?"

"Eveline," Robyn said, leading him down the hallway. "All I know is, it was important to talk to her." The encounter had left her feeling full, even though their conversation had only added more questions to the ones Robyn already had.

Key's hands were empty. "Where are the apples?" Robyn asked.

"I gave them away," he answered. Adding thoughtfully, "I think you're onto something with that idea."

As they entered the storeroom, Robyn informed Key, "Eveline told me we can take anything that we need from here."

"Um," Key said, when they saw the room. "Wow. Anything?"

They were surrounded by shoe boxes. Columns of them, stacked on shelves stretching six or eight feet high. A couple of quick glances showed that the boxes actually did contain shoes. Behind that were crates piled with tubes of hair gel, boxes of hair color, and massive bottles of conditioner. Hair products galore, ordered by the dozens. The room clearly held the overflow supplies from both the braiding salon and the neighboring shoe store.

Robyn stared at the inventory with her hands on her hips. "What are we supposed to do with a thousand stilettos and a vat of industrial-strength detangler?"

"Build a torture chamber?" Key suggested. His voice made it sound like he was already standing in one.

Robyn laughed. "Let's call that plan B."

"There's no lock on this door," Robyn said. "I think that means we can come back anytime." She picked up a copy of the shoe catalog.

"We don't need this," Key mumbled. "The image is seared on my eyeballs." But he took it anyway, stuffing it into his back pocket.

Robyn unfolded the scrap of paper from Eveline and showed the message to Key:

*398.26 ML*

"That's a call number," Key said. "For a book in the library."

>>>→

The sun sank lower in the sky. In the distance, the towers of Nottingham Cathedral turned to shadows against the red-gold-purple skyline. Robyn and Key rushed to meet Laurel back at the tree house before true dark. The library would have to wait until tomorrow—feeling their way through the night woods would be hard enough, let alone finding the carved arrows.

Laurel was already waiting when they arrived. The rice was a tad crunchy, perhaps, but it did the trick. They shared a can of beans along with it, dividing the food into bowls Key had woven out of strips of thick green leaf. Under the circumstances they all were grateful for a half-warm meal.

As she did the previous night, Laurel snuggled close to Robyn under the thin blanket they shared and dozed off immediately. Robyn wondered at the small girl's willingness to trust so instantly. She rested her cheek on stacked hands and tried to close her eyes.

Key sat gazing through the plastic ceiling at the moon. Robyn wanted to ask him why he would bother to look at the moon if he wasn't able to read anything from it. But the words never made it to her lips, as she slipped off to sleep.

At first light, the trio headed down to the library. Passing the wall of Wanted posters in the entryway, Robyn was reminded of her recent afternoon in jail. Once again she felt grateful that the guards hadn't processed her; otherwise, she'd have ended up fully identifiable in the system. Laurel, too, glanced nervously at the display. Key didn't even give it a glance; he just proceeded through the vestibule and held open the door. Robyn and Laurel stepped aside for a frazzled-looking mother with a squirming toddler in one arm and a bag of books on the other exiting the library. The kid shrieked and wiggled, as if trying to escape over his mother's shoulder. His waving arms strangely reminded Robyn of her mother, on the security video, moving in the MP's arms as they lugged her out of the house.

The blinking posters punctuated the memory, sending a surge of energy through Robyn. Mom was still alive somewhere. Apprehended. And Dad—he'd left Robyn instructions and she had done nothing so far but fail him.

Perusing the wall, Robyn's eye fell on the poster for Floyd Bridger. Though she had only seen him briefly, Robyn knew she would never forget his face. Especially with that notable Y-shaped scar on his jaw. There could be no confusion. Beneath his face, they had a list of his crimes: theft, assault, resisting arrest, political agitation, inciting rebellion . . . and murder.

Murder? Wow! If Bridger had really done all these things, he sounded like a seriously bad guy. But he had seemed so kind and thoughtful that day in the square. His eyes, as the MPs dragged him away, had looked anything but scary— they looked scared. Robyn's gut feeling told her to remain on his side.

*Where was Bridger now?* Robyn wondered. Clearly, the MPs had not yet caught him. Robyn felt good for a moment, knowing she had helped him get away. She wished there had been something she could do for Nyna Campbell, too.

Gazing elsewhere along the wall, Robyn noticed for the first time the bold display of APPREHENDED suspects. She did a double take: one of the pictures was of the mother and children she'd run into last night! The banner beneath the picture read, APPREHENDED: THEFT OF GOVERNMENT PROPERTY. The date stamp was last night.

# ≪CHAPTER THIRTY-TWO≫

## *Unintended Consequences*

"Oh no." Robyn clamped her hand over her mouth. The MPs must have caught the woman with the stolen items Robyn gave her.

She'd gotten an innocent homeless family arrested! But here in public, Robyn had to control her reaction to the terrible news.

"What?" Key said, responding to her soft gasp.

Nor could she fully explain to Key what was troubling her. Not with people passing through the vestibule behind them. "This happened last night," she whispered pointedly, nodding toward the screen.

Three innocent people! Because of her recklessness. Robyn felt horrified, ashamed.

Key draped an arm across her shoulder. "Next time, we do it my way," he said. "They might not even notice anything missing."

Robyn nodded, trying to swallow the horrible knot in her throat. Key's plan sounded slow and boring, but if it worked, well, fine. Robyn never wanted a mistake like this to happen again.

She forcibly tore her attention from the APPREHENDED list. She couldn't afford to let guilty feelings affect her behavior. It wouldn't do to appear suspicious in such a public place. Together they moved farther into the library.

Key knew his way among the books. He turned and wound smoothly until they landed in the correct section. Trailing behind him, Laurel touched the spines of the books in a strange, almost sad, way. The small girl drummed the fingers of one hand against her mouth, running the others along the book spines.

"This is where it should be." Key slid his finger into a gap on the shelf. "But there's nothing here."

"Oh." Robyn's shoulders slumped. She struggled to contain her dismay. No book. Another dead end. She was no closer to finding her parents. No closer to understanding Dad's message.

Robyn crouched down on the floor. She leaned against the books and closed her eyes. Her parents had placed all this faith in her, and all she'd done was let them down.

There were real people—a mom—in real trouble now, too, because of her. It made Robyn's stomach ache. Those two boys? Robyn knew what they must be going through. If her own mom was alive, like Eveline thought, she was probably somewhere behind bars. Somewhere horrible.

》》》—→

"I just want to sit here a while," she told the others. "You guys can go. I'll meet up with you later."

She expected one of them to say okay, and then to hear footsteps leaving. When she heard nothing, she opened her eyes. Laurel was sitting cross-legged right next to her. Key lay on his side, sprawled across the aisle, looking relaxed but alert. His bent knees rested near her hip, and he had his head propped up on his palm down by her feet. He gazed solemnly at her, completely still.

"It's okay, guys. Just go," Robyn said. She needed some time alone. Everyone she was trying to help, she ended up letting down. Key and Laurel should get out of the way before they got hurt too.

Laurel leaned in, inches from Robyn's face. "What is wrong?" she said, very seriously.

Robyn laughed. She couldn't help it. The comically-intense, concerned expression on Laurel's face raised her spirits considerably.

Key also cracked a smile. Laurel leaned back, surprised and confused. "What?"

"I—" Robyn began. Laurel obviously cared, and she wasn't going to leave Robyn alone. *I've never had a friend before*, the girl had said. Robyn hadn't, either. At least not the kind of friend with whom you could break out of jail, share a tree-house bed, and plan criminal activity. Exactly the kind of friend Robyn had always wanted.

Robyn decided to speak the thought that had been forming in her mind. It was a little bit crazy, maybe, but it could solve everything at once. "I want to help the woman from last night. She's in jail because of me."

"How can we help her?" Key said.

"She's going to disappear," Laurel added.

"I can't let that happen," Robyn insisted. "We have to get her out." *Her . . . and my backpack*, she thought. She needed the hologram back, so she could fix it. The rest of Dad's message had to be important.

"Out of jail?" Key said, skeptical.

"We broke out once," Robyn said, glancing at Laurel. "How hard could it be to break back in?"

"You want to break back *into* the jail?" Laurel's eyes bugged wide.

"Um, I'm thinking NO," Key said.

"Even if we could get inside, I don't think we'd ever get the warden away from her desk," Laurel said. "She just sits there, reading those magazines." She pantomimed page turning and affected a glassy-eyed stare.

Robyn laughed. "Yeah. I think it would take a drastic act of fashion to get her to budge."

Laurel cracked up. Key didn't get the joke. He just lounged there, watching them ham around. Robyn reached over and grabbed the shoe catalog out of his back pocket. She smacked him lightly on the hip with it, then held it up.

"Hey, Laurel." Robyn grinned. "What size do you think the warden takes?"

# CHAPTER THIRTY-THREE

# Special Delivery for the Warden

"This is definitely a bad idea," Key muttered as he and Robyn approached the door of the Sherwood Jail. "Why did I agree to this crazy scheme?"

"This genius scheme, you mean?" Robyn grunted with effort. The warehouse dolly was proving harder to maneuver than she had expected. "What are you complaining about? At least we have a plan this time."

Half an hour ago, they had made a rather large withdrawal from the braid shop's storeroom. Now they pushed the wide load slowly along the sidewalk, each controlling one handle.

Of considerably more concern to Robyn was the fact that her MP uniform pants were falling down. The rope she was using as a belt, though hidden beneath her shirt hem, didn't seem to be doing its job effectively.

Obviously the pants were meant for a grown adult man, so they'd had to be altered. Key knew how to sew, so he had hemmed the camouflage pants. His tailoring skills did not extend to taking in waistlines. Robyn knew which end of the needle the thread went in, but that was about it. And if she got pantsed walking through the door of the jailhouse, the jig would definitely be up.

The third uniform had been hopelessly large, so Laurel remained outside, near the back door, ready to cause a distraction if the plan failed as miserably as Robyn feared it might.

"Ready?" Key said to Robyn. The jailhouse loomed in sight. At the very least, Robyn knew, their actions were being captured on some surveillance camera or other.

"Ready as I'll ever be," she answered. She stepped in front of the dolly and marched confidently in through the door of the jail. She held it open as Key attempted to roll the box through the door. The warden didn't look up from her desk.

The guard beside her, Burle, said, "Hey, what's going on?"

Robyn had been hoping someone else would be on duty today. Someone less likely to recognize her.

As planned, the box was just slightly too wide to fit through the jailhouse door. "Burle, can you give me a hand here?" Key called loudly, jamming the box against the door frame. "Warden, did you enter some kind of sweepstakes?"

They had decided to create a commotion right away and not give the guard much time to recognize them.

Burle came to the door. "There's a box out there," he announced.

*Way to illuminate the situation, Burle,* Robyn thought.

"Sweepstakes?" the warden said. "Wait, what's this?"

"It's addressed to you, Warden," Key said. "Return address is some kind of fashion surplus?"

The warden heaved her bulk off the high stool and lumbered toward the door. *The good news,* Robyn thought, *was if that was her top speed, they could definitely outrun her.* She had feared the warden might turn out to be secretly fast, like her dad's friend Bill, who was the size of a refrigerator but moved like lightning.

Keeping her face lowered beneath the camouflage cap, while Key kept Burle and the warden distracted, Robyn hurried to the warden's desk. She punched the door-release button and raced across to the room with the cubbyholes. One quick scan of the wall—her backpack was still there! She grabbed it and slung it over her shoulder.

Next she ran back to the warden's desk. Clear, except for the usual magazine. Robyn's heart skipped. She yanked open the top drawer, hoping . . . *Whew!* The massive ring of keys was right there. Robyn breathed, relieved.

The second drawer contained routine office supplies. Robyn grabbed for the biggest, firmest object—a desk stapler. As she lifted it, her gaze fell upon the warden's computer screen. It was open to an interdepartmental memo titled "Pending Prisoner Transfers: Black Farms Ridge to Centurion Gate." The header was followed by a long list of people's Tag numbers.

Robyn gasped aloud, causing Key to look over his shoulder at her. Robyn stared, frozen, at the screen.

She knew her mother's Tag number just about as well as her own. It was right there, in bold black type on the warden's list.

She punched down on the screen, but that was all there was. No more information. Robyn wanted to try harder—a database search for prisoner records? There was a search field right on top of the screen. Robyn's fingers itched to try it. From the doorway, Key glared daggers at her. He jerked his head, as if to say, "Get on with it!"

Clutching the key ring, Robyn raced to the panel that controlled the cell block hallway door and buzzed herself in. She wedged the stapler in the gap to keep the door ajar. She would not be able to buzz herself back out again. If the exit plan failed, Robyn needed an escape option other than the vent.

Robyn slid into the hallway. The prisoners shied away as she passed. To them, she must have looked like a real MP trainee, not like a friend. She found the family in the last cell, the same street-rat cell Robyn and Laurel had occupied.

"It's you," the mom whispered. "You're . . ." she took in the uniform, obviously confused. Robyn placed a finger to her lips and motioned the three out into the hall. They stood patiently while Robyn ran down the row, unlocking the other cells. As long as she was here, she wouldn't just save one family. She wanted to let them all out.

Robyn led the prisoners through the hallways to the alarm-laden back door. The one she and Laurel had stumbled upon in their own escape. The hinges, positioned outside the door, had been awfully easy to remove this morning.

The area was under heavy surveillance. Laurel had stood on Key's shoulders and held a tree branch down over the nearest camera's eye. Meanwhile, Robyn had pulled the bolts from the hinges using the wrench in Dad's pocketknife and plenty of elbow grease. A low-tech solution to a high-tech problem. A literal back door.

Assuming Robyn had done the job well enough, the door should come open backward. They hadn't tried it, for fear of setting off an alarm too early.

Now came the moment of truth. Robyn stood at the head of the pack of escapees and lifted her foot. She ignored the electronic keypad, and the wires, and the push bar. She kicked forward at the hinge side as hard as she could. Shocks ricocheted up her leg. Three kicks later, the door lurched open. Not wide enough. Robyn slammed her shoulder against it for a final push. Ow.

No alarm went off. The electronic-lock side of the door remained intact enough that the door wasn't registering it was opened! The wires stretched taut, but there was enough slack in the lines to allow a gap. *Bad, bad security*, Robyn thought. *But great for escaping.*

"Go," Robyn urged everyone. They bent beneath the wires and squeezed one by one through the slim opening and raced off down the block. Robyn was supposed to follow. That had been the plan—but they were expecting an alarm. Instead, she waited. The prisoners ducked by her one by one.

Many whispered thanks. Some shed tears. Others pressed at her hands and her shoulders, and their eyes spoke what their tongues could not.

"Who are you?" some wondered.

"I'm Robyn," she whispered. "You're fugitives now. Good luck."

Robyn waited until the last man had slid through. She jammed her backpack through the gap, where Laurel could see it and pick it up. Then she ran back toward the front of the building.

She nearly collided with two figures approaching from the opposite direction. The pair came hurrying out of the hallway leading from one of the blocks of solitary cells.

One of them was a gaunt teenage girl with golden skin and black spiky hair tipped with red. She grabbed the arm of the young MP walking beside her.

Robyn drew herself up, prepared to act the part of a real MP trainee and bluster her way through the encounter. But she recognized the other person. It was the same MP trainee who had arrested her in Sherwood Forest!

His eyes widened in recognition, too. The jig was up!

# ≪CHAPTER THIRTY-FOUR≫

## *Familiar Faces*

Robyn and the young MP stared at each other for a long tense second. Robyn was sure that at any moment he would sound the alarm and take her back into custody. *Run!* Robyn's mind screamed. But she felt locked in place.

Instead his gaze flicked away, over Robyn's shoulder.

"The door's already open," he said, puzzled. He lightly shoved the spiky-haired girl's shoulder. "Go. GO!"

The girl darted past Robyn, swirling a slight wind as she passed.

"This never happened." The young MP vanished down the hall he had come from, leaving Robyn alone and confused. Was he letting her go?

No time to dwell on the mystery—Robyn raced back to the front of the jail. She pulled the stapler and returned to the computer on the desk.

"What are you doing?" Key whispered, meeting her in the center of the lobby. "Didn't you get them out?"

Past him, the warden squeezed into the doorway, ripping through the large box to examine each and every pair of shoes. A confused-looking Burle juggled an armful of shoe-box lids.

"They're out," Robyn whispered.

"No alarm?"

Robyn shrugged.

"*Ooohh*," cooed the warden. Her voice sounded like an echo, which was understandable, considering the top half of her had utterly disappeared into the giant box.

"Time to go," Key whispered, tension in his voice. "The distraction is about to be over." Their shoulders bumped as they rushed to stand side by side at attention. *So much for the computer search*, Robyn thought longingly. At least she had another clue now. Centurion Gate. What did that mean?

"Warden, what do you want us to do with these?" Key inquired, in an official-sounding voice. "Is there somewhere you'd like them delivered?"

"That won't be necessary," she said, surfacing from the box with a blue satin pump in one hand and a wad of toe-filler paper in the other. "Just put them in the trunk of my car." She touched her PalmTab, and the trunk of a beige car parked along the street popped open.

"Sure thing," Key said. The warden retrieved the matching blue pump, then Key and Burle rolled the dolly down the sidewalk toward the car. Robyn eased past the warden and followed.

"Hey," the warden said to her.

Robyn looked back, trying not to raise her head far enough to let the warden see her face, which was tricky, since she was being directly addressed.

"On second thought," the warden said. "Put these in, too." She handed Robyn the blue pumps. The jailhouse door banged shut between them. Robyn breathed a sigh of relief, just a moment too soon.

Hurrying after Burle and Key, Robyn felt her pants continuing to slip. One step later, they dropped over her hips and fell down her thighs.

## ◄CHAPTER THIRTY-FIVE►

## *Wardrobe Malfunction*

As Robyn's pants slipped down, she quickly spread her legs to stop them from falling. She wore black leggings underneath; it's not like anyone would *see* anything. But no self-respecting MP—or thief, for that matter—loses her pants.

"Hey," said Burle. He wasn't the quickest on the uptake, but Robyn's rope belt was a pretty obvious giveaway. "That's not regulation," he added.

Robyn pitched the blue pumps into the trunk alongside the other shoe boxes Key and Burle had unloaded. She grabbed the camo pants by the waist and hoisted them.

"I, uh, left my belt in my other pants," she said. "Pretty stupid, eh?"

Burle just frowned. "Yeah," he said, but his big dumb face contorted like he was trying to puzzle something out.

Key took the dolly from under the now-empty box. "Well, thanks, man," he said. "See you around."

Robyn backed away and fought the urge to run. She didn't look back, though she was tempted. The sound of a car trunk slamming behind them allowed her to breathe a sigh of relief. Burle was going about business as usual.

Once around the corner, they began to jog. "You need to learn to tie a better knot," Key muttered.

"Maybe you need to learn to sew better," Robyn retorted.

Key acted offended. "I hemmed the heck out of those pants," he said. "You didn't hold up your end of the bargain."

Robyn nodded toward her fist full of fabric. "Well, I'm holding it up now," she said. They laughed, racing back toward the storeroom.

Robyn's pulse still raced and her head felt light. It had been nerve-racking and scary but FUN pulling one over on Burle and the warden.

The escapade had been exciting, but the tidbit of information about Mom was almost worse than nothing—now Robyn knew the information existed, she just couldn't access it. Mom might be alive. Dad, too. But maybe the prisoner database contained records of everyone captured, even the dead.

No.

*I expect that they're alive,* Robyn reminded herself. *I expect to find out what happened to them. I expect to see them again.*

Robyn and Key met Laurel at the braid shop's storeroom. Laurel handed over Robyn's backpack. "Thanks." Robyn unzipped the pouches and checked off the items inside: the device Barclay had given her. Dad's envelope. The broken silver hologram sphere. All present and accounted for. Even the plastic bag that had once held the bacon was there. She breathed a sigh of relief.

She looked up to find Key staring at her. "What is that?" he said.

"What?" She wasn't sure she wanted to tell Key about the hologram yet. Laurel didn't even know.

"That bag. You wasted a bunch of time inside getting it. It'd be nice to know if it was worth it."

"It's my bag," Robyn said. "They took it when they put me in jail. I wanted it back."

"The plan was to break the people out. You could have mentioned there was something else you wanted inside."

"It took two seconds to grab it."

"Time matters. You left me hanging out to dry with Burle and the warden. And what were you looking at on the computer for so long?"

Robyn shrugged. "It wasn't that long."

"Felt like it from where I was standing. Every second you goof around is a second they could recognize me."

"Recognize you for what?" Robyn retorted. "I thought you weren't on a Wanted poster."

Key turned away angrily. "Forget it," he said.

They changed out of the MP uniforms and tucked them into Key's bag. "I'll get these back to the tree house," he said, then stalked off.

The glow of the successful jailbreak dimmed a bit for Robyn in the wake of his anger. She didn't regret grabbing her bag, though. She'd do it again.

Robyn and Laurel set out toward their statue stash to grab some food for dinner. As they walked, Robyn relayed her version of the jail break-in for Laurel, and Laurel told her side of the story, waiting nervously across the street. ". . . and then your pants fell down!" She giggled. "I thought you were a goner for sure."

Robyn rolled her eyes. "Yeah, yeah. How about we not keep that as part of the story next time we tell it."

"But that's the best part!"

Laurel led Robyn into an alley and pointed up to the fire escape. The ladder was suspended about eight feet off the ground. Laurel took a running start and made a surprisingly effective vertical leap for someone of her height. She grasped the bottom rung and pulled herself up.

"Come on," she called.

Robyn mimicked the difficult jump. Good thing she was already a gymnast in training, or she wouldn't be able to keep up with this girl.

"I thought we were getting food," Robyn said as they climbed.

"I want to brush my teeth first," Laurel told her.

"On a rooftop? I thought your stuff was in that yard in Getty."

"Oh, I have toothbrushes everywhere."

They rolled over the lip of the roof. From up here, Robyn could see a lot of Sherwood, high rises and brownstones, the towers of Nottingham Cathedral, and the pointed tops of the pine trees in Sherwood Forest. The rest of the Notting

Wood lay beyond that, punctuated by glimpses of the raised expressway that bordered the neighborhood.

Laurel led Robyn to one corner of the roof and pulled a small cloth satchel from a hiding spot between the back of a vent shaft and the edge of the building.

"How many stashes like this do you have?" Robyn wondered aloud. Laurel shrugged, unpacking toothbrush, toothpaste, and half-empty water bottle. The rest of the pouch was full of small cloth-wrapped objects, which Laurel did not disturb.

"Here, Robyn. Do you want one?" Laurel held out a red-and-white toothbrush in clean plastic packaging that promised to reduce plaque and fight gingivitis.

"Sure," Robyn said. She had always hated to brush her teeth at home. Every night her parents had made her do it. But after not brushing for several days, they were starting to feel significantly fuzzy.

Laurel squeezed toothpaste and the girls stood on the black tarry rooftop, brushing. They spit into the rain gutter. Laurel used a bit of the bottle water to rinse the brushes. Robyn would have liked a little water to rinse her mouth, too, but she was quickly learning that life on the streets as a fugitive meant sacrificing certain comforts.

Laurel re-hid the pouch and the girls descended the fire escape. Bad timing, though. As they dropped into the alley, an MP happened to be passing along the street.

"Here, what's this?" he said, pausing what was probably a routine patrol. He began marching toward them. "You two!"

Robyn and Laurel glanced at each other. Understanding arced between them. It was as if they'd been partners in crime for years. *Best to split up*, the look said. "Meet back in the woods," Robyn whispered. They ran to the mouth of the alley and took off in opposite directions.

An MP came running toward Robyn from the other direction. "Hey," he shouted. "Stop right there!"

*Not again*, she thought. *I'm not going down so easy this time.*

They seemed to be coming from everywhere. She turned and darted off in the opposite direction, back the way she came. She dodged through another alley and found herself running alongside the boarded-up old Nottingham Cathedral. The graffiti-covered expanse of plywood seemed to taunt her, like a colorful grin.

*Perfect*, Robyn thought. *I've picked the only block in all of Sherwood with absolutely no opportunity to hide.*

"You there!" called the MP. "Halt!"

Robyn refused to halt. The MP seemed to be gaining on her. What if she couldn't lose him? She peeked over her shoulder as she tore around the corner of the church—and slammed straight into another person.

A dark hand clamped over Robyn's mouth. Strong arms yanked her back into the shadows.

## ≪CHAPTER THIRTY-SIX≫

# *Secrets in the Cathedral*

Robyn struggled against her captor. "*Shh,*" a male voice whispered in her ear. "There's a grid patrol coming." He drew her back, all the way against the sealed church wall. The corrugated metal sheets thundered behind him. So much for silence.

Then he pulled Robyn straight through the wall. Darkness closed around them. Robyn gasped, as the hand dropped away from her mouth and the guy released her. Robyn spun around.

A young man maybe a few years older stood in front of her with his hands extended like a barrier between them. "I'm not going to hurt you. I swear, I only wanted to help."

Robyn blinked, her eyes adjusting to the dim light inside the church. "Did you really just pull me through a wall?" she asked, incredulous. They were standing in the church sanctuary. The ceiling swooped into high arches above a cavern of shadowy air. The only light filtered through high, narrow stained-glass windows. Every regular window was boarded tight.

"There's a loose panel," the guy said. "You just have to know exactly where to pull. And they were coming up too fast for me to explain."

"I would have been fine," Robyn said. "You didn't have to grab me."

The guy shook his head. "Trust me, there wasn't time. The MPs have the grid-search protocols worked out tight as a drum around here. Two were coming from the other direction, too."

Robyn's heart trilled. *If that was true . . .*

"I saw you from the choir loft." The guy pointed to a set of stairs at the side of the sanctuary that led to a narrow balcony. "Come up and look," he said.

Robyn's mood wavered between annoyed and curious. Who did this guy think he was? She followed him. "Who are you?"

"I'm Tucker Branch." He bounded up the stairs and onto the landing with a flourish. "Denizen of the Nottingham Cathedral."

Curiosity won. Robyn climbed the stairs after him. "And you decided to save the day. Just for the heck of it?"

Tucker shrugged. "I figure, anyone who's running from the MPs like that is probably a friend of mine." He led her to one of the boarded-up windows, which had a plank missing. From this vantage point, she could see the MP who had been chasing her standing at the intersection with his hands on his hips. Four MPs approached from opposite directions, searching every inch of the block.

"Are you some kind of criminal?" Robyn asked. Not that she was judging.

Tucker smiled broadly. "Actually, I'm in seminary." He pointed to a wooden table in the loft with a pile of thick old books resting on it. Several were open along with notes; it looked like he'd been studying.

"You're studying to be a priest?"

"A minister."

"And in your spare time you take in fugitives?"

"Helping the wayward is pretty much a full-time job," Tucker said.

Robyn looked down at the searching MPs. "How long until they leave?"

"Less than five minutes to search the block. So I'd give it twenty or so for them to clear the whole area."

Robyn nodded. So she was stuck here for a little while. "Thanks, by the way." Tucker had saved her hide. She really hoped Laurel had gotten as lucky, and made it back to the woods.

Tucker leaned against the wall and crossed his arms. "Forgive me for saying so, but you don't seem like the typical fugitive. What happened?"

Robyn sighed. "Kind of a long story,"

Tucker smiled. "It always is." He stood, just waiting to see what else she might say.

"To be honest, they started chasing me for no good reason." Which was actually true. Coming off a fire escape wasn't necessarily a crime. "Although, I may have previously done a few things that are chaseworthy."

"Or else, why run?" Tucker said.

"I'm Robyn," she said. Tucker acknowledged the introduction with a slight nod but said nothing further. The strange, old quiet of the cathedral took over. "This is a weird place to study, even for a priest."

"Minister." Tucker's expression turned wistful as he gazed out into the dim, dusty cavern. "I grew up going to this church," he said. "I'm doing my thesis on its history."

"So you come here to write?"

"Right."

Robyn felt a stirring inside her, despite the stillness. She smoothed her hand over her pocket, where Dad's map rested safely. She had to take advantage of this unexpected development. "Mind if I look around?"

"Sure," Tucker said. "I'll show you the place."

Adjacent to the cavernous sanctuary, through a set of doors on the left-hand wall was the church house. The church house was a three-story building with lots of small offices, meeting spaces, and Sunday-school rooms. They had a dining room and industrial kitchen on the first floor and a smaller house-size kitchen on the second floor, near the office suite.

Everything looked broken down, unused in years, except for the second-floor kitchen, which had some snack items laid out on the counters. Macaroni-and-cheese boxes. Crackers and bread.

"The kitchen still works?" Robyn asked.

"Yeah," Tucker said. "You want something? Help yourself."

Robyn didn't need to be told twice. She reached into the cracker box and pulled out a sleeve of round crackers and tore it open. She munched on them as they walked around.

Returning to the sanctuary, it seemed even huger than before. Cobwebs. Dust. Chipped wood furnishings. Cracked stained glass. Plywood. "It's in pretty bad shape," she commented. "What's going to happen to it?"

"I don't know. It's been a landmark in the Nott City skyline for so long that they're not going to tear it down. But no one cares enough to pay to fix it up, either."

They walked to the front of the church. Dirty stained-glass windows lined the wall above the altar. It must have been really pretty in its prime, with light streaming through. But where was the light coming from? It couldn't have been an outside wall; the building didn't end there. Around behind the altar was a small fellowship room and a preparation room for the ministers. Narrow stone-walled hallways on either side of the altar led to those back rooms.

There seemed to be a hole in the church. An open cube in its floor plan.

"What's on the other side of this wall?" Robyn asked. She put her hand against the stones. The crevices were sealed with mortar, yet she felt a slight breeze. The whiff of cool air drew her closer to the place.

"Nothing, really," Tucker said. "It's kind of a hole in the construction. People used to complain about why they put a wall here. Always having to walk around it. They said they did it to allow light to flow through the stained glass."

Robyn followed the wall back to the stained glass and peered through. "It's a courtyard," she said. "There must be a way to get in there." The gut-tugging feeling grew stronger.

"In theory," he agreed. "I mean, I found a possible entrance. It's hidden in the choir loft, back where we started."

"Upstairs?"

"I know that sounds strange, but I think there's a staircase that winds down into the yard. You can kind of see it." Tucker directed Robyn to peer at an upward angle through a lighter-colored pane of the stained glass. "See those metal-looking dark lines? But the door is locked."

"Show me," Robyn said. The insistence in her own voice shocked her. The desire grew strong, though inexplicable.

They climbed back into the choir loft, skirting past Tucker's massive mound of books. Studying to be a minister must be serious business. At the front of the loft, alongside the high stained-glass windows above the altar, was a black-painted door.

"The keyhole has been removed, see?" He pointed at a dark circular indentation about where a doorknob should have been. But there was no doorknob, either. "It must be permanently bolted."

"No," Robyn said, though she couldn't explain her certainty. "I think that this *is* the keyhole." She pushed against it with her thumb. It didn't budge. She took out Dad's pocketknife—her knife now, she corrected herself—and sliced through the layers of black paint. She peeled back the gummed-up disk of latex, revealing an oblong silver flap.

"I've never seen a keyhole like this." Tucker's voice came alive with wonder.

The shape was—to Robyn—both unusual and familiar. She pushed back the flap by inserting her thumb into a curved cavern just large enough for it. The keyhole came to a point inside. Two grooves along the outside edges seemed ready-made for a special kind of key.

Robyn glanced up at Tucker. She didn't really know him. He might be what he claimed to be—a friend—but really, he could be anyone.

*To succeed in this journey, you will be required to trust,* Eveline had told her. Tucker had saved her from the MPs, after all. He had helped her get this far.

"I-I might have the key," she told him.

# ≪CHAPTER THIRTY-SEVEN≫

## *The Moon Shrine*

Robyn brought the moon pendant out of her shirt. She bent forward and slid it into the keyhole until it clicked into place. The door swung open, jerking her along by the neck. She found herself standing on a two-foot-square landing atop a staircase of rusted, black-painted metal. It felt even less secure and enclosed than a fire escape, but it was similar.

The key slid back into her palm, and Robyn straightened to survey her surroundings. The courtyard below was about twenty feet wide, along the stained-glass wall, and almost as deep.

"This is amazing," Tucker exclaimed. "I have to get my notebook!" He dashed off.

Robyn descended into the courtyard alone. The steep stairs rocked with each step. She steadied herself using the narrow handrail on the wall. There was no second rail; just the open courtyard air. Diagonally across the courtyard, a second, dingy beige staircase led up into the opposite wall.

Gravel stones of black, white, and gray covered the ground. Robyn looked up—the space stretched clear to the sky.

What was this place?

At the center of the gravel stood a flat, wall-like monument, built of solid black stones, with a single row of white stones accenting the middle. It was smooth to the touch. Maybe the same kind of stone as the moon necklace? The wall looked old and weathered, with jagged edges like you might see on ancient ruins. The whole thing wasn't more than seven feet tall. A base of the same black stones pushed out about two feet at the bottom. An altar, perhaps.

But an altar to what?

From a stone lip jutting out of the wall's top edge flowed a segmented cloth curtain. It did not look weathered, but fresh and vibrant in the sunlight. Robyn stepped forward and touched it. This, this was the place that had drawn her. She could feel it, pulsing energy at her, strong and warm as the sun itself.

The curtain was segmented into six pieces, none wider than Robyn's palm, though each was thick and heavy as a giant piece of fettuccine. The silky fabric strands felt smooth, but Robyn sensed texture at the same time. Strange.

She pushed the curtain segments aside. A row of small blocks in the black wall were etched with moon silhouettes, from a blank space that represented a new moon to a full circle. Slivers, crescent, half, gibbous, full. The crescent was centered and appeared largest.

Beneath it, on the single row of white stones, was another set of markings: doming curves and circles.

They looked to Robyn like the pattern of the rising and setting sun. Flat line of the horizon to a bright noonday sun and back again. The circles grew rounder and higher and then returned again.

Robyn heard a knock from above. The black door was closed again. She bounded up the stairs to let Tucker in.

"You trying to lock me out?" he said, looking hurt.

"I left it open," Robyn said, puzzled.

"Well, it didn't stay open."

Robyn shrugged. "Sorry. I don't know."

Tucker poked in beside her. It took him about four times as long to get into the courtyard, because he kept stopping to write things down.

"You're going to fall down the stairs if you're not careful," Robyn warned him.

But Tucker was too busy writing to answer. In the silence they both heard the door softly slough shut, of its own accord. They looked up at it.

"What is this place?" Robyn asked. Tucker's frantic note-taking indicated a level of understanding that exceeded her own.

"I-I didn't tell you everything I know before," Tucker admitted, lowering the journal. "Most people don't have time for strange old stories."

"What else?" Robyn said. "Tell me everything." Dad had led her to this place. She couldn't imagine the reason, but if there was any chance that following his clues could lead her home again, she would do anything.

"It's just a legend," Tucker said. "I mean, I thought so, but then, here we are . . ." He gazed around in awe.

"A legend?" Robyn prompted. "You mean the moon lore?"

"Oh, I have whole books about the moon lore," he said, waving his hand. "I meant the legend of the Nottingham Cathedral courtyard." He had a nerdy, excited tone of voice.

Robyn nodded for him to continue.

"This church was built over two hundred years ago," Tucker said. "It was commissioned by well-to-do business-men from the Castle District, who had long since turned their back on the old ways. This site used to be a temple of the moon. No one even knows when the original shrine was built; it was just always there."

Robyn shivered. She could feel the ancient truth of it, standing here.

"The church's commissioners ordered the moon temple razed and built the cathedral on top of it, believing it would end people's devout adherence to the moon lore and draw them into the church. They might even have thought it would end the civil wars, once everyone followed the same system."

"You can't change what people believe that easily, can you?" Robyn wondered.

"No," said Tucker. "The civil wars only got worse, and the moon lore followers went underground for decades. The old legends have been surfacing again in recent years, but not like it once was. It's almost become a fad."

"Like a horoscope that people read for fun but don't really believe in?"

"Exactly," Tucker said. "But the workers who built the church truly believed in the ancient moon lore," Tucker said. "So they preserved this most sacred shrine in secret, against the will of the church elders. It's all going in my paper," he told her. "I never thought I'd actually find it!"

Robyn felt sure it was fascinating . . . to someone. But it didn't answer any of her questions. So many bits and pieces, but none of them made any sense. None of them brought her closer to finding her parents. She suddenly felt exhausted.

"I suppose I'll be going now," Robyn said, with a last look over her shoulder at the moon shrine. Part of her wanted to stay, but being here hurt her heart.

"I should to get back to work, too," Tucker said.

They returned to the choir loft. As Robyn walked away, the door clicked shut behind her, as if on a slight breeze.

"I guess it has a mind of its own," Tucker said jokingly. "Too bad. I was hoping to go back in there to study." His gaze dipped down to the key around Robyn's neck.

Robyn smiled and covered the pendant with her hand, a silent answer to the question Tucker was too polite to ask outright. The key was meant to stay with her. She knew it as sure as anything.

Something was happening here beyond her understanding. Whatever she had thought about the moon lore—*it's a myth, it's old-fashioned*—she was rethinking it now.

# ≪CHAPTER THIRTY-EIGHT≫

## *Chazz's Challenge*

"Where are you headed?" Tucker asked Robyn as they crossed the choir loft.

Robyn thought about how to answer without saying too much. Tucker continued anyway.

"If you feel like giving me a hand, I've got a lot of stuff to carry down to T.C.," he said. He led Robyn toward a pile of canvas grocery sacks full of what appeared to be medical supplies. "You should come anyway and talk to Chazz. He knows all about the Crescendo and the moon lore."

"The Crescendo?" Robyn asked.

Tucker passed her a portion of the bags by their handles. A hesitant look crossed his face. "Oh, I just assumed . . . because of the pendant . . ." He cleared his throat. "We should just go," he concluded. "Chazz will want to meet you."

Robyn remembered Chazz well enough. The old guy had kind of given her the creeps. She recalled him leaning back in the rainbow chaise, with his hands clasped in front of him, staring intensely at her.

Robyn followed Tucker out of the cathedral. The bags weren't too heavy, but there were a lot of them. It seemed the least she could do, considering he had saved her from the MPs and shown her the moon shrine. She had been right about the rectangle symbols on Dad's map. But the questions she had about these places only grew bigger.

T.C. wasn't a far walk from the cathedral. "Whoa," Robyn said. Last time she was here the parking lot portion of the fairground had been totally empty. Now it was occupied by a trailer, a couple of vans, several red-awning tents, and a big crowd of people. The trailer and vans were painted light gray, with big red plus signs emblazoned on the sides of each.

"What's going on over there?" Robyn asked.

"It's clinic day," Tucker said. "Volunteer doctors and nurses come down one day each month to take care of people." They headed toward that end of the lot.

The tents bore labels like Blood Pressure Screening, Foot Care, and Ear-Nose-Throat. A banner on the trailer said "Women's Health." Tucker nudged his way around the clusters of waiting folk. Two smock-clad women behind a folding table smiled at him. Each held a blood pressure sleeve in one hand and wore a PalmTab on the other.

"Hey, Tucker," they said. He showed them his bags. "Great. We can use that stuff over by the vans."

Robyn and Tucker carried the bags there. Two teenage boys sitting in the van's sliding-door opening doled out sandwich-size plastic bags containing small bandages, gauze pads, headache medicine, and small tubes of ointment. While Tucker handed over the supplies he'd brought, Robyn took one of the pouches the other boys offered. She put it in her backpack. Even in normal life, she could barely go a week without needing a bandage for some reason or another. It was bound to come in handy.

"This is a great idea," she told Tucker.

"Yeah," he agreed. "People really need it. Especially now that the clinics are converting to BioNet. Not too many people around here are in the network. And they like it that way."

Robyn knew about the BioNet. It was like the InstaScan checkout system—a way for doctors, clinics, and hospitals to keep track of patients. But it had never occurred to her what it would be like to not be in the system.

"Great, there's Chazz," Tucker said, pointing across the lot. Robyn looked in that direction. The older man slouched his way across the lot toward the cardboard city, clutching a paper bag. "Chazz!" Tucker waved. He tapped Robyn's arm. "Come on, I'll introduce you. Chazz!"

Chazz still appeared to be moving in the opposite direction. Tucker called out again, and pretty loud. "Hey, Chazz!" They caught up with him and Tucker tapped his shoulder.

"You again," Chazz said, pivoting reluctantly. "The one with the questions. I done told you, I said all I got ter say about it."

Tucker was not deterred. "I want to introduce you to my friend. This is—"

"Robyn. We've met," Chazz said, giving her a once-over. "You the one I told to get outta Dodge. Still here, eh?"

"I have no reason to run," Robyn lied. He was making her nervous with that piercing stare.

Chazz's stern demeanor cracked. His hollow laugh echoed off the blacktop. "Every one of us got reason to run, missy. Ain't most of us got the means, is all."

"Tell him about the key," Tucker said, nudging Robyn's arm.

"What key?" Chazz's gruff voice sharpened.

"It's nothing," Robyn said as casually as possible. She didn't trust this old guy, even if Tucker and Laurel considered him something of a friend. The skeptical gaze Chazz pointed at her let Robyn know that he didn't trust her, either.

"Oh, it's really neat," Tucker started. "To the door I was telling you about—"

"No," Chazz said, cutting Tucker off. He kept his eyes on Robyn, though. "I don't know what you think you found, but I ain't interested. I got nothing for you."

"But," Tucker persisted. "It's something to do with the moon lore."

Chazz turned away, weaving in between the cardboard walls.

"He's a bit stubborn at times," Tucker admitted. "I guess you have to catch him in the right mood. He does know all there is to know about the moon lore."

"Would it hurt him to just tell us?" Robyn grumbled. She felt angry all of a sudden. She hadn't even wanted to talk to

Chazz in the first place, but if he had the answers she was seeking . . .

Robyn tore after him into the cardboard city. She kept her eyes on the ground, since things jutted out into the walkways—narrow edges of blankets and duffels and suitcases and other belongings. In some stretches the pavement was spotless; in others litter like coffee cups and takeout containers rolled about, creating obstacles.

Chazz muttered as he walked. "What do I care? Waste of time, following the moon." Robyn could hear him but not see him. The path between the boxes wound and wove. She followed the sound of his voice until the path opened up into a clearing. A bare circle of pavement, with a fire pit at its center, ringed in by the walls of the tent city.

Chazz was headed across the clearing. "Nothing good ever came of it. Good way to wreck your life, chasing it." He poked his fist at the sky, as if to punch something. "You think you're the One? You ain't the One." He disappeared beyond the far side of the clearing.

"You could just tell me," Robyn yelled after him. "What do you care, right?"

A small campfire burned low in the rock-ring fire pit. The familiar wood scent nearly brought tears to her eyes. Memories of all the good times around a backyard fire with Mom floated back at her. The taste of roasted marshmallows and hot dogs. She stopped running, not wanting to go forward, or back. She closed her eyes and breathed it in.

When she opened them Chazz stood in front of her. Robyn flinched.

"No." He spoke in the familiar low, insistent tone that chilled her and made her want to back away. "You find the curtain, you come talk to me. You find the Elements, you come talk to me. Until then, you leave me the hell alone." He spun around and stalked off.

"I found it," Robyn said softly.

Chazz froze, with his back to her. "You lie."

"I found the curtain," she told him. She could hear Eveline, loud and clear. *If you are to succeed in this journey, you will be required to trust.*

Silence. Silence, apart from the soft lap and crackle of the campfire.

Robyn swallowed hard. This would be the moment. Chazz would turn, and he would tell her everything she wanted to know, and more. She was sure of it. She clenched her fists and held her breath. Ready.

The older man breathed a long sigh. He looked up at the late afternoon sky as the sun began its descent behind the trees. When he finally spoke, his voice came more gently than she'd ever heard it. "It doesn't matter, Robyn. You are not the One." And he wove away between the cardboard walls, leaving her alone with the fire and its scent and its whisper.

Robyn stared into the small patch of flames. Tucker appeared beside her.

"The One?" Robyn said quietly. "What does that mean?"

"In the moon lore, *the One* is the leader of the people," Tucker answered. It echoed something from Dad's hologram.

The flames licked and snapped. "What's the best way to put out a fire?" Robyn asked.

"Sprinkle dirt on it," Tucker answered. "But we don't put this fire out."

They returned to the open lot. What had been a fairly calm scene a few minutes ago was no longer. Chaos ensued.

Under one tent several doctors hosted basic medical visits, right out in the open. Back to back they stood, examining sprained wrists, plucking out splinters, and asking people with sore throats to say *ah*.

Now, on the far side of the tent, a big line of people jostled and argued and seemingly competed for the attention of one of the doctors.

"What's going on over there?" Tucker said.

"Let's find out," Robyn answered. They walked toward the commotion.

Standing alongside the doctor, a large, pretty girl in a red-and-orange dress held up her hands to the crowd. "Please step back," she said. "Please. We're doing everything we can."

The girl had a very silky bob of dark brown hair and hazel eyes that sparkled. Robyn gasped. It was Merryan Crown—a classmate from Robyn's school in the Castle District!

# ≪CHAPTER THIRTY-NINE≫

## *Trouble in Tent City*

"H-hi, Robyn," Merryan stammered. Her plump cheeks reddened. "I didn't know you volunteered, too."

"Merryan? What are you doing here?"

Robyn was alarmed. Not only was Merryan from Castle District—she was Governor Crown's niece!

Merryan gripped Robyn's arm and pulled her to the side of the table, her eyes wide and frightened. "Please. You can't tell anyone you saw me here, doing this. My family really doesn't approve of me coming here."

Her frightened insistence baffled Robyn. "Who am I going to tell?" Robyn answered. It wasn't as if she could go back to Castle District anyway. "I don't care where you go."

"You promise? I'll get in so much trouble."

"Not as much as I will," Robyn answered. "I mean, I'm supposed to be dead, or something."

"What?" Merryan relaxed her grip. "You haven't been in school. I thought you had already left on vacation."

"Vacation?" Robyn spat the word out like poison. "Not exactly."

"Oh." The pretty girl shrugged. "I thought you were going to be gone all month like the others."

"What others?"

Merryan rattled off the names of a dozen classmates, all children of Parliament members. Her father's friends, in fact.

Robyn's pulse sped up. "They're all missing?" Why hadn't she realized she wasn't the only kid affected by the disappearances?

Merryan's tone turned confused. "They're on the diplomatic trip. With their parents." She added wistfully: "It sounds so exciting. When do you actually leave?"

Robyn shook her head. "What are you talking about?" Merryan was acting like she didn't know about the disappearances. Had Castle District people been told something different?

But the conversation was interrupted by the jostling people clustering around the table. Merryan held up her hands again. "Please. Please wait your turn!" she cried. People pushed and shoved, trying to get closer.

Behind the table the doctor said, "That's it, I'm afraid."

The crowd simmered around the announcement. "I'm very sorry. It's all we have for now," he added. After a few moments of clamoring, the people accepted the truth—the medicine was finished.

"Stingbugs again?" Tucker asked.

Merryan nodded. "A lot of people are sick."

"From stingbugs?" *That doesn't make any sense*, Robyn thought.

"Stingbug infections," the doctor clarified. "They carry bacteria that can cause a bad blood infection."

"I've never heard of that," Robyn said. Stingbugs were annoying, but no big threat.

The doctor continued: "It's common for people in Sherwood to eat a particular herb from the woods that helps naturally repel the stingbug. If you eat it regularly enough, the bugs can smell it on your skin and they don't bite you."

"Bitterstalk. But the woods are off-limits now," Tucker added.

Robyn looked down at the skin of her arms. She'd had plenty of stingbug bites in her life, but she'd never gotten a blood infection. The bites simply swelled into a round red knot and itched for a few days before fading. The people in line for the antibiotics had similar bites, but red and purple lines spidered out from the knots on their skin. Some of the infected people stumbled and staggered around, appearing dizzy and nauseated.

"I'm sure you are vaccinated, like me," Merryan told Robyn. "Everyone in Castle is. But not here. Here they rely on bitterstalk."

Dad used to eat bitterstalk. Robyn found it too tangy, but Dad loved it. *It's an acquired taste*, he would say. *Yes*, Robyn always agreed, *but why would anyone want to acquire it?* Dad would just smile.

Now she understood—it had been protecting him.

"How long will they be sick?" Robyn asked.

"Weeks, without treatment," the doctor answered. "Longer for some. And it depends on the bite. How big and where. Arms or legs, not so bad. Head and neck, worse. Abdomen—the worst of all. It can spread from there to the organs, and then—" he shook his head, as though hopeless. "But the antibiotic starts to clean the blood within a day or so."

It sounded bad.

"Anyway, bitterstalk can't cure the infection. What we need now is medicine." The table was full of small pill bottles, yet the doctor shook his head in dismay. "Other antibiotics are less effective. We don't have nearly enough to go around for the people that are already sick. And the bugs will keep on biting."

"I volunteer at Sherwood Clinic," Merryan said. "They have lots of the pills there, but they're so expensive."

"I bring as much as we can spare from my pharmacy," the doctor said. "But it isn't much. People in Castle rarely get this infection."

That didn't seem fair. She was safe, and Merryan, too. The crowd of bitten people thinned as they headed back to their living spaces. Disoriented. Dejected. Robyn swallowed hard. "There has to be a way to get them some medicine," she murmured.

"What did you say?" Merryan asked. She had resumed her other volunteer duties, with a clipboard in hand jotting something down.

Robyn looked at her. Compared to Merryan, all clean and pressed and pretty, Robyn felt exactly like the grubby, homeless urchin she was rapidly becoming. A few days ago, Robyn would have called Merryan stuck up, annoying, prissy, all kinds of things like that. Seeing her here, down in the depths of Sherwood, of her own accord, dealing so kindly with the rough-edged folk of T.C. was pretty shocking. Still, Robyn wasn't about to tell all.

"Nothing," Robyn said. "You and me—we were never here. Is that the deal?"

For a moment it seemed like Merryan was about to say something. Then she just shook her head and smiled. "Deal."

# ≪CHAPTER FORTY≫

## *Called on the Carpet*

The room was white and the floor was slippery. The warden trembled in her sensible shoes. She stood silent. Alone. Waiting.

Sunlight streamed in through the slats in the blinds behind the sheriff's desk. The desk itself was a giant screen, angled slightly to favor the person sitting behind it. The warden tried to ignore the images flashing by, but there was really nowhere else to look.

"Warden," said the sheriff as she strode in through sliding doors that led to her private conference room.

"Yes. Hello, Sheriff Mallet." The warden admired the sheriff's sense of fashion. Mallet didn't bind herself to the uniform code the warden and the MPs were required to follow. She wore a crisp peach suit with a deep-orange blouse and narrow, heeled boots.

She took her seat behind the desk. The warden remained standing. There were no other chairs in the room.

"All the prisoners?" Sheriff Mallet's tone conveyed her disdain. "Explain."

"Not all. Only one from solitary," the warden stammered. "W-we think the others were a diversion she created to mask her escape—"

"Stop." Mallet dismissed the warden's explanation with a wave of her hand. "I don't need to hear your excuses."

"It was out of our hands," the warden blurted out. "They—"

"I said stop."

The warden clamped her lips shut and lowered her gaze to the floor.

"Seventy-five low-level prisoners . . . and one Crescent." Mallet glared. "Unacceptable."

Mallet had been down to the jailhouse to survey the damage personally. The warden was wrong about one thing: the Crescent girl in solitary hadn't masterminded the jailbreak. Not a chance.

Boltless hinges. A kicked-open door. This was not an inside job. Someone had broken in from outside.

Someone bold and brazen enough to stage a daytime jailbreak, right under the nose of the warden and guards, in full view of a half dozen security cameras, none of which managed to capture a clear shot of the perpetrator's face. Just the crown of her head and that strange, elaborate braid.

Someone who, Mallet feared, would go on to cause more trouble in Sherwood. She ran a hand along the rim of her desk now, thinking.

"It won't happen again." The warden couldn't keep herself from speaking into the silence. "We'll change the doors . . . it hasn't been in our budget to date, but we can . . . It will never happen again."

"Oh, I know it will not." Mallet pressed a button on her screen. "Come and take her now."

The sliding doors opened. Two beefy MPs stormed into the room.

"But—" The warden flinched in surprise as the guards surged forward and seized her roughly by the arms. Her feet slipped on the slick white floor as they pulled her toward the door.

"Put her in Sherwood Jail. Solitary."

"No!"

"Look at the bright side, Warden," the sheriff said, gazing coldly across the desk. "Cell block security is out of the MP's hands, remember? You shouldn't have any trouble getting out."

Mallet flicked her wrist. Her guards dragged the warden off.

## ≪CHAPTER FORTY-ONE≫

## *Wires in the Tree House*

Laurel bounced across the tree house with one giant leap and threw her arms around Robyn. "You were gone forever," she cried. "I thought they got you!"

"I had to hide out for a while," Robyn told her. "But I'm here now."

Laurel's spindly frame belied her strength; the hug was like a vise around Robyn's torso. The almost-violent affection felt strange and lovely. Laurel's words were a smaller, fiercer version of a scolding she might get from her mother for staying out in the woods too late. The truth sunk in for Robyn: she had been missed.

"Everything okay?" Key asked.

Robyn's hand automatically went to the black pendant. Until she understood the significance of the moon shrine, she didn't want to let anyone else in on the secret. Key was interested in the moon lore, like Tucker. He might want to go see it and discuss theories. Robyn wasn't ready to talk about what it meant.

"Yeah," she said. "I'm okay."

Key's expression said he knew she was holding something back.

"There's trouble in T.C.," she said, to change the subject. "Stingbug infections."

Laurel nodded knowingly. "No one can get to the bitterstalk."

"Crown doesn't understand the full consequences of cutting off access to the woods," Robyn said, repeating what the doctor had told her.

"I think he understands them just fine," Key said, with the characteristic bitterness that accompanied talk of Crown.

"There are always guards near the biggest patches," Laurel said dejectedly. "I haven't had any in weeks."

"See?" Key said. "He knows."

Crown couldn't get away with this. It was basic cruelty. Robyn put her hands on her hips. "We'll go to Sherwood Clinic tonight," she said, "and get them the medicine they need."

Laurel shook her head. "Getting medicine . . ." she said. "It's not like getting food."

"All the clinics are locked down tight. As a drum." Key agreed. "You can't even walk out of there with medicine if you don't have a Tag. I mean, you physically can't. There's something in the door that scans you before it opens."

"InstaScan?" Robyn said, feeling discouraged. She always used to like InstaScan. It made things easy, but now she realized it also provided very tight security.

"Getting in is easy. Getting out is the problem," Laurel said. "Like always."

"People need help now," Robyn answered. "We can't wait. The medicine is just sitting there. We have to find a way."

The three sat quietly for a while, thinking. Robyn's hands itched to toy with something. She reached for the hologram sphere in her backpack. She pulled the halves apart and studied the connections again. The wires were so delicate. The cords from her circuit board were much too thick to be helpful. None of the ones from Barclay's box appeared to match, either.

"What is that?" Laurel asked.

"It's a hologram." Robyn glanced at Key, and admitted, "It's why I needed my bag back."

"A hologram," Key said. "Who made it?"

"My dad," Robyn answered. No harm in giving the basic facts. She was careful not to push the halves all the way together. She didn't want to accidentally play Dad's message in the tree house. She would look at it again later, when she was alone.

As she fiddled, Robyn thought about the map. The arrows, the strange message about gathering the Elements. The flames on the map did represent T.C., apparently. She simply hadn't seen the campfire the first time through. Was she supposed to gather fire somehow?

"If a small flame is burning, how do you put it out?" she asked, remembering Eveline's suggestion again.

"Blow it out," Laurel answered at the same time as Key said, "Pour water on it."

One question, three answers so far. Eveline was wrong, Robyn decided. That was no help at all.

"I don't know about the clinic," Key said finally. "But until we figure it out, let's keep on with the food. I think we can go bigger."

"How do you mean?" Robyn asked.

"Last time you just grabbed whatever was available and on top," he said. "We can get more organized."

"Food is food," Laurel said. She popped open a can of peaches to punctuate her statement.

"Why do we need to get more organized?" Robyn said. "It worked pretty well on the fly."

"Aim for a different target, maybe. One they're not expecting. The trucks from the market, for one thing," Key said. "Apparently they drove most of them to bigger storage compounds in other counties. Didn't even unload. They're just sitting there."

"So?" Robyn said.

"We could take them back," Key said.

"The trucks?"

Key nodded.

"Where are these compounds?" Laurel asked.

"There's a couple way out in the boonies of Block Six, the warehouse district. Some here in Sherwood, and plenty in Castle itself. We could go in at night, and take a lot more stuff at once. Maybe a month's worth of stuff, not just a couple of days."

"What's the security like?" Robyn asked, plucking and twisting at the hologram wires. She spotted the bad connection. One thin wire had been sliced and frayed by the edge of the broken sphere. It held together by threads. No wonder the image had failed.

Key leaned forward. "Less security than the jail, apparently. Some guards, but no walls. Big fences to scale—things like that."

"Not a problem," Robyn said. "So let's check it out. For sure."

"Well, we have to find them first. All I have is a list of compound numbers: 211. 760. 410—"

"The 410 Compound? I know that place!" Robyn exclaimed. "That's where they're keeping the other food trucks?"

"One of the places, yeah."

"It's in Castle District. I used to go there all the time," she said.

"Cool," Key said. "That makes it easier than I thought. Wanna go now?"

Robyn returned the hologram sphere to her bag. The three friends ventured out into the forest. They had only just pulled the camouflage off the bike when they heard voices in the forest nearby. MPs must have been patrolling deeper than usual.

The friends hid in the trees until it seemed the coast was clear, then they cautiously made their way forward.

"We're going to need a new hideout sooner or later," Key told Robyn. "Something inside of Sherwood."

"What's wrong with the tree house?"

"Come on," he said. "We can't keep dodging the woods patrol. There are more than there used to be. It's only a matter of time before they catch one of us. Especially with that loud-as-heck bike leading them straight to us."

"Hey." Robyn had barely used the bike yet. "The wheels are going to be really useful. Especially since we have to go all the way to Castle and come back with a month's worth of stuff."

A month sounded like such a long time to Robyn. Time moved slower than ever. It was hard to believe only a few days had passed since the Night of Shadows, when her parents disappeared. Harder still to believe that a month from now, she still might not be home. She didn't even have any leads on her parents' whereabouts, beyond the cryptic reference to Centurion Gate. It bothered her, not knowing.

Was Dad still alive? Had Mom been moved yet?

The map, the pendant, and the hologram remained her only connection to them, and it wasn't enough. She felt like she was letting her parents down.

Her spirits lifted thinking of a return to the 410, though. Barclay would be there, like always. Maybe she could get a wire to fix the hologram. Then she'd finally have some answers.

"I think we're okay in the tree house," Robyn told Key. "It's pretty deep in the woods and hard to notice." She didn't add that, from here, she could get home without much danger. Moving into Sherwood felt like leaving behind the chance that things were ever going to go back to normal.

# ≪CHAPTER FORTY-TWO≫

## *Bigger Than a Bread Box*

They parked the bike in the woods behind Loxley Manor and struck out for the 410 on foot. Sneaking through the darkened streets of Castle District, Robyn felt at home. And with Key and Laurel by her side, the adventure seemed brighter than ever.

The 410 was still under heavy guard. Though she was happy not to be alone, Robyn felt more conspicuous with Laurel by her side. The two girls scrambled up the fence and vaulted over to the trailer top. Key moved off somewhere in the darkness, toward the other side of the lot. Dressed in his MP uniform, he would go to the truck gate and get it opened for them. *If he could.* That was the plan. And Key seemed confident he could talk his way into anything.

Robyn had bacon in her pocket, in case Waldo and friends were on duty. A little rummaging in a diner Dumpster had gotten them all the meat Robyn thought they needed. She brought the pouch to her hand as she and Laurel lowered themselves onto the gravel. But the dogs did not come.

*Waldo?* Robyn thought. *Are you here?* She realized she had been halfway looking forward to seeing that flop-tongued little bacon lover again. Had the MPs brought in dogs just for the Night of Shadows? That didn't make much sense.

Robyn stuck the pilfered bacon back in her pocket. Had she gone hip deep in rancid scrambled eggs for no reason? That was annoying.

She led Laurel through the maze of junk toward the far side of the lot, where the trucks were parked. There were dozens of plain box trucks, like the ones they had seen MPs loading market wares into. But the market had many kinds of stalls—not just food stands.

"Which do you think has food?" Laurel whispered. Nothing would be worse than successfully stealing a truck and having it turn out to be full of potted plants or baskets or something else from the market.

Robyn shrugged. "Ones closest to the edge?" she guessed. The trucks would have been brought in very recently. The girls tiptoed down the line of the trucks' cargo doors. They slid one open a crack and met with the musty fabric smell of carpets and drapes.

Nope.

They left the door ajar, to avoid making further noise, and moved on.

The second truck was full of men's clothing. The third, a mix of pottery, clothing, and jewels. These were all things a normal thief could make use of for money, but they were no good to three kids just trying to survive.

By the time they cracked the seal on the fourth truck, Robyn was worried. What if Key's information was wrong? What if all the food had gone to the depots, after all, and only the merchandise from the dry-goods and hardware stalls came to the compounds? And how many more trucks could they risk opening? The sliding sound was bound to alert someone eventually.

"Yes," Laurel said as she breathed the scent of fresh bread that assailed them. This was the truck they needed!

Plastic-wrapped loaves of bread from Rennison Bakery. Bushels of fruit from Tommie's Orchard. Root vegetables lolling about in mesh pouches on the truck floor. Perfect.

Laurel immediately reached in and took an apple in each fist. Robyn eased the door closed and made sure it had latched.

"This is the one. Let's get out of here," she said.

Robyn and Laurel hurried to the front of the chosen truck. They scooted along its length and mounted the metal running board. Robyn tugged open the driver's-side door.

The small courtesy light in the ceiling lit up like a beacon, illuminating Robyn's startled face.

## ≪CHAPTER FORTY-THREE≫

## *A Dangerous Detour*

The girls leaped inside and Robyn yanked the door shut, but not all the way. Just far enough to put the overhead light out. Not far enough to latch it and send a slamming sound echoing over the gravel.

The previous driver had been much larger and taller than Robyn. And she wasn't short. But with the bench seat pushed all the way back like that, she was able to fold her entire body into the space between the seat and the pedals. Laurel did the same on the passenger side, clutching her apples like treasure. If anyone looked through the windshield, they wouldn't even see the girls' heads.

Robyn pulled the panel from under the ignition slot and reached for the wires underneath. She and Dad had built a solar engine together once. She knew how it worked and how to start it without the key.

It was almost time, but not quite. Key might not be in position yet. Huddled beneath the steering wheel, she pulled in her arms and legs, ducked her head and closed her eyes.

*If I can't see them, they can't see me.*

A memory washed over her then, unwelcome but warm. She'd been terrible at hide-and-seek as a small child. She'd hide behind anything—big couch, small table, thin lamp, whatever—and just close her eyes. Her dad loved to stomp around near her, pretending he couldn't find her, until his antics made her giggle aloud. Then he'd scoop her up and tickle her until she curled up tight in a ball of laughter. Much later, she realized he could see her all along, but he'd played her game because he was a good father. She missed him . . . hard.

If he could see her now, would he play along? She was doing what she had to. Would he be proud?

Robyn's eyes snapped open. She strained her ears, listening for the guards. As long as they were here, she wanted to try to get the spare wire she needed to fix Dad's hologram.

They'd come here for this truck full of food, but if she could leave with something else, too . . .

Robyn reached up and flipped the cabin light switch, so that the light would not come back on when she opened the door. She was pushing her luck now, for certain. It had already been pushed to the breaking point. But with Dad's last message to her at stake, no risk was too great.

"Wait here," she told Laurel. "I'll be right back. And I'm going to need to borrow this." She plucked the second apple from Laurel's fist. The girl whimpered over the loss.

Robyn climbed down from the truck. The guards appeared to be circling the other side of the compound, but she knew she had to move quickly.

She wove through the junk piles to his usual spot.

"Barclay," she whispered. "Barclay?"

The sheet metal shifted. "By the moon, girl!" the man exclaimed brusquely. "What do you think you're doing back here? How many screws you got loose in that pretty head?"

Robyn grinned and held out the apple. "No loose screws. Loose wires, though. I need something ultrafine. Do you have anything?"

"It's for this hologram sphere." She pulled it from her pack and showed him. "Right here."

Across the yard, guards began shouting. Robyn's heart raced.

Barclay sighed. "Girl, you always come with a pack of trouble, don't you?" he said.

"Do you have anything? Fast. I have to go."

"Let's see what we can do," Barclay said. The sheet metal moved farther. Robyn found herself staring into a box six inches deep full of electronics and wires and gadgets. Barclay pushed it out toward her. "Take what you need."

"You've been holding out on me," Robyn grumbled. "How long have you had all this?"

"Heh." Barclay laughed. "If I gave you all the goods at once, how's I gonna be sure you'd come back to visit me?"

Robyn plucked free several of the finest wires she could see . . . and the voltage adapter she'd been waiting for. "I'll come back," she promised. "And next time I'll have more food."

"You better," Barclay said.

Robyn raced back across the lot. Something had happened. The guards were running rampant! Footsteps seemed to come from all directions. Floodlights snapped on, one by one, high overhead. The yard was suddenly lit as if it were daylight. Uh-oh!

Robyn hurried around the corner of one of the tin-roofed huts. She tossed a desperate glance through the curtainless window. The room appeared empty, lit only by the glow of a vast computer console. About a dozen monitors and various blinking machines filled one whole wall of the hut. It seemed like an awful lot of tech for a junkyard, Robyn thought. But she needed a place to hide. She slipped inside.

Instantly, she knew she'd made a terrible mistake. The console wasn't empty, after all.

## ≪CHAPTER FORTY-FOUR≫

## *An Uneasy Alliance*

In the large pilot's chair sat a teenage girl with spiky black hair, dyed deep red at the tips. She swiveled around at the sound of the door, and Robyn realized why she hadn't noticed the girl. She was short to begin with, and she held herself hunched low in the chair, no doubt to avoid being spotted through the window.

Robyn's eyes narrowed. "You." It was the girl from Sherwood Jail!

"It's you," the girl at the computer said back, at almost the same time. She sounded more relieved than upset, unlike Robyn. The girl spun back to face the computer, as if dismissing Robyn as any threat whatsoever. Somehow, that smarted.

"What are you doing here?" Robyn demanded. It felt like righteous anger, seeing her own act of trespass being trespassed on.

The girl's fingers flew over the keys, flitting from switch to switch on the console. "Oh, like you're supposed to be here, either," she retorted. "Do you even know how to work a computer system?"

"Of course I do!" Although Robyn snapped at the girl, her confidence flagged as she witnessed her proficiency.

The computer emitted a series of beeps and whines. "Ha!" the redheaded girl chortled. She pulled a flat gray card out of one of the slots on the front of the console. A portable hard drive. "I got what I came for."

"And what's that?" In spite of herself, Robyn was curious.

The girl smiled and waved the portable drive. "Everything."

"Everything?"

"Everything in this part of the system, yeah."

"They've broken up the data pretty well, but I'm going to get it all. We're going to find out where they took everyone."

"Took everyone?" Robyn echoed.

"Everyone they disappeared." The girl waggled the drive in Robyn's face once more, then clipped it to a chain around her neck and buttoned it inside her corduroy jacket. *Who wears corduroy in the summer?* Robyn thought, though it was ridiculously beside the point.

The corduroy was but another layer between Robyn and the problem at hand. Her parents were among the disappeared! If there was information on the disk that could help find them . . .

But the girl was headed out the door. Robyn had to act fast. As the girl's hand turned the knob, a great chorus of shouts and crunching gravel arose outside the trailer.

"Intruder alert! Intruder alert!" A blue blinking light strobed from somewhere inside the lot.

The girl's eyes flashed with fear. She released the doorknob and crouched below the curtainless window.

Robyn, too, splayed herself low on the floor as the shouts rose and receded and flashlight beams cut into the room, painting the ceiling in haphazard arcs, like Grand Opening floodlights airbrushing the night.

The redheaded girl glared at Robyn, her catlike eyes widened in fright. "They're probably looking for you. You've ruined everything," she said, her voice cracking.

"They could just as easily be looking for you," Robyn retorted. But the girl's fear made her seem less annoying, more innocent. Now they had a common enemy, which would make them de facto friends. If there was one thing she'd learned in the past few days, it was that friends could help get you out of big trouble. She'd still be in prison if it wasn't for Laurel, or she'd have got caught outside Nottingham Cathedral without Tucker to show her to safety. But under this girl's hostile stare, a sudden burst of friendship didn't seem likely.

Allies, then.

"We're in this together at the moment," Robyn said. "I don't want to be caught any more than you do."

Cat eyes. Glare.

"My name is Robyn," she tried. "What's yours?"

"Scarlet," the girl whispered, with a resigned sigh, as if to say, *We're about to die; what's the harm in telling you?*

"I can give you a way out," Robyn offered. "In exchange for sharing whatever you just downloaded."

Scarlet perked up, though her eyes remained skeptical. "What way out?"

Robyn hesitated. If she told Scarlet the plan, what was to stop her from getting in her own truck and just following Robyn's lead?

"You'll have to follow me, and trust me," Robyn said. "Just like I have to trust that you'll actually share what you know with me once we're away."

Scarlet nodded. Robyn reached for the doorknob. The coast seemed clear, as if the chaotic search had moved to the other side of the compound. But no sooner had Robyn stepped onto the gravel than a small figure went running full speed past her.

"Laurel," Robyn blurted out, unable to stop herself. "What are you doing?"

"Run!" Laurel cried, her small eyes bugged wide. "They're coming!"

## ≪CHAPTER FORTY-FIVE≫

## *Pedal to the Metal*

"Follow me." Robyn led the way straight across the lot back toward the truck. There was no point in sneaking—the guards were onto them now. From various points around the lot they shouted to one another, clearly racing around searching for the intruder. Laurel or Key must have been spotted, or one of them tripped some kind of alarm.

Robyn opened the driver's door. "Get in."

Scarlet and Laurel clambered in quickly and scooted along the bench.

"Get down and hold on," Robyn suggested, pushing Laurel's shoulder. The other girls hunkered down in the cavity beneath the dash, curling their fingers into tears in the cloth-covered seat.

Robyn grasped the ignition wires and took a deep breath. She had learned that staying ahead of Crown's military police force required a perfect balance of stealth and brazenness. The stealthy part was over. Time to be brazen.

"Where's Key?" Robyn asked, pausing.

"You don't have the key?" Scarlet said. "We have to go. Now!" But Robyn just looked at Laurel.

"I don't know," she answered. "He should be waiting at the gate." But their careful plan was foiled. With intruders on the compound, surely there was no way Key could get the gate open for them without giving himself away.

Robyn eased herself forward on the seat. Perched on the front edge, with both legs stretched out, she could reach the clutch and accelerator comfortably. She wouldn't be needing the brakes.

Robyn drew another deep breath. Three. Two. One. She tapped the wires together. The truck rumbled beneath her, vibrating to life with a noise that meant they were no longer silent intruders. The headlights snapped on, cutting a white swath across the gravel, illuminating the fence. Robyn clutched and shifted into drive. The truck lurched forward. It was not her first time driving, but the truck was huge. It felt like a beast with a life of its own beneath her.

The guards began to shout. They didn't sound too near, but Robyn was sure they would be in a minute. She aimed to be long gone.

She accelerated, steering the truck out of its row and onto a long open stretch of gravel. She maneuvered the giant steering wheel until the truck lined up facing the distant exit gates. The gates stood high and tall, topped with barbed wire, connected by chains and padlocks. Robyn took a deep breath. There could be no hesitation. Out the passenger-side window, Robyn saw two guards sprinting toward her. The popping sound of long guns rang out.

"We've definitely worn out our welcome," she murmured.

Robyn slammed the pedal to the metal. The truck lumbered forward, gaining speed with every rotation of the enormous tires. Not the greatest pickup, but understandable, considering it was weighed down with a full load.

"Come on," she shouted. "I need more speed."

She got it. The truck churned up gravel, heading straight for the gates. They showed no sign of opening. What had happened to Key? He was supposed to be near the gate. She had thought he'd be in sight by now. So she could see he was okay.

Robyn steered the truck at the gates anyway. No wavering. No apologies. Beside the gate, the door to a small guardhouse opened. A tall MP darted into her path and waved his hands overhead.

"You better move, guy," Robyn called, though there was no way he could hear. Her heart raced. She didn't want to hurt anyone. Her fist wrapped up in the dangling chain, sounding the truck's horn. *Beep. Beeeeeeep. Beeeeeeeep.* Her foot on the pedal didn't let up. *Beep. Beeeeeeep. Beeeeeeeeeeeeeeeeeep.*

*Oh no.*

The truck was a matter of feet from the fence before the guard dove out of the way.

At the moment of impact, perhaps unwisely, Robyn closed her eyes. The entire truck shook. The metal on metal contact gave a sickening crunch. The truck slowed. Scarlet shrieked. Robyn opened her eyes, fearful that she had failed. But the fence snapped and twisted, and in seconds, Robyn's stolen truck was whipping down the paved thoroughfare.

She hated leaving Key behind, but that was the plan. After opening the gate, he was supposed to drive the bike back to Sherwood. With his MP uniform disguise, he had a better shot at getting out on foot than any of the rest of them. They couldn't afford to wait.

Robyn glanced in the rearview mirror. The gate guard stood among the fence wreckage, leaning against the twisted metal poles. The other two were still running along the road after her, but they were losing speed and breathing heavily.

"Winded already?" she scolded, as if they could hear. "That's what you get for smoking, boys."

Laurel giggled.

"By the moon," Scarlet groaned, clambering out of the foot well and strapping herself into the passenger seat. "You sound like an after-school special."

At that, Laurel laughed even louder.

"Look at them. They can't run worth a lick," Robyn said. Not that she was complaining.

Scarlet said something in response, just as sirens began to wail in the distance, drowning out whatever little quip she might have offered. Robyn stamped on the accelerator, hoping against hope that they would make it to Sherwood alive.

# ≪CHAPTER FORTY-SIX≫

## *Who Needs a Driver's License?*

Ahead, the road split into a Y with a narrow left option and a wider one on the right. The left-hand road appeared to head straight into the woods. It would probably dump out in Castle District. So Robyn took the right-hand turn. The road ran close to the edge of the woods. Nothing but a three-foot concrete edging wall separated the boulevard from the tree line.

Robyn was sorely tempted to pull the truck over and make a run for it among the trees, but they had to get back to Sherwood or they'd be walking for hours. And there was no way Robyn was going to lead her pursuers to the edge of the woods. The last thing she needed was to clue them into where she might be hiding.

"Where are you taking us?" Scarlet asked, her voice rising in alarm. "I want to go to Sherwood."

"We are." These might have been unfamiliar roads, but as long as she kept driving in the correct general direction . . . and Robyn had a pretty keen sense of direction.

"Not this way," Scarlet cried. "This is the skyway. It goes straight to Notting District!"

Robyn would have shrugged if she hadn't needed all her upper body strength to keep control of the massive wheel. "So, I guess we'll go to Notting and double back."

"Bad idea," Scarlett shouted. "Get off this road. Get off it now!"

The urgency in her voice left Robyn with little desire to argue. She yanked the wheel hard right, skidding through a gravel access driveway labeled Emergency Vehicles Only. It sure felt like an emergency, and the appropriate vehicles would surely be coming up fast and furious, any second. The truck's real wheel missed the driveway altogether. It bounced over the curb and down onto the frontage road with a tire-squealing skid.

"*Whee!*" Laurel cried, bouncing around on the seat. The little girl seemed to be enjoying the ride. Robyn could not say the same. The frontage road was pitch-black and narrow.

"Why aren't there road signs?" Robyn cried, peering into the dark.

Scarlet clung to her seat-belt strap. Through gritted teeth, she muttered, "There ARE."

But Robyn felt helpless to do much but watch the road and maneuver the wheel. The truck steamed down the frontage road at a breakneck pace. To her left, the concrete median grew taller and taller, until it stopped being a wall and became massive concrete pilings holding the skyway aloft. The pillars continued as far as she could see, eventually obscured behind the tall buildings that rose alongside.

"The skyway is thirty miles, end to end," Scarlet explained. "If they're smart, they'll have a barricade waiting at the other end." She reached suddenly for Robyn's backpack, resting in the foot well. The zipper had come open and a wire from the Barclay box poked out.

Scarlet nudged the gap wider and pulled the box free. "By the moon," she murmured. "Where did you get this? Does it still work?"

"I don't know," Robyn answered. Her voice shook as the truck jounced along. "What is it?"

"You don't know what it is?" Scarlet said. "It's a modem. Very old. Could be very useful . . ."

"How?" Robyn asked, eager to know what value lay in this thing she'd been carting around for days. It had felt important when Barclay gave it to her, but—

"Uh-oh," Laurel exclaimed.

A couple hundred feet ahead, the road dead-ended in a T. Left or right?

Robyn slammed on the brakes. "Read me the signs," she said. "I can't see them. Kinda busy over here."

Scarlet jammed the modem back into the backpack. "City Fairgrounds to the left, downtown Sherwood to the right. Go right!"

But Robyn stepped on the gas and hung a left. "Fairgrounds it is."

"If you're trying to spite me, this isn't really the time," Scarlet grumbled. "We're going to end up in the middle of nowhere."

"This is the plan. They won't be expecting it," Robyn said confidently. She hope, hope, hoped the MPs were far enough behind them that the girls could get everything useful out of this truck in time.

Robyn pulled the truck through the pair of concrete pillars that read City Fairgrounds. She braked hard along the blacktopped stretch of parking lot and swung around so that the tail of the truck was close—a little too close!—to the cardboard huts of T.C.

She didn't bother to cut the ignition; just threw it into Park and leaped out of the cab. Scarlet, too, vaulted free. She made for the gates, retracing the truck's path. And carrying Robyn's backpack.

"Hey," Robyn called after her. "That's mine!"

Scarlet paused, but the sirens weren't waiting for anyone. "They could be here any second," she complained, still backing away. "We have to go!"

"I have to get the food out of the truck," Robyn answered. "You have to stay. Help me."

Scarlet chewed her lip. "You saved my life," she said. "I know I still owe you." But the girl was already several yards away. "Tomorrow. Ten a.m. Behind the library." She tossed the backpack at Robyn and kept on moving.

Robyn let her go. There was no time to waste on negotiation.

She slipped her backpack on her shoulders and ran to the back of the truck. Laurel had opened the cargo door as far as she could reach. After all this, they refused to go back into the woods empty-handed. Sirens wailed through the streets of Sherwood, no doubt looking for them.

## ≪CHAPTER FORTY-SEVEN≫

## *Vanishing Act*

Robyn jumped onto the bumper and shoved the door open all the way. The truck was full to bursting with all manner of delights. Jars of jam and honey. Barrels of fruit. Piles of potatoes and bundles of veggies. Sacks of bread. Robyn had never seen so many loaves in one place in all her life. She didn't waste a second. She stood on the edge of the truck bed and called out over the cardboard city. "Who wants food! Free food for all! Come and get it!" Heads popped up all over T.C.

Laurel stood slack-jawed at Robyn's side. "Whoa," she said, and took a breath.

"Run around and wake people up," Robyn urged her. "We have to get all the food out. Now." There was no question that the MPs would catch up with the truck soon enough. But Robyn was not about to let a good night's haul go to waste.

Key rode up on the green scooter. He was okay! Robyn grinned in relief. Key braked hard right next to the truck and leaped off the bike, shouting, "What the heck are you doing?"

"Feeding people," Robyn said, though she thought it self-evident.

"Are you trying to get us all killed?"

Robyn knelt on the bumper and dragged bread boxes forward. "Just help me, would you?"

Key leaped into the back of the truck and started pushing the loaves of bread out onto the blacktop.

"You are crazy," he said. "What's the point of making a plan if you're not going to stick to it?"

"We were already inside," Robyn protested. "What was I going to do, not take the truck?"

"The plan was going perfectly. You were at the truck. I could see you. I was going to open the gate. And then you decide to detour." He was angry.

He had seen her? He had been ready? Guilt sank into Robyn's chest. "But—" *I needed those wires*, she wanted to say. Instead she blurted out, "What's the big deal? I only needed a minute."

More quickly than Robyn could have hoped, people emerged from their boxes. A growing crowd converged on the truck. The shabbily dressed and just-woken people snapped out of their exhausted daze and snagged bags of bread by the armload. When each person had all he or she could carry, they disappeared back into the cover of the cardboard city.

Key helped her hand things down to the people. They worked efficiently together, but the silence between them was less than friendly. "I would have been fine," Robyn said, "if you two had just waited in place for a minute. *I* didn't set off any alarms. I was coming right back."

"You could have been caught. And then what?"

"I broke out of jail once," Robyn retorted. "Twice, kind of."

"Yeah, so what are the odds they'll put you in minimum security again?" Key argued.

Robyn felt like crying. "I was doing what I had to," she said. "You ruined it."

"*I* ruined it?" he said. "You're the one taking crazy chances. Risking everything, for all of us."

"Laurel didn't have to follow me," Robyn told him. "That's how the alarm went off, isn't it?"

"Why do you think she did that? We're a team," Key said tightly. "We're supposed to look out for each other."

*We're family,* Dad used to say. *We look out for each other.*

Robyn looked at the sky, which was slightly overcast. Maybe she didn't want to be part of a team right now. She wanted to be part of a family.

But minute by minute, her parents seemed farther away. Robyn touched her chest, feeling for the moonstone pendant. She scanned the skyline for the hulking towers of Nottingham Cathedral. She could see the tops of the twin spires, as usual.

The T.C. residents grasped for the food they offered. "Thank you," Robyn heard whispered over and over. "It's a miracle! We are blessed, indeed." The sleepy people giggled in delight at the sight of so much food.

When the truck was empty, Key emerged, holding several bags of bread by their plastic necks. The swirl of sirens seemed nearer than ever. Key said, "They'll tear up T.C. if they find this truck here."

"I'm on it," Robyn said. "Make sure you hide all the food. And the bike. Meet us at Nottingham Cathedral. Southeast corner."

Key looked puzzled, but nodded.

Laurel jumped into the truck cab with Robyn. The smaller girl wore a grin from ear to ear. "That was the best thing ever!" she exclaimed. "Did you see how much food?"

Robyn gunned the engine and tore out of the Fairgrounds. No sooner had she turned onto the main road than an MP jeep with sirens blaring fishtailed into sight behind them.

Laurel stared into the rearview mirror. She whimpered and her voice turned listless. "We're caught."

"Not yet," Robyn said. On the skyline in the near distance, she had her eye on Nottingham Cathedral. She steered the truck onto the street she knew led to the church and accelerated harder. "Hold on," she told Laurel. "And get ready to leap out on my command."

Laurel gripped the door handle. As they passed the church, Robyn braked and took the final corner. The truck screeched to a halt.

"Now!" Robyn cried. The girls jumped out of the truck. "This way," Robyn called, and Laurel joined her. They raced to the side of the old church. Robyn pulled the loose plywood sheet and they slipped behind it, hopefully unseen.

# ≪CHAPTER FORTY-EIGHT≫

## *Sincerely, Robyn*

Through the cracks in the plywood, Robyn and Laurel watched as a jeep with three MPs rolled into the lot. They got out and paced around the abandoned truck, looking pleased and puzzled at the same time.

"They're calling it in," Tucker said, coming up the stairs to the choir loft with a handful of slices of individually wrapped cheese. "Reinforcements will be here soon."

"We're safe in here, right?" Laurel sounded nervous, but she didn't waste a second slapping together a cheese sandwich.

"Safe enough," Robyn said.

Tucker joined her at the sliver of a window. The MPs stood with arms crossed at the front of the truck.

"Someone's going to hang for this," Tucker mused. "Mallet can't afford the appearance of a mutiny, however small."

Robyn's heart skipped. She thought about the mom and boys she'd rescued from Sherwood Jail, serving time for a theft they didn't commit. "I did this," she said. "I don't want anyone else going down for my crimes. Not ever again."

She started down out of the loft toward the loose plywood sheet.

"You're not going to turn yourself in," Tucker said, following her. "That's insane."

Robyn's mind clicked around the problem. "No," she said. "I'm just going to take credit. You have any paper handy?"

Tucker reached into his back pocket. "Uh, no, but I have these." He held out a big pad of bright-green sticky notes and a marker.

"Good enough. Thanks!" She scrawled a quick note and headed for the door.

"You're not going back out there!" Laurel exclaimed.

"I have to," Robyn said. Laurel should understand how she felt, especially after the jailbreak. It was worth the risk to avoid another mistaken arrest.

Tucker sighed. "All right. I'll distract them," he said. He straightened his clerical collar and edged out of the building. "Officers, what seems to be the trouble?"

He conversed with the MPs, standing alongside the truck's front bumper. After a brief exchange, Tucker pointed away from Robyn. "I saw someone running that way a minute ago," he said. Two of the MPs tore off around the corner in pursuit. Tucker chatted up the remaining man, shifting his stance slightly so the MP faced the direction Tucker wanted him to—away from the truck.

When his back was turned, Robyn ran up and placed the note in plain sight, right inside the lip of the empty truck bed. The bright-green color ensured it wouldn't be missed.

*To whom it may concern:*

*This food was confiscated from its rightful owners, the people of Sherwood. Consider it confiscated back.*

*If you think you know me, you do not.*

*If you think you can catch me, you cannot.*

*Sincerely,*
*Robyn*

Robyn drew the arrow on an impulse. It felt right. It was a symbol of the rebellion—wasn't she a rebel now, too?

As she ran out from behind the truck, the MP talking to Tucker spotted her. He pointed, and cried out, "Here, what's th——"

Tucker elbowed the MP in the face. He dropped like a sack of rocks. Out cold. Tucker hurried to Robyn's side.

"Minister, eh?" Robyn said, raising her eyebrows.

Tucker shrugged. "Some days it's easier to preach than to practice."

They ran around the corner, back into the church.

The air rang with sirens once again as the area around the empty truck lot filled with more clusters of police. They strung up crime-scene tape, scanned for fingerprints, tweezed Robyn's note into a clear plastic bag, and puzzled over it.

"Are you sure that was a good idea?" Tucker asked. "Now the sheriff is really going to be gunning for you."

"I'm already a fugitive," Robyn said. "I'd rather they come after me than the people in T.C., or worse—someone totally uninvolved."

The Wanted poster went up within the hour:

# WANTED

**Name:** Robyn (last name unknown)

**Height:** 5'7" (5'9" in boots)    **Build:** Thin, athletic

**Hair:** black (last seen braided)    **Eyes:** unknown

**Skin:** light brown

**Status:** Hoodlum, thief, traitor

**Last known whereabouts:** Sherwood

**Considered dangerous. Apprehend on sight!**

—Nott City Department of Justice

# ≪CHAPTER FORTY-NINE≫

## *Hubris*

There was no such thing as a coincidence. Mallet knew it. She'd always known it.

A brash young thief by the name of Robyn?

The mistakes she'd made in purging the Crescent rebels were coming back to haunt her. Her own hubris.

What danger could one girl, one small child, pose to her? Plenty.

Crown had made clear the need to purge the rebel leaders. At the time, the order to take along their families had seemed irrelevant.

Now Mallet knew different. It was the children he had wanted, as much as the dissident Parliament leaders themselves.

The Crescent rebels followed the moon lore, which promised a leader would one day rise to bring unity.

Of course, the existence of "the One" was a myth, Mallet knew.

The rebels' belief in it was not.

And belief could turn a myth into action. She had seen it in the square a few days ago, when the crowd responded to her dire threats with rustles and hisses. A leader, propped up by legend, could wield unspeakable power. But that power belonged with Crown.

Mallet tapped her desk screen. The Wanted poster surfaced instantly. She keyed into the banner across the top, for MP eyes only. *#1 Most Wanted.* Charles Lorian and Nessa Croft could wait. Their agitation had already been stifled by the recent purge. Mallet had more pressing concerns today.

She leaned back in her chair. It was not necessary at this time to report the trouble in Sherwood to Crown. It would only highlight her failure. It would only reveal that she had lied.

Better to wait until the hoodlum Robyn was in hand.

# ≪CHAPTER FIFTY≫

## *Sherwood's Most Wanted*

When Key arrived, he had one of Robyn's fresh Wanted posters in his fist. Laurel let him in through the plywood gap, and he stormed up to where Robyn was sitting at the front of the church and slammed the page down on the altar.

"No one was supposed to see us!" His voice burst angrily. "They're plastering Sherwood with these things as we speak. On ACTUAL PAPER."

Robyn picked it up and studied it. "It's no worse than the previous one," Robyn said. It didn't even have a picture of her, just a description that the MP who spotted her must have given. Once he regained consciousness. Or maybe the gate guard. He'd probably gotten a look at her, busting through the compound fence. Scarlet's and Laurel's heads had been below the dash—no reason they wouldn't think she'd acted alone.

"It's way worse," Key informed her. "Out there, it's definitely worse. They're practically hunting for you."

"I can't help that," Robyn said.

"You could have warned me there'd be a cordon of cops out front," he said. "Why did you want to meet here?"

"I-I didn't think it would be safe for us to leave," Robyn stammered. "With all those MPs right out there."

"Oh, but it's perfectly safe for me to wander through them," Key thundered. "Do you ever think about anyone other than yourself?"

"I did what I had to do."

"You didn't have to do any of it," Key argued. "You could have just got out." Robyn had seen him annoyed with her before, but she was surprised by how angry he seemed.

She jumped to her feet. "Going inside the compound was your plan to begin with. It was always going to be risky."

"You left the truck and went somewhere. Why?" Key demanded.

"They have a lot of electronics in the 410," Robyn admitted. "I thought I might be able to—"

"What were you thinking?" Key exploded at Robyn. "You could've gotten us all caught. They sent a perimeter patrol around outside the fence," he informed her. "I almost got caught waiting for you. Laurel almost got caught inside." He pointed at the other girl, who sat in the front pew with her knees tucked tight against her chest, watching silently.

"I told her to wait in the truck," Robyn protested. "I didn't ask her to come after me." She turned to Laurel. "I didn't want you in danger."

Key scoffed. "Like she was going to let you run off on your own. You put us all at risk! And for what? Some wild goose chase."

"It's not!" Robyn swung her backpack down. She thrust it forward. "There's something important in this message from my dad. Maybe I can find my parents now. Or at least know what they would have wanted me to do next."

Key's expression turned cold. "Right. You don't care about us, or anyone else. All you care about is yourself."

How could he say that, after what she'd just done in T.C.? Robyn clutched the backpack in both fists. All her hope rested in that little sphere, and it wasn't even working. Every time she got a little closer to finding the truth, something pulled her further away.

"You don't understand what it's like!" she shouted, looking between them. "Either of you." She stared at them, realizing there was no way they could understand. "If either of you had parents, maybe you would get it," she added.

Key's face grew still as stone. He uncrossed his arms and took two steps closer. Robyn already regretted her words, but she couldn't take them back. It was true. She wanted to find out what happened to her parents more than anything, and she had put her friends at risk because of it. But her desperate heart wasn't about to stop looking.

"Your parents are not here," Key reminded her. "We're here. But, I don't think I want to be here anymore. Not with someone like you."

Giving Robyn one last look, Key turned around and strode away.

Robyn turned to Laurel and was surprised to see tears rolling down the brave little girl's face. Laurel unfolded herself and stood up. "I thought we were friends," she whispered. Then she turned and followed Key.

The door hinges groaned lightly and the slap of the loose plywood was just barely audible. Then the sounds faded. Robyn stood in the cavernous sanctuary alone.

## ≪CHAPTER FIFTY-ONE≫

## *And Then There Was One*

"Tucker?" Robyn called. Her voice echoed in the cavernous cathedral. "Tucker?" No answer. Where had he gone?

So Robyn climbed into the choir loft, headed for the moon shrine entrance. Tucker must have been working when they arrived. A granola bar wrapper and a still-sweating glass of ice water rested on the table, in the only clear space among Tucker's nest of papers, files, and notes.

She trailed her fingers along the edge of his pile of books. Tucker must really like to read. Robyn also enjoyed a good story, but she preferred to hear books read out loud, or to watch something on screen. Books with pictures were okay, too, but sitting still long enough to read one wasn't Robyn's specialty. She flipped through a couple of the thinner tomes. *History of Nottingham Cathedral. Prayer and the People. The Church in Nott City. The Plight of the Poor.* No pictures. Tiny print. Bo-ring.

Robyn quickly moved along. She didn't need to see Tucker. She needed to see the moon shrine. She keyed in using the pendant and climbed down the rickety stairs, feeling relieved, as before, when her feet touched down on the pebbles. The door drifted shut behind her.

The courtyard was dark. Thick clouds bunched overhead, blocking out moon and stars. Robyn went to the mysterious curtain and fingered each of the six strands, still curious. She knelt on the altar, clutching the crescent-shaped necklace.

*Dad.* She pleaded with him in her heart. *Where are you? Why did you lead me here? What am I supposed to do?*

She swept the curtain aside and studied the etched shapes in the stone. The row of moon phases. The arc of the rising and setting sun.

The two largest shapes, positioned in the center, one above the other, stood out to her more now than the first time. A black crescent moon. A round white sun.

Robyn placed one hand over each. The black moon was cool as the moonstone it was etched in. The sun, surprisingly, felt warm. Robyn pressed her palm more firmly against the etching. Yes, the spot had grown faintly warm. It reminded her of . . .

She yanked her hand away and gasped. "Mom?"

Robyn brushed aside dirt and pebbles and lay down on the preserved altar. It was clean, and safe, and—at least for now—hers. She closed her eyes and tucked her body tight, willing the wall to shed answers upon her. For all she knew, she was the first to find this spot in a hundred years. She didn't know how, she didn't know why, but it had something to do with her parents. There was something of them here. She could feel it.

A chilly breeze swirled down from above. Robyn awoke, shivering, curled in the same spot on the altar, with her back against the curtain. The clouds overhead had cleared. The entire courtyard was bathed in soft moonlight. The moon itself was small and high in the sky, circled by drifting sheets of dark clouds, but its glow seemed bright all around her.

Robyn unfolded herself and stretched. How long had she slept?

A rolling tumble of thunder echoed in the distance. The air smelled cool and damp. Ready for a storm. Robyn felt reluctant to leave the shrine, but knew she had better get back to the tree house before the sky opened.

As she got to her feet, she glanced over her shoulder at the mysterious, glowing curtain, wishing she could—

Wait . . . the curtain was glowing?

## ≪CHAPTER FIFTY-TWO≫

# The Curtain in the Moonlight

Robyn scrambled away from the wall. The strange curtain was indeed glowing. Not everywhere, though. Most of the curtain remained plain silver, but now glowing diagonal lines crisscrossed each strand. Perhaps reflecting the moonlight?

*It is a moon shrine,* Robyn chided herself. She supposed it made sense that the curtain would respond to moonlight.

No longer afraid, but curious, Robyn crawled closer again. The glowing lines were not actually lines. The silver streaks formed slanted cursive words. Big, single words woven in various angles across each curtain strand. Tilting her head, Robyn could make out some of them.

DARKNESS

LIGHT

BEACON

DAUGHTER

HOPE

PLACE

MOON

ANCIENTS

There were many more. Most were ordinary words on their own, but together they added up to nothing. Just nonsense. Woven, slanted nonsense.

She got up and looked around the shrine. Maybe in the daylight there would be some kind of clue she hadn't noticed before? Robyn paced around on the gravel, drawing the diagonal between the two staircases. She climbed the second staircase, which ended in another door. This door had a keyhole, too, but her moon pendant did not fit. This hole was rounder.

Robyn believed that the moon shrine had something to do with *both* her parents. Could it be that the white stone pendant her mom wore was the second key? And where did the door lead? Looking up, it appeared to be positioned below the bell towers.

Robyn didn't have much time to study. The curtain's glow dimmed as dark gray clouds rolled back across the moon. Robyn sensed the gathering storm. She'd better get back to the tree house before it started to rain.

On her way through the choir loft, Robyn noticed Tucker's glass and wrapper were gone. He must have come back up for a while, not realizing she was here. How long had she been asleep?

The mound of books looked more or less identical to before, in fact—

Robyn gasped—*Tucker's books!* She began riffling through the stacks. What if, in his research, he'd stumbled across the book Eveline had told her to find? That seemed likely, in fact, since Tucker seemed to have every possible book about churches in Nott City. *What was that call number again?* Robyn tried to remember.

She sifted through the books looking at their spines. Finally she stumbled upon a number that looked familiar. An old leather-bound volume that looked all but hand-written. Yeah, that was probably it. It wasn't even too thick, Robyn noted with relief.

Thunder crashed again, closer now. Time to get moving. Robyn wasn't about to sit here and read through the whole thing anyway. She tucked the book in her backpack.

She didn't want to disturb Tucker's notes, but she saw a blank stack of his neon-green sticky notes. That would work.

Robyn scribbled on the top note:

*Hi, Tucker—*

*I borrowed a book on the moon lore. Will bring it back!*
*Robyn*

Tucker had several more notepads; he probably wouldn't miss this one. She stuck it in her backpack.

Robyn exited the cathedral and headed toward the woods. She avoided major streets, sticking to alleys and small roads as usual. But it didn't prevent her from hearing the announcement.

"Attention, Sherwood Citizens!" It was Sheriff Marissa Mallet's voice. But where was it coming from? It seemed like everywhere.

Robyn slowed and looked in through the window of a barbershop. The men seated around the room angled their necks up to focus on the high-mounted small screen above one mirror. Mallet appeared there, much the way Governor Crown had done in previous days.

"A message for one among your number. To the hoodlum known as Robyn: dissent will not be tolerated. You believe you are one hiding among many. We will find you. You say you are working on behalf of the people. It is the people who will suffer for your actions. Consider yourself warned."

The screen filled with a shot of Robyn's Wanted poster. She ducked from the window and scurried on toward the woods. Mallet's voice followed her, from speakers mounted high on street lamps. Robyn had never heard of such a thing. When had those been installed?

Robyn hurried to reach the woods. Despite Mallet's threat, she felt safer than usual crossing under the trees— she figured the MPs would not want to patrol under threat of a rainstorm, even in search of Sherwood's Most Wanted.

A cool breeze blew. Dead leaves drifted down from the branches overhead. Their gentle rustling was everywhere. Rain was imminent. Robyn hurried. She climbed the spiral stair and tucked inside the flap.

The tree house was empty.

# ≪CHAPTER FIFTY-THREE≫

## *The Moon Lore*

Where were Key and Laurel? They should have made it back by now. Were they all right? Robyn's heart slowed. After the terrible things she had said—were they even coming back?

When the rain began, it sounded like more leaves rustling. Robyn had to listen closely to be sure of what she was hearing. Fat droplets plunked against the wood.

The radio hissed and hummed and soon Nessa Croft's voice filled the small room. Robyn curled up close to the speakers, grateful for the moment to feel a little less alone.

". . . Have you heard about the market truck heist?" Nessa Croft was saying. "The taunting hoodlum Robyn just jumped to Number One Most Wanted, displacing our own Charles Lorian and, of course, yours truly . . ." The broadcast cut in and out. The old technology struggled to carry its signal through the raging storm.

". . . fast work, I'd say. Keep it up, little one. The hope of the ancients is alive in you . . ." Nessa's voice reached through to Robyn, warm and strong and sure.

". . . caught in the Elements . . . a good and safe night to all. All breath and blood and bone, for Sherwood. Zero one thirty."

The radio fell silent. *Breath and blood and bone.* The refrain hung in the air. What did it mean? People said it so often that it had to be about more than those three words alone. Robyn huddled in the corner with a blanket. She lit the lantern and opened the library book.

## The Moon Lore: A Love Story

The story begins when the universe was young, when Shadows lived one place and Light another. These forces were so powerful, so enchanting, and so opposite, that the universe was sure they would fight to the death if they ever met. The universe tried everything it could think of to keep them apart. Light was sneaky— it never stayed where you put it—so the universe captured it and tied it into a ball. But in the deep, dark cosmos, Shadows were everywhere, and they could go anywhere. The Shadows and the Light eventually met, and instead of fighting, they fell in love.

Shadows and Light ran away to one corner of the universe and tried to hide. Shadows untied light, and the two were joined. For a while they were extremely happy. Their child, the Earth, danced between darkness and light, relishing in both equally.

When the universe discovered the breach, it cursed the two lovers, casting them into exile. The curse ensured they would live side by side, but never meet. The universe tied the Light back into its ball and tossed it into the sky, just out of reach of its daughter, the Earth, who lay cradled in the deep arms of the night. The Earth herself was cursed to spin and twist, seeking the attention of both its parents at once. But wherever there was Light, Shadows faded. In order for the Shadows to return, the Light must be blocked out.

In time, the Earth's own children, humans, forgot what their grandparents had taught them, about the pure love between Shadows and Light. They fought bitterly, just as the universe had predicted.

The children of Light built great palaces, their halls lined with blazing bulbs, where Light's glow burned all day, and all through what should have been night. They forgot the power of Shadows.

The children of darkness burned quiet fires into the night and watched the shadows dance. They never forgot the Light, for the Earth's mother, the sun, rose every morning to remind them—but they alone cherished the return of their grandfather each night. As a gift, Shadows gave them the moon, a precious orb that could only be seen in darkness, but which held the glow of the sun. It was the closest possible thing to a reunion of Shadows and Light. These children worshipped the moon and prayed to the universe to end the curse and bring the children of Shadows and the children of Light together under one banner as offspring of the Earth.

But as the centuries wore on, the divide only deepened. The children of Light, unable to see the missing half of themselves, developed an insatiable craving for power. The children of Shadows craved unity, but this hope only led them deeper into despair. They fought back.

Witnessing the enmity between her children, the Earth's heart broke. The Earth bore additional children, by the hundreds and thousands, some dark and some light, but none imbued with the true spirit of Shadows or the true spirit of Light. The Earth hoped that without the ancient spirits yearning inside them, the children could find peace. But these soulless children simply joined in the fight.

The once beautiful Earth began to crumble. Storms, fires, earthquakes, floods—all were desperate cries for her children to return to her bosom . . .

# ≪CHAPTER FIFTY-FOUR≫

## *Storm*

*Storms, fires, earthquakes, floods . . .* Robyn did not want to read anymore. Not while she was alone, and so high up in the rain and the dark.

A pocket of night, Mom used to call it, when a storm darkened the sky in the afternoon. Robyn could picture the delicate tremble of her shoulders as she spoke. Of course, now it was actually night, but it still felt like a pocket of something.

Mom was afraid of storms, but Robyn secretly loved them. At least she did when she could look out from the safety of her bedroom window. The tree house rocked with each gust of wind. The boards beneath her were solidly built, she thought, but still it was not a comforting feeling. The air itself churned as the rain tumbled down.

Dad, on the other hand, found water from the sky almost holy. *The tears of Earth's mother,* he would say. *Her sorrow helps us live.*

It sounded like something out of the moon lore, Robyn now realized. Dad said things like that all the time, things that confused her. But Robyn hadn't had time to be confused back then—she'd always pushed confusing things aside. She liked easy things, things you could do and things you could touch. A somersault was easy, or a back handspring. Of course it could be hard to actually perform one well, but it wasn't hard to understand what it was. Building things was easy, too, or making electronic gadgets run. There was always a right way—an answer that was clear.

Unlike now. Now Robyn was just confused, with no way to push aside what she didn't understand.

Laurel tripped in the door, sputtering like a drowned rat. Robyn was startled—over the sound of the storm, she hadn't even heard the footsteps. Laurel was back, after all. Robyn felt hugely relieved.

Laurel carried something large, metal, and awkward in her arms—it looked like a pot or bowl. "Wet . . . wet . . . wet . . ." The girl coughed and trembled.

"It's like a shower," Robyn told her, trying to put a positive spin on it. Eyeing Laurel's dripping T-shirt and jeans, she added, "Or a washing machine?"

"Not if you don't have soap," the younger girl grumbled. She set down the pot and shook out her limbs like a dog.

"Hey," Robyn cried, as droplets pummeled her.

Laurel stripped off her soaking shirt and shorts and rummaged in the cardboard box that held their few items of clothing. She wriggled into a sweatshirt and a pair of leggings that would have been a better fit on Robyn. She squeezed her hair in her fist, up and down the length, until the steady stream of water faded to drips.

"Where's Key?" Robyn asked.

"I don't know."

So he hadn't come back with her. Robyn lowered her head. "Oh." She hoped he was hunkered down somewhere warm and dry, not caught out in Mother Nature's melee.

When Robyn raised her head, Laurel was glaring at her. "I do have parents," she said stiffly. "I just don't know who they are."

"I'm sorry," Robyn said. "That was really mean of me to say."

"I would look for them if I could," Laurel whispered. "I don't want to go back to being by myself."

"Me either," Robyn said.

"I don't think friends should leave each other behind," Laurel said. "Next time you try to follow the clues, don't leave me behind."

"I promise," Robyn said. "And next time I'm mean, just yell at me."

"Okay." Laurel threw her arms around Robyn, hugging her tight. "But don't be mean."

Robyn laughed. "Right. That's what I meant to say. And if I do find out what happened to my parents—when I find them, I mean, you can come home with us." Robyn knew her parents wouldn't mind. Once they met Laurel and heard her story, they could never turn her away. "It'll always be you and me."

"I brought dinner," Laurel said. She pushed the pot toward Robyn, who could now smell the wafting warmth of rice and something else. Meat?

Robyn's mouth watered. "Awesome. Thanks!"

"Steam grates work wonders," Laurel added. "But I would've done it tomorrow if I knew it would rain."

The girls huddled under Key's warm wool blankets and scarfed down two-thirds of the steamed rice and canned meat Laurel had prepared. They stared out the window at sheets of water so thick, the space between the trees appeared almost white.

"Are we going to float away?" Laurel whispered.

"I don't know," Robyn answered. "Where do you want to float to?"

Laurel leaned her head on Robyn's shoulder. "Someplace that feels like home," she said, drawing out the *o*, so the word sounded round as a hug.

"Yeah," Robyn agreed. But the dreamy distant hope in Laurel's voice felt light enough to be washed away by the rain. For Laurel, a true home was the stuff of fantasy. For herself, Robyn feared, it was a thing of the past.

## ≪CHAPTER FIFTY-FIVE≫

## *Key Returns*

Robyn tossed and turned that night, but Laurel slept soundly. And late. Robyn sat in the tree house, fiddling with the hologram and listening to the remnants of the rain dripping off the leaves outside. One of the fine wires Barclay had given her seemed like a right fit, but now the hologram wouldn't even start. No matter how she held or rubbed or squeezed it, nothing happened.

She examined Barclay's modem. Knowing what it was helped a lot—it looked basically functional. Modems were very old technology, like the TexTers, like the radio. It was how people used to access the web and the Nott City databases long before the wireless technology that was ubiquitous now. But there wasn't much she could do with the modem until she had a place to plug it in. Robyn couldn't imagine how something so old that it wasn't even wireless could be useful at all. Scarlet had seemed excited about it, but for now, Robyn put it aside.

She used the circuit board to test the TexTer batteries. They were charged and ready. She fiddled with the devices to learn how they worked.

When Laurel finally woke, Robyn had gotten the TexTers working. You could type a message into one, and a few seconds later it would show up on the other. The messages had to be short. Just barely a sentence or two. Robyn wondered about the range of the devices, but she imagined it could cover most of the city. The signal bounced through old cell towers stationed around the city. These towers were everywhere, just now defunct. No one ever bothered to take them down when they became obsolete.

"Check this out," Robyn said. She held up one TexTer.

Hi, Laurel!

Laurel looked at the screen but did not react. "Is it working?"

"Looks like it."

"Cool." The small girl rolled over and yawned, rubbing her belly in a great big circle.

Robyn smiled. "You hungry?" She offered Key's cold portion of the rice and meat from last night to Laurel.

"Not really," Laurel said. She rolled back over and closed her eyes. That was strange. They were always hungry. Last night it had been all they could do to save the food. Granted, it was less appetizing now, but . . .

Footsteps on the stairs. Key was back.

He ducked through the tree house flap, and frowned.

"Oh," he said. "I didn't think you'd be here."

Robyn shrugged. "Well, we are here." She should apologize, and she knew it. But Key was glaring daggers at her. He hadn't come to make up. He had stayed out all night and come back late trying to avoid her.

"I got the TexTers working," she said tentatively, holding one up. "We can use them on our next shopping spree." The smile she offered him felt forced.

"You mean so you can let me know before you ditch the plan to go rogue?" Key snapped.

Robyn's chest heated up. "Plans change, Key."

"*You* change plans, you mean. And leave the rest of us hanging."

He was partly right, and she knew it. But she didn't feel sorry. "I needed the wires," she said, her voice rising. He had to understand. "My parents—"

"This is way bigger than you and your parents, Robyn. They're gone. Get over it."

"They're not gone," she shouted. "You don't know." She grabbed the hologram sphere and held it up. "My dad left me these instructions. I have to know what I'm supposed to do."

"None of us know what we're supposed to do," Key shouted. "We figure it out. Together."

"Find the shrines. Gather the Elements." She echoed. "I don't know what it means, but—"

Key scoffed. "We're all trying. What makes you so special?"

"Trying what?" Robyn answered. "Who all?"

Key's expression hardened even further. "It's the moon lore. You either get it or you don't."

Robyn rose to her feet and faced him. "Tell me what you know," she demanded. Had Key been holding out on her? "Do you know about the shrines and the Elements?"

"I know enough to know not to waste time with someone who's only out for herself," Key shouted. "Someone crazy enough to rub the MPs' noses in it." He waved a small stack of green sticky notes, exactly like the ones Robyn borrowed from Tucker. "Taking solo credit? How selfish can you get?"

"I'm not out for myself," Robyn shouted back. She had done it to *protect* the others. "I—"

"The moon lore's about all of us," Key said, but didn't stop to hear Robyn's response. "The Crescendo is about all of us. All of Sherwood."

Robyn stamped her foot as her frustration burst forth. "What is—"

Laurel was crying. "Stop yelling," she said, in a tiny voice. Her eyes filled up with tears.

Robyn and Key shut their mouths and turned to her. The small girl lay listlessly on the floor of the tree house. Her body shook with sudden sobs.

"What's wrong?" Robyn blurted out, barely able to lower her voice. But Laurel was shaking, speechless. Robyn and Key glanced at each other. Their fight, for the moment, did not matter. Something else was very wrong.

Laurel began coughing and retching. Acting fast, Key kicked the rice pot closer to her. She lifted her head and threw up in it. She wrapped her arms around the pot as the short gagging sounds continued.

Robyn knelt beside her. "I didn't know you weren't feeling well," she said, patting Laurel's back. "I'm sorry."

Laurel caught her breath and said, "We're going to be late."

"Late?" Robyn frowned. Was the girl delirious? She pressed a hand to Laurel's forehead, like Mom had always done when Robyn herself was sick. Blazing hot skin.

"She's really sick," Robyn said, looking up at Key. "What should we do?"

"You'd better go, or you're going to be late," Laurel said again. She flopped back onto the floor. Her shaky, shallow breaths frightened Robyn.

Key knelt beside them. "Laurel," he said gently. "Where does it hurt the most?"

Laurel lifted one pale hand and laid it on her stomach.

"Let me see." Key held her wrist and moved her fingers aside, then raised the hem of her shirt several inches.

He sucked in his breath hard.

"No," Robyn whispered. Laurel's stomach was a mass of red infection lines. It radiated out from a single sting-bug bite about an inch above her belly button. *Bites to the abdomen are the worst*, the doctor had said. *The infection just spreads and spreads.*

# ≪CHAPTER FIFTY-SIX≫

## Stingbug Stomach

"We need to get you to the clinic," Robyn insisted.

"Fugitives can't go to the doctor," Laurel said, and Robyn knew she was right. "You're going to be late. Go see the girl. With the MO-DEM." She said the word so hugely that Robyn smiled, in spite of the circumstances.

"That's right," she said. "It's close to ten!"

"Go. Don't be late!"

"Not without you," Robyn said. But it was clear the younger girl wasn't going anywhere. Not under her own steam anyway.

"We have to get her to a doctor," Key said. "We can't care for her in the woods like this. We don't even have running water."

Robyn did have to go meet Scarlet. She had to know what the modem could do. There was no telling how long the girl would wait for her if she was late—if she even would wait at all. But she couldn't abandon Laurel. She had promised never to do that again.

Robyn gave Key the keys to her bike. "Let's take Laurel to the cathedral," she suggested. "Tucker may know what to do."

Robyn helped Laurel climb onto Key's back. He carried her down the stairs. They climbed on the bike—Key driving, Laurel pressed against him, with Robyn clinging onto the back. It was still a tight squeeze for three on the long seat, but this was a bona fide emergency.

Key zipped them along through the woods and burst out onto the streets of Sherwood. He was a pretty good driver. Robyn's arms stretched around Laurel's sides, holding her upright, and gripping fistfuls of Key's shirt for balance. The smaller girl slumped against Key's back, and her body slid every which way in the momentum of each turn. The illness was taking over.

"Slow down," Robyn cried, as Laurel's body pitched to the side and Robyn nearly lost her to the pavement.

Key complied, daring to glance over his shoulder. "You okay?"

"Just get us there," Robyn said. "But take it easy."

Key pulled the bike to a screeching stop in front of the cathedral. As he climbed off the bike, Robyn fought to keep Laurel upright. Based on Laurel's slack limbs and cheeks, her closed eyes, Robyn wasn't sure she was even conscious.

"I've got her," Key said. He handed Robyn the bike key and scooped Laurel into his arms. Key wasn't such a big guy, but Laurel looked tiny and fragile cradled in his arms like that. "Here," Robyn tucked one of the TexTers on Laurel's waistband. "They're working now. If she needs anything . . ."

Key nodded.

Robyn checked both ways then pulled aside the loose plywood to let them into the church. She didn't follow.

Robyn hopped on the scooter and raced toward the library. She jogged the bike into the alley behind the building. It was empty. No one in sight.

But she wasn't that late! Ten minutes, tops. And there had been an emergency. Surely Scarlet could have taken that into consideration. Robyn kicked the bike stand angrily. She ran a hand over her head. There was no point in being upset. If she had it to do over, she'd still help Laurel before anything. She leaned against the bike seat and thought about what to do next. Her path and Scarlet's seemed to cross accidentally often enough. Maybe if she just went about her day, the meeting would happen anyway, purely by accident.

"I wasn't sure you'd show," Scarlet's voice said.

## ≪CHAPTER FIFTY-SEVEN≫

# *Thoroughly Modem*

Scarlet had taken a page from Laurel's book, apparently. Robyn looked up in the direction of the sound of her voice and saw the black-and-red-haired girl hanging upside down from the top rung of the fire-escape ladder.

"I'm glad you're still here," Robyn said. "I had a bit of an emergency."

"I would hang around all day to get another glimpse of that modem," Scarlet said. She dropped down from the fire escape. Her moves were smooth and measured. More like a graceful ballerina than the scampering monkey that was Laurel.

Robyn patted her backpack strap. "It's right here."

"We have to go inside," Scarlet said.

Robyn started around the building.

"No, no." Scarlet indicated the back door. "Through here."

"That's a staff entrance," Robyn said. It had an electronic keypad lock. "You need some kind of code to enter there."

"Not if you're a hacker," said Scarlet. "Just try it."

Robyn levered the handle. The door came open.

Scarlet waved her hands with a cheesy grin behind them. "Surprise. That's what I did while I was waiting for you."

"Cool." Robyn was impressed. "Wish I'd known you a few days ago." Her foot and shoulder practically still smarted from her efforts to smash the jailhouse door down.

They sneaked into the staff section of the library and hunkered down in an empty office. Empty of people, that is—the room was full from wall to wall with wires and consoles. "This is the server room for the library," Scarlet said.

"That's a lot of wires," Robyn said.

"Yeah, especially since everything is pretty much wireless at this point," Scarlet answered. "BUT, the wires still work. And that is where the modem will come in handy." She plugged the modem into a console and began clicking away.

"Ha," she said, moments later. "Yes. It is one big back door."

"What does that mean?" Robyn asked.

"It means—" She turned the computer screen toward Robyn, who found herself looking at patron records for the library. With a click of the keyboard, they could see who had checked out books.

"This is just an example," Scarlet said, waving her hand. "The library system is mostly public anyway. If we can get it onto a terminal where there's real information, we can get in without anyone seeing us."

"Like in the compound last night?"

"Yeah, except last night I was hacking directly through their system. Like trying to break in through the front door. Sooner or later they always catch on to what I'm doing."

"And this modem makes it different?"

Scarlet nodded. "The government monitors these systems like crazy. Everything's wireless, but it's almost impossible to hack into." She raised the modem. "With this device, I can access their systems in a way that they don't monitor, through the wired connections. No one monitors those anymore, because no one uses them."

Robyn nodded. "Like sneaking in the back door." A high-tech version of the way she had gotten into Sherwood Jail—by skipping the high-tech keypad and going for the old-school hinges.

"Yeah," Scarlet said. "If you hook this up to the Nott City ID databases, you can track people's Tags, the way the government does," Scarlet said. "For one example."

"So," Robyn mused, "You can tell where people are? You can find them?" Her heart skipped with excitement. Could Scarlet really help her track her parents?

Scarlet nodded. "Yeah, but not just that. You can also make them think you—or someone else—isn't where they really are. Know what I mean?"

"Yeah. What about the prisoner database?" Robyn asked. "Can you get into that?"

"Not from here," Scarlet said. "The NCID databases are one closed system. You can't hack in from here without them knowing. We'd have to get to a physical terminal that runs the system, and then we can come in with this baby." She tapped the modem lovingly. "They might never know the difference."

"How about something in the BioNet database?" Robyn asked. Her wheels turned around the situation. "I need to get into Sherwood Clinic."

Scarlet looked troubled. "That is a complicated system, too, but yeah. If you got physically into the clinic, and hooked to their servers. That's what I'm talking about."

"Getting in is easy. It's getting out that's the issue," Robyn said, as Laurel had observed earlier.

"Getting out with what?"

"Medicine. For the stingbug epidemic," Robyn answered.

"Oh," Scarlet nodded knowingly. "Yeah. Give me a couple of days and I can figure out—"

Robyn shook her head. "I need it now."

"Like, right now?" Scarlet said.

"Yes," Robyn said. "Laurel, my friend from last night? She's got it bad. I have to help her."

Scarlet sighed. "If we get caught in there—"

"I know," Robyn said. "But I have to try. Do you want to come, or do you want to just show me?"

Scarlet looked offended. "Show you?" she said. "Like transfer years of experience and knowledge to you in one magical psychic mind meld?" She stared into Robyn's eyes. "Not possible."

Robyn stared back, willing herself not to smile. "Okay, then. So you're coming?"

# ≪CHAPTER FIFTY-EIGHT≫

## *Through the Back Door*

It had seemed like a great idea when they were hunkered down in the relative safety of the library. Now, standing on the street in front of the Sherwood Clinic, Robyn wasn't so sure. It wasn't as life threatening as breaking into the 410 Compound. The security here was all digital—no guards apart from an older, uniformed man on a stool inside the door who appeared not at all ready to take down any threats. He barely blinked as people strolled in and out through the cage of the sliding doors.

Would the gloves she wore prevent the BioNet from reading her presence? Just walking though the waiting room could trip the sensors. They were set to scan the incoming patients for acute conditions. Electronic triage, her mother always called it, so that the sickest people would be sure to get served first.

Robyn's heart was racing. Was that a medical condition? She wondered if she would get flagged for nervousness. She tried to control her breathing.

For Laurel. For the others suffering in T.C. She had to take the risk. Robyn took a deep breath and stepped between the doors. When the glass slid shut behind her, she had to remind herself to breathe. Not breathing was definitely a serious medical condition.

The glass in front of her opened. "Welcome to Sherwood Clinic," the greeter said, in a flat tone of voice. "Waiting to your left. Billing to your right."

Robyn nodded to him as Scarlet followed her in through the doors. They scooted down the hall toward the Billing Department. The medicine stock would be kept back by those offices, too, Robyn assumed.

She strode confidently down the hallway, though neither she nor Scarlet was familiar with the building. They had done enough reconnaissance to note the presence of all the exterior doors on the building—and the fact that all were equipped with InstaScan double doors, including the staff-only exits. There could be no easy stealing of medicine from this clinic.

Doctors and nurses, clinic volunteers, patients, and lab techs roamed the halls. Robyn and Scarlet blended in well enough. They wandered until they reached a room labeled Pharmacy. It was an active pharmacy—with staff at high tables counting pills into vials and patients waiting in curvy plastic chairs.

"Maybe there's a storeroom," Robyn suggested. Otherwise, they'd have to come up with some kind of diversion. Pulling a fire alarm was not out of the question, but it would be messy. Not the way Robyn liked to roll. Stealth was the key, in her mind. Not like the great truck-through-the-gate debacle that landed her as one of Sherwood's Most Wanted.

The girls continued down the hall and soon discovered a second entrance to the pharmacy. The door had a digital keypad lock. Through the window, they could see lines of plastic bins with pill boxes, medicine vials, jars of ground herbs, tubes of cream, and bottles of antiseptic solution.

Scarlet went to work on the keypad. Robyn leaned a shoulder against the wall, covering Scarlet's hacking effort from the eyes of passersby. In a matter of seconds the lock clicked free. Robyn found herself grateful that she hadn't come to the clinic alone, which was strange—she'd never minded going solo in the past. There were plenty of heists she could certainly pull off on her own, but it was amazing to see how much more she could do with help.

They slipped into the pharmacy and combed the shelves for the medicine they needed. The sounds of the transactions at the front of the room made the risk of capture seem closer than it had in the hallway. The pop of pill caps and the register's *ching* and the soft voices discussing pill side effects and timing routines. How often did the pharmacy techs come back to get a new medicine? Were the squeaking sounds of comfortable shoes on tile heading their way?

"Here," Scarlet said, pointing to a large bin on the second-to-bottom shelf. There was plenty of stingbug medicine. Dozens of bottles, each with a barcode.

"Can we just take them out of the bottle?" Robyn said. There were plenty of plastic bins around that appeared to be uncoded.

"The pills themselves must be coded, too," Scarlet said. She opened a bottle and they stared down at the small orange pills. "Otherwise it would be too easy."

"How do we get them out?" Robyn asked.

"I see two options," Scarlet said "Recode the bottles into something that we can leave with, or else try to jam the doors open."

"Doors," Robyn said. "Isn't that easier?"

"Easier. Faster. And riskier," Scarlet said with a shrug. "If it doesn't work, you're screwed."

"*I'm* screwed?" Robyn said. She'd thought they were in this together.

"Yeah," Scarlet said. "To keep the doors open, I'll have to stay at the terminal with the modem plugged in. While you get out with the pills."

*To succeed in this journey, you will be required to trust.*

Robyn sighed. She had come this far, and the fact was, she couldn't do it alone. "Let's do it," she said.

Robyn and Scarlet returned to the hallway. Robyn's backpack bulged with pill vials. They had stuffed it to the max, but it wasn't too heavy. They found the room with the building's computer servers and luckily it was empty. They ducked inside. The machines hummed away, and Robyn could see servers for the BioNet database, the InstaScan system, the medicine coding, and more. The other side of the room contained shelves of digital medical equipment, all hooked into dozens of charging stations.

Scarlet crouched under the main desk, looking at the setup. Robyn knelt beside her, keeping her head low, lest anyone glance in the window and see them.

The central computer was attached to a single power cord that disappeared into the wall and probably led to solar panels on the roof. Otherwise, it was completely wireless. But as Scarlet predicted, the terminal still had a wired connection socket that wasn't being used.

She plugged Barclay's modem into the server and attached a handheld tablet of her own to the modem. "This is the oldest thing I could find," she commented. "New PalmTabs don't even have any ports."

As Scarlet clicked away at the miniature screen, Robyn's focus drifted. She opened her backpack and studied the tiny raised tracking chip on the pill bottle. Should they recode them instead, after all? The coding server appeared to be right there . . .

Footsteps in the hallway snapped her back to attention. Voices sounded from immediately outside the room. They grew louder as the server room door swung open.

# ≪CHAPTER FIFTY-NINE≫

## *A Medical Miracle*

The first person through the door was Merryan Crown. She wore a red-and-white volunteer smock and was accompanied by a short, thick-haired doctor. The doctor held a long MedTab clipboard in his hand and he was studying something on it while giving Merryan a series of instructions. ". . . bone splint and a medium blood pressure cuff—the one in room 22 has been acting up," he was saying.

Merryan made it around the desk first. She gasped and drew back at the sight of the girls crouched there. Her expression widened in recognition. She glanced between Robyn and Scarlet and the powered-up computer and Robyn's backpack, bulging with pill bottles. She paused in the space between the desk and the wall, such that the doctor behind bumped into her.

"Oh! Sorry, doctor," Merryan exclaimed, taking him by the arm and gently spinning him around. "I forgot. One of the nurses asked me to tell you something. Mrs. O'Leary, down in room 42, was complaining of some new aches and pains. She's not sure the cream you prescribed is strong enough. The nurses are sure she would feel better and perhaps we can get her out of here sooner if you could just . . ."

Merryan chattered away alongside him until they were well out of the room.

"That was close," Scarlet breathed. She raised her screen and started typing again. "Was that a coincidence, or did that intern girl really cover our butts?" she asked with wonder.

"Not a coincidence," Robyn murmured.

Moments later Merryan returned. This time, she closed the door behind her before she raced around the desk.

"Robyn? What's going on?" She reached into the bag and picked up one of the stingbug med bottles. "Are you *stealing* these?"

"What are you doing here, Merryan?" Robyn snapped, all the while knowing she should be nicer to the girl who just saved her skin.

"I-I work here." She fingered her clinic volunteer badge.

"Just get out of here," Robyn told her, "and pretend you never saw us."

Merryan didn't go. "You know, I heard what you said back in T.C.," she said. "When I saw you in here, I knew . . . I thought . . . maybe I could do something to help."

"Well, you showed up at exactly the right moment," Scarlet said, still typing away. "That was awesome."

Merryan blushed. "Did you think it was convincing?"

"Very," said Scarlet.

Merryan looked at Robyn. "It's not right what they're doing, keeping people out of the woods so they can't get bitterstalk." Her broad shoulders shivered. "It's just the worst thing."

"Nowhere near the worst," Robyn muttered.

Merryan gave her a quizzical look. But there was no time to explain.

"We have to get out of here," Scarlet said. "I'm in, so I can jam the door signal now, but it might only last for a few seconds. You should get over there and wait."

"What about you?" Merryan asked.

"I can go out the front," Scarlet said. "It's getting the pills through that matters."

"Hang on—" Robyn said. "Will the clinic notice them missing?"

"Eventually." Merryan shrugged. "I don't know how long. Could be hours. Could be days."

Robyn pulled the green sticky notepad out of her pocket.

"What are you doing?" Scarlet asked. "You're wasting time."

"I always leave a note," Robyn explained. "I can't let them know who I am, but I want them to know it was me."

Scarlet cocked her head, confused.

"I don't want anyone else to get arrested for something we did," Robyn clarified.

*Dear Sherwood Clinic,*

*Looking for the stingbug antibiotics? People needed them. You must be so happy to have been able to help.*

*Sincerely,*
*Robyn*

She handed the note to Merryan. "You want to help? Put this in the pharmacy, okay?"

"Side door," Scarlet said. "Go now. Run."

Robyn did. She tore down the hallway, mindless of the heads that turned. She got to the side doors, nearly breathless. When they opened, both at the same time, and quivered in the walls, she darted through the opening. Free and clear and into the sunlight.

She'd made it!

Robyn ducked into the alley across the street to wait for Scarlet. Instead, it was Merryan who came out through the doors. She glanced left and right.

Robyn waved and held up her hands in question. Merryan darted across the street. "Scarlet says to tell you she needs to borrow the modem. She'll get it back to you."

Robyn felt a burst of annoyance. "She could have asked me."

"I-I tried to stop her," Merryan said. "She just took off."

"It's not your fault." Robyn kicked at the ground. She continued aloud, though the next thought should have remained quietly in her head. "I hope she'll really return it. Otherwise how am I ever going to find Centurion Gate?"

Merryan's face paled. "Centurion Gate?"

# ≺CHAPTER SIXTY≻

## *Centurion Gate*

"Where did you hear of that?" Merryan asked. "No one is supposed to know about Centurion Gate."

"What is it?" Robyn asked. She tried to make her voice sound innocent, not desperate. She wasn't sure she succeeded.

Merryan's mouth formed a small round O. "I-I can't tell you," she said. "I'm not even supposed to know."

"But I already heard of it," Robyn protested. "It's not like you'd be telling me for the first time." She led Merryan into the alley, making her way toward Nottingham Cathedral. If Scarlet was gone, she was long gone. And Robyn couldn't very well stand around in front of the clinic with a bag of stolen meds.

Merryan took a deep breath. "What do you know about it already?"

"Just that it has something to do with the missing Parliament members, and . . ." Robyn glanced around and lowered her voice. "Crown."

Merryan's expression turned confused. "Missing?"

"Is Centurion Gate a prison?" Robyn asked. "Is that where Crown took them?"

"Took who?" Merryan said.

Robyn fought the urge to shake her by her shoulders. "The Parliament members. There's no diplomatic trip, Merryan. Crown kidnapped them."

"He didn't take them anywhere," Merryan said. "What are you talking about?"

Right. Merryan didn't know the truth. Well, if she was going to be hanging around Sherwood, it was time she knew. "Crown. When he took over the city and ousted the dissenters in Parliament."

Merryan frowned. "Are you talking about the restructure?"

"I'm talking about the Night of Shadows," Robyn said. "When Crown took over the city."

"Why do you make it sound like that? He's not as bad as people around here think," Merryan said. "Everyone in Sherwood seems to hate him."

"He's exactly that bad," Robyn informed her. "Haven't you seen his broadcasts? All he does is threaten people."

"For people in Castle, it's different," Merryan explained. "People like the changes he's making."

"He kills people!" Robyn cried. Merryan looked about to protest, so Robyn added, "Or throws them in prison if they don't go his way." Merryan closed her mouth and looked at her shoes. "He's taking our food and being generally horrible," Robyn continued, lowering her voice because other passersby were starting to look at them.

"I know he's not the nicest person," Merryan admitted quietly. "But I'm sure he doesn't kill people."

The announcement videos Robyn had seen said otherwise. "Or throw them in prison . . ." Robyn paused. Her eyes narrowed. "But you already know about Centurion Gate. Where is it? One of the prisoners there is—"

Merryan's cheeks turned red. "It's not a prison," she insisted. "It can't be. I mean, it's right . . . ," her voice trailed off.

At the edge of the cathedral, Robyn checked for onlookers, then let herself and Merryan inside.

As their eyes adjusted to the dim church, Robyn tried again. "Who told you not to talk about it?"

"No one had to tell me," Merryan said, glancing around the sanctuary in awe. "We don't discuss anything that goes on inside the governor's mansion with anyone outside."

"The governor's mansion?" Robyn echoed. "What?"

"Well, I live there," she said. "With my uncle."

Robyn's stomach became a sinking, tightening knot. "How could I forget? You're Crown's niece." How had she expected Merryan Crown to actually help her or the people of Sherwood? And, adding insult to injury, now Robyn had just let her into the cathedral! What had she been thinking?

"I can't help that," Merryan blurted. "No one can change what she was born into."

"Tell that to your uncle," Robyn said, not too nicely. Merryan's words hit a little too close to home. Robyn, too, felt like she was born into something she couldn't get out of. "The people of Sherwood can't help being poor any more than you can help being rich."

"You act like you're so much better than everyone," Merryan said. "I used to think you were cool. I always wanted to be your friend. But now I see you're just mean. I don't know what I was thinking."

"Fine," Robyn snapped. "I never wanted to be friends with you anyway."

Merryan spun back toward the door and ran off. Robyn could only hope that their secrecy pact would stay in place.

# ≪CHAPTER SIXTY-ONE≫

## *Shower*

Tucker came down from the choir loft moments later and found Robyn standing in the same spot, looking after Merryan.

"You okay?" he asked.

Robyn supposed he'd heard everything from up there. There was no point in answering. Clearly nothing was okay.

"How's Laurel?" she asked. Tucker's bleak expression told it all. They climbed to the church house, where Laurel lay on a thin mattress on the floor of one of the old offices.

Robyn retrieved one bottle of pills from the bulging pack. Tucker brought a tin cup of water from the kitchen. Robyn shook Laurel's shoulder to wake her. They helped the younger girl sip and swallow the pill.

Robyn held up the rest of the bottle. "This should be enough for her, right?"

Tucker nodded. She poured the rest of the stingbug medicine bottles onto the floor. "I want to stay with her," she said. "Can you get this down to T.C.?"

"Happy to," he answered. They both looked down at Laurel as she curled back into herself and slipped off to sleep again. Tucker gathered the pills into a plastic bag.

As she walked with Tucker back to the sanctuary, Robyn said, "I don't think Laurel and I can go back to the place we've been staying. Is it okay if we . . . ?" She let her voice trail off.

"You want to stay here in the church?" Tucker grinned. "Are you asking my permission? You know I don't actually live here, right?"

Robyn was surprised. "You're always here."

"I work a lot," he says. "And it's close to T.C. People there need me from time to time."

"So we can stay? You don't mind?"

Tucker shrugged. "I've always thought that churches were meant for whoever needed to come to them."

Robyn wondered if he felt the same way about the moon shrine. She still wanted to be close to it. Something in there called to her, on a deep level.

"You just have to be very careful that no one sees you coming or going," Tucker said, as he headed for the exit himself.

"Yes," Robyn agreed. She glanced through the stained glass above the altar at the moon shrine courtyard. She wanted to go out there, and yet the thought of looking upon the glowing curtain seemed too heavy and painful right now.

Instead, while Laurel slept Robyn explored the run-down old church, looking at every fixture like a treasure. Whole walls were missing in places, but it would suit her purposes just fine. There was running water in the kitchen, and in two bathrooms. One was on the second floor, near the kitchen, and the other was in the basement, along with an old staff locker room with shower stalls. Robyn used the toilet in each room, just because she could. It was a far cry from squatting in the woods.

She pulled out the hologram sphere. "Breath, blood, bone," it said. Taunting her. She wanted to play it again, to feel the closeness to Dad. To hear his message.

Alone in the basement quiet, she pressed the sphere halves together and waited for Dad's image to appear. She stared expectantly into the space above her hand. Nothing happened. No matter how she held or squeezed or rubbed the halves, nothing.

The new wire must've made matters worse, not better. Robyn tightened her fist and fought the urge to fling the thing across the room. Frustrated and sad, she tried again to think about what she knew. Shrines, like the one in the courtyard. Elements that came from the moon lore: wind, water, earth. One who can lead us . . .

Robyn set the hologram sphere aside and looked at herself in the mirror over the sink. The glass was stained and smudged and dirty, but she was even more so. Her hair was a fuzzy mess. She hadn't been sleeping with her silk cap. Not to mention all the running and ducking and diving through the woods. Her braid might have started off as a tight and hardy thing, but it could only take so much torment. Wearing the beret had helped a little bit, but her scalp was itching. It was time to wash her hair.

Robyn removed the rubber band from the tail of her braid and began to unwind it. Soon her hair was free, flopping and swelling in a misshapen dome around her head and shoulders.

The shower had working toiletry dispensers mounted on the wall, which was a blessing. The water flowed warm and Robyn scrubbed herself clean. She soaked her hair and combed the thick, snarled strands with her fingers. Getting the tangles undone would be easy; it just took time. But Robyn was nervous about trying the braid all by herself.

She could do it, but Dad usually watched and often helped her. She tried to focus on what he had told her when they celebrated the first time she completed it without help. *"See? You don't need anyone but you,"* Dad had said that day.

Maybe he had been talking about more than just the braid. Robyn struggled hard to believe that. All the friends she had just almost made were disappearing. Key had left in anger. Laurel was too sick to do much of anything right now. Scarlet had stolen from her. Even Merryan hated her. Robyn didn't really want to be alone, it was just how it was. And it was easier. No one to worry about. No one to hold her back. No one to laugh with. No one to make her cry.

Robyn leaned into the shower spray and let the water rush over her face. All the water in the faucet, and all the water in her heart.

The familiar braid shouldn't have been any harder than usual, but without Dad to watch and make sure she was doing it right, it seemed harder. Robyn kept second-guessing the twists and loops and crosses. When she was done, she stared into the dirty mirror.

It didn't feel like a victory. It only felt sad.

*Mom, Dad*, she thought, her heart twisting.

And just a breath later: *Laurel. Key.*

Robyn dried her face on paper towels from a dusty dispenser. She slid the moon pendant chain back over her neck and patted it close to her heart. She looked at her clean, freshly braided self and realized that not everything she wanted was entirely out of reach. She had gotten the medicine. Laurel was on her way to healing. Maybe Merryan would keep her secrets, after all. Maybe Scarlet would return. And Key had helped her out this morning, even though he was angry with her. They were still a team, even when things got rocky.

If only he would come back.

# ≪CHAPTER SIXTY-TWO≫

## *Bitterstalk*

Sheriff Marissa Mallet sat behind her desk screen nervously waiting for the video connection to open.

Governor Crown's pale, thin mustached face appeared on her screen. "Sherwood is out of control," he said, without preamble. Rumors of the medicine heist at Sherwood Clinic had spread far and wide. Through the people of the county, through the web of MPs working all over the city, and apparently right up the ladder all the way to the governor.

"Sir—"

Crown did not wait. "Get your house in order, Sheriff."

"I'm taking care of it, sir," Mallet said, with all the confidence she felt. "The situation is well in hand."

"It had better be." The connection cut off. The governor had never been a man of many words.

Mallet sat quietly and rubbed her forehead. If this kept up, the hoodlum Robyn would cost her the longed-for promotion to deputy commissioner. It was time to squash this interference, once and for all.

The intercom light lit up. Her assistant's voice came through the speaker. "Sheriff, there's something you need to see."

"What is it?" Mallet snapped.

"I'm sending them in." The intercom shut off and the sliding doors opened. Two MPs entered, holding the elbows of a short, wavy-haired teenage boy. The boy walked calmly between them, not struggling. Not pleading for mercy. Unusual.

"We caught him stealing bitterstalk out in the woods," one MP reported.

Mallet glowered at them. "And instead of throwing him in jail, you brought him to me, because . . . ?"

The other MP swallowed nervously and stepped forward. "He had this on him." He tossed a square pad of green sticky notes onto the sheriff's desk.

Mallet fingered the notepad as she examined the would-be thief. Male. Too short. Perhaps a couple of years too old, as well. "You are not Robyn."

"No," he said.

"But I'll bet you know where she is. Who are you?"

"Call me Key," he said.

# ≪CHAPTER SIXTY-THREE≫

## *The Elements*

Robyn came out of the shower room, and paused. The formerly still basement now echoed with a slight hum. She heard a voice. It sounded like it was coming from down the hall.

Tucker?

But it was a female voice, she thought. And too deep to be Laurel's. Had someone else entered the cathedral with Tucker?

Robyn tiptoed through the basement hallway. She peeked into the room where the sound originated.

It was a young woman with dark hair that sprung out from her head in ringlets. She sat facing the door, leaning in to speak to a bulky handheld microphone that looked like a spiderweb. She glanced up, startled as Robyn appeared in the doorway.

". . . Nessa Croft. Signing off. All breath and blood and bone, for Sherwood. Zero four forty." She clicked a button on the radio transmitter in front of her and smiled. "Hi, there."

"You're Nessa Croft?"

"Yes," the young woman said. "And you must be Robyn."

As they locked eyes, a surge of kinship arced between them. "You're Most Wanted, too," Robyn said. Not the first thing she would have thought she'd say to Nessa Croft. But there was something comforting about laying eyes on another high-level fugitive.

Nessa laughed. "I'm down to number three now, thanks to you."

"You broadcast from here?"

"I broadcast from a lot of places," she said. "They try to trace my radio signal."

She carried a carved wooden arrow sewn against the straps of her radio bag. She packed the portable equipment carefully away.

"Why does everybody talk about breath and blood and bone?" Robyn held the hologram sphere. "You always say it in your broadcast."

"The Elements?" Nessa said. "They're all we are. They're everything we have. That's what we have to put into this fight."

"Elements?" Robyn echoed. "Wait, I thought the Elements were earth, air, and water?"

"Yes." Nessa shrugged. "In the moon lore, it's the same difference. We are the earth. The earth is part of us."

Robyn shook her head. "I don't understand."

"Earth is flesh and bone; air is our breath; water, our blood." Nessa said. "It's in all of us."

"Oh," Robyn said. "So—"

"But on top of that," Nessa continued, "each of our spirits aligns with an element. It drives us. For me, it is air." She laughed lightly. "I guess it's fitting, then, that I use the airwaves to do my work. To serve the Crescendo."

"What is the Crescendo? People keep saying that, too."

"The Crescents' work isn't finished. They want to come back to fight Crown, but they are getting on in years. They can't do it again; not alone. We are rising *together*. The next generation. You and me. Many others."

"We are the Crescendo?" Robyn said.

Nessa nodded. "Everyone who wants to be." She reached out and touched Robyn's cheek. "Follow your heart, little one. Soon enough, the people will follow you. The fire is alive in you. Anyone who knows the moon lore will see it."

"Fire?" Robyn said. "But, is fire one of the Elements? Blood, breath, and bone are only three . . ."

"Fire is the spirit, the soul. It breathes, it bleeds, it bolsters. It's not one of the Elements." Nessa slung her radio bag over her shoulder. "Fire is not constant, or inevitable. It's . . . a blessing of sorts. And few are so blessed as you."

She blew Robyn a kiss and disappeared through the door.

# ≪CHAPTER SIXTY-FOUR≫

## *The Braid and the Prophecy*

Robyn went back upstairs. She found Laurel sitting up, leaning against the wall. "Are you feeling better?"

"A little," Laurel said. Her voice sounded weak, but when she opened her eyes, she looked much stronger already. The medicine must be powerful, to bring about a reversal so quickly.

Robyn put her arms around the younger girl, so happy to see her looking better.

"Your hair is really wet," Laurel said, patting the damp spot on Robyn's shirt. The tail of her braid was dripping down her back. "Yeah, I just took a shower downstairs," Robyn explained.

Laurel jumped to her feet so fast Robyn nearly toppled backward herself. "There's a shower!" she exclaimed. This sudden burst of energy was promising.

"Yeah." Robyn led the way, keeping her arm around Laurel to steady her. "It's one of the things I wanted to show you here."

When Laurel laid eyes on the working shower in the basement, Robyn thought the girl might implode from enthusiasm. "An inside shower!" she screeched, prompting Robyn to grin enormously.

"Can we keep it?" Laurel pleaded, bouncing up and down.

Robyn nodded. "We can stay here as long as we keep it secret," she said.

Of course, all Laurel wanted to do after that was take a shower, so Robyn used the time to scout around the church for things they could use. She found the pile of thin, dusty cot mattresses in a basement closet and dragged a second one up to the room on the second floor where Laurel had lain. She positioned the sleeping pallets against adjoining walls so they each would have a personal area to occupy.

Key had been right about needing to move, Robyn realized. As temporary digs went, the church wasn't so bad at all. The kitchen was right across the hall. Definitely a step up from the tree house. Even though it was farther from her real home.

Good enough for now, Robyn decided, looking around the dilapidated church. But she wouldn't miss this place one bit when it was finally time to go home.

When Laurel came up later, sparkling clean and beaming, Robyn told her, "There's something else I want to show you."

Laurel's energy was nearly spent. Robyn moved slowly as she led her friend through the secret entrance to the moon shrine. Laurel was immediately delighted by the glowing curtain.

"It's pretty," she said, tilting her head.

"I don't know," Robyn said. "There must be a meaning. Do you think it's some kind of code?"

"Code?" Laurel echoed.

"Yeah," Robyn said. "What do you think the words mean?"

Laurel sighed dejectedly. She sat down on the gravel and lowered her head. "Oh. I don't know. What does it say?"

"Your guess is as good as mine," Robyn answered. "It's a mess. And why is it cut into strands like that?"

"Six strands. What are there six of?" Laurel mused. "Six districts, if you don't count Castle."

"The moon lore might not," Robyn agreed. "It's older than the lines around the city."

"Six days and six nights before the day of rest," Laurel offered.

"Maybe we need the moon lore book," Robyn said. "But I left it in the tree house." Key's tree house. Who knew what he might have done with their things by now?

"Yeah, it must be something significant to the moon lore," Laurel agreed. "Is six a special number? We could go to T.C. and ask Chazz. He knows lots about the moon," she suggested. "Or you could ask the old lady. What was her name again?"

"Eveline." Eveline, with the braid. The braid, which was important. Robyn stared at the divided curtain, as realization slowly dawned. "My braid has six strands."

Laurel leaned to look around behind Robyn. "Really? It looks like way more than six."

All the writing on the curtain was etched at a slant. "If I braid it, maybe we'll be able to read it!" Robyn exclaimed.

Laurel clapped her hands. "Oh, try it!"

Robyn did, but very quickly she realized it wasn't going to be that easy. After several failed attempts, she released the cords. "I'm used to doing it behind me," she said, frustrated.

"I don't know how you do it at all," Laurel said, gnawing on a piece of licorice that must have come from Tucker's kitchen stash.

"On my own head, it feels different." Robyn pantomimed the motion of reaching back and over.

"Try it that way," Laurel said. She scooped the ribbons into her arm and swept them over Robyn's head.

"That's brilliant," Robyn said, and reached for the ribbons above her. The cloth strips were much thicker and wider than sections of her own hair, but Laurel was right, the motion came much easier. Especially since there was no need to worry about picking up and adding extra pieces, like she had to with her hair.

"Wow," said Laurel.

Robyn stepped back to survey her handiwork. "Yeah. Wow."

"That's so cool," Laurel said. "What do you think it means?"

## ≪CHAPTER SIXTY-FIVE≫

# A Message in the Moonlight

Braided, the glowing strands no longer spoke total nonsense:

OFFSPRING OF DARKNESS, DAUGHTER OF LIGHT

GIFTING THE PEOPLE, BEACON INTHE NIGHT

EMERGE AFTER SHADOWS, HIDING HER FACE

HOPE OFTHE ANCIENTS, DISCOVER HER PLACE

BREATH BLOOD BONE, ALL ELEMENTS UNITE

BLAZE FROM WITHIN, INSPIRE THEIR FIGHT

SUN FINDS HOME, IN ANCIENT RUNE

DEEP INTHE CRADLE, OFTHE CRESCENT MOON

Each line had six words, one on each strand of the braid. But the rhyming message as a whole still didn't make a whole lot of sense to Robyn.

As they stood there, the curtain began to relax and unravel. Robyn reached down and caught the ends. She looked around for something to tie it in place with.

"I don't think it ought to be tied," Laurel commented matter-of-factly. And Robyn agreed.

So Robyn stood reading and rereading the message out loud until they both practically had it memorized. Then she remembered the sticky notes in her pocket and copied the phrases onto that, just in case. When she released the bottom, the strands slowly separated.

The girls left the moon shrine and returned upstairs. By the time they reached the pallets Robyn had prepared, Laurel could barely keep her eyes open.

Robyn recited the moon lore verse in her head again as she lay down. *What does it mean?* she wondered, but the wondering was no longer so deep or so empty. *The one who can lead the people . . .* , she thought. *Offspring of darkness, the daughter of light. The hope of the ancients. Could it be . . . ?*

And then she, too, fell asleep almost immediately, thinking of twisting rhymes, of suns and moons, of the mysteries of the universe, and the mysteries of herself.

# ≪CHAPTER SIXTY-SIX≫

## *Vengeance*

Deep into the night, Sheriff Mallet sat at her desk, scrolling through Wanted posters.

In the dark, slow, single-digit hours, she made a decision.

She clicked into the corner of her screen that sent messages to her senior MPs. She typed the instructions deliberately.

Moments later, her second in command appeared on the video screen. He wore rumpled sleep clothes and had clearly stumbled out of bed to answer her summons.

"All of them?" he grumbled, then cleared his throat. "Really?"

"Yes. And bring the bitterstalk boy," Mallet said. "The one that goes by the name Key." She did not know who he really was yet. His Tag had been surgically removed.

The senior MP was clearly uncomfortable. He blinked and rubbed his eyes. He pulled his lip and sighed. Mallet waited.

"Meaning no disrespect, Sheriff," he said. "But are you sure you want to do this?"

Mallet smiled slightly. His protests didn't matter. He would do her bidding. They all would. They understood what would happen if they refused.

"It is as I ordered." Mallet confirmed. "And I will be there to observe. We move in at first light."

# ≪CHAPTER SIXTY-SEVEN≫

## *The Sun Pendant*

"Robyn. Robyn?" Merryan burst into Nottingham Cathedral, shouting. Robyn rolled off her sleep pallet. The sun was barely up. It was too early in the morning.

"Robyn! Are you here?" Merryan's voice trembled with urgency. Something was wrong.

Robyn raced downstairs. Merryan stood in the center of the sanctuary, looking this way and that. Her round cheeks were a high red.

"Oh, Robyn. Good." Merryan hurried to meet her.

"What are you doing here?" Robyn asked. "What happened?"

"Anyone can decide to be different from their family," Merryan said, breathing like she had run here all the way from Castle District. She held out a small brown sack, wrapped tight with a rubber band. "This is for you."

Robyn accepted the package reluctantly. Merryan Crown said she wanted to help, but what did she really understand of the situation? Probably about as much as Robyn had known before the Night of Shadows.

When Robyn opened the pouch, she gasped. It was a gold-chained necklace with a pendant of white stone. Mom's sun pendant!

"How did you get this?" Robyn demanded.

"Last night . . . I didn't believe you . . . about Centurion Gate . . ." Merryan said, all rushed and breathless.

"Merryan, where did it come from? You have to tell me."

"You recognize it, don't you?" Merryan said.

"My mother never takes this pendant from around her neck," Robyn said. "I never saw her without it." Her breathing came fast and shallow. *Please, no.*

"Yes, she wears it," Merryan said. "She asked me to give it to you. Centurion Gate . . . it's the dungeon in the governor's mansion."

"My mother is a prisoner in Crown's castle?"

Merryan's eyes blurred liquid. "It seems so," she said. "I'm sorry—I didn't believe you. I didn't know."

Robyn felt weak in the knees. *Mom.* She held the necklace in her palm. It began to warm.

Robyn's eyes stung with tears. She blinked hard, refusing to let them fall. She was not a crying kind of girl. She hated to cry.

Robyn's heart cried out what her lips could not. *Mom . . . alive!*

The plywood clattered, and Tucker stormed into the cathedral, looking just as breathless as Merryan had moments before. "Big trouble in T.C." he reported. "The MPs are down there tearing the whole place apart. They're looking for anyone with stingbug meds and threatening to arrest everyone else, until Robyn turns herself in."

# ≪CHAPTER SIXTY-EIGHT≫

## *Hologram Help*

Robyn and Merryan raced out of the cathedral, following Tucker toward T.C. When they reached the edge of the fairground, the scene before them was total chaos. MPs stormed through the cardboard shelters, driving people out into the clearing where the medical tents had stood just a few days ago. They systematically tore apart the tent city, leaving no hut uninvaded.

The lot was surrounded. As the search ousted people from their sleeping spaces, they tried to run, but rings of MPs caught and corralled them in a large crowd. A row of dark canvas-walled trucks stood waiting.

Sheriff Mallet herself stood in the bed of a pickup truck, shouting over the crowd. "You would do well to surrender, Robyn," she called out. "Or more of your friends will pay the price."

Robyn, Merryan, and Tucker crouch-ran up to the high stone pillars that bridged the road into the fairgrounds. As they approached, Robyn spotted a familiar black-and-red haired figure already hiding behind the low stone wall that ringed the edge of the fairground.

At the sound of their footsteps, Scarlet glanced over her shoulder, alarmed. When she recognized Robyn, she went back to observing the MPs' raid. Robyn, Tucker, and Merryan knelt alongside Scarlet.

"They've discovered the missing medicine," Scarlet said immediately. "And figured out where we took it."

"Wasn't that big a mystery," Tucker grumbled. "We should've been more careful."

Shame sliced through Robyn. She had only been trying to help. Not just help Laurel, but all of T.C. Instead her actions had once again only brought more hardship.

News of the market truck heist had spread far and wide among Sherwood residents. The numerous Wanted posters and the MPs' obvious wrath against the mysterious bandit "Robyn" had fueled speculation in the community. The sudden appearance of much-needed medicine only added to the growing legend.

"I'm so stupid," she muttered. "How could I let this happen?"

Merryan laid a hand on Robyn's shoulder. "You were trying to help," she said. "People appreciate that."

How could they appreciate it, given what was happening right now? Every few minutes, Mallet's MPs loaded another small cluster of people onto one of the trucks.

"She's bluffing. She can't arrest everyone," Scarlet said. "There aren't enough trucks for that."

"They could come back," Robyn said, as one truck, now

crammed with prisoners, drove off through the gates. The four friends ducked low and pressed their backs against the pillar, hoping to remain unnoticed. The large vehicle steamed past without slowing.

"You see, people of Sherwood?" Mallet screamed. "The Robyn you look to doesn't care about your needs. She will stand in the shadows and let you take the fall for her mischief." She paced along the tailgate. "Ask yourselves: What kind of hero is that?"

A low hiss rose up from the crowd. A familiar sound of protest Robyn remembered. Was it protest against the MPs? Or against her?

"Silence!" Mallet motioned for more people to be placed into the trucks.

"We have to do something," Robyn said. Low in her gut, she felt the certainty that Mallet would indeed arrest all of T.C. to prove her point. Even if it took all day. Even if it required filling every truck in her fleet.

"We need to make them think you're here, and surrendering," Scarlet suggested.

"A decoy?" Tucker suggested.

"Yeah, but none of us look enough like Robyn," Merryan said. Tucker was too tall. Scarlet, too short. Merryan, too round. "We need someone her same size."

"Like a hologram," Robyn said glumly as the MPs rounded another small cluster into custody.

"Yeah, exactly," Scarlet said. She quipped, "You have one of those handy?"

"I do." Robyn handed Scarlet the device. "But it won't start." What did she have to lose by sharing it now? It was broken.

"Wow, it's triple coded," Scarlet said, turning the sphere over. "That'll take forever to crack. Who does it belong to?"

"It's mine," Robyn said.

Scarlet looked puzzled. "Then why won't it start?"

"I don't know."

Scarlet handed it back. "Trigger it, and let me take a look."

Robyn held the sphere tight. "See? Nothing."

Scarlet rolled her eyes. "Well, you're just holding it, so no wonder. It needs all three from you." She added, "Breath, blood, and bone."

"No, that can't be." Robyn started to protest. The first time she had opened it, in the woods, all she had done was touch it. No—she had blown some leaves off it. Her fingers had been scratched and bleeding.

Robyn groaned in exasperation. How could she have been so stupid? The directions were written right there on the sphere itself. But it was a bit extreme, wasn't it, asking for actual flesh and blood?

She dragged her pinky finger against the rough edge of the stone pillar until she felt the sharp sting of drawn blood.

The sphere began to glow.

"Give it here," Scarlet said. But Robyn's gaze gravitated toward the image of her father rising from her palm.

"First I need to listen," Robyn said. "The sphere was broken before. I never heard his whole message."

"We don't have *time*," Scarlet insisted. She plucked the sphere from Robyn's hand.

Robyn fought the urge to grab the sphere and run. Dad was speaking now, but over the sounds of the MPs scuffling in the fairground, it was too hard to hear his voice.

Scarlet laid the sphere on her tablet and poked away at the screen alongside it. Dad's image disappeared. "Okay, I can record you. Go," Scarlet said.

"Wait—" Robyn panicked. "Did you delete my dad?"

"No," Scarlet said. "There's plenty of room. I'll start it again. Stand up and say something . . ."

Robyn stood behind the pillar and spoke the recording. She didn't think, or plan, or know what was coming next. She didn't have to. The words poured out, unbidden. She could feel a thrum in her chest that was almost musical.

When she was done, Scarlet stopped the recording and clicked away at her tablet screen. Merryan and Tucker stared up at Robyn with wide eyes and parted lips.

"What?" she said, suddenly self-conscious.

"That was really cool," Merryan breathed.

"You are definitely going in my paper," Tucker said.

Robyn knelt beside them. Her body felt flushed and full, an energy pulsing through her veins, beating harder even than the pulse of her own blood.

"I can give it a one-minute start delay," Scarlet said, tapping away. "Long enough for you to start it and get out of sight."

"Great." The sphere would only open for Robyn. She was going to have to start it herself.

"The MPs will all run this way when they see me," she said. "They won't be watching the crowd. By the time they realize it's a hologram, maybe we can get some people to safety in the woods."

The others agreed. They ran off toward the woods side of the fairgrounds. Robyn gave them several minutes head start, then climbed the pillar, rubbed and blew on the hologram sphere, then set it up top. It rested easily in the grout groove between the stones.

One minute to get as far away as possible. Robyn scrambled down the pillar. It was no harder than climbing out her bedroom window. It reminded her of simpler times.

From the truck bed, Mallet called out, "All right, Robyn. If you won't come forward to save these strangers. Maybe you will to save a friend."

Robyn's heart stilled. She paused in her crouch-run and dared to look over the wall. In the back of another pickup, two MPs lifted a bound prisoner to his feet. He had been lying down, out of sight.

Robyn glanced back in horror at the top of the pillar. The hologram was already set—but now she knew she couldn't flee to the woods with the others. Key was in danger!

# ≪CHAPTER SIXTY-NINE≫

## *Elements Gather, All to Fight*

Robyn ran on as the hologram came to life high above. In an instant, the MPs' attention was all on the pillar where she appeared to stand.

"Here I am!" her synthetic voice boomed. Scarlet had set the volume ultraloud. "But you'll never catch me."

It occurred to Robyn, as she raced along the wall, that they had never actually tested the hologram—had the new wire she put in place actually fixed the projection problem properly?

*It's going to flicker*, she thought worriedly. *It's going to die, and the jig will be up.*

But the image held true. "Sheriff Mallet, leave the people of Sherwood alone. They have done no wrong. It is me you want. I'm here to surrender."

"Get her!" Mallet ordered.

A collection of MPs abandoned crowd control and dashed across the lot to surround the pillar.

"You can have me, but you can't have Sherwood. You can bring me down, but you can't bring down Sherwood. Take me, and the people will take care of the rest."

The MPs circled the pillar. They were large guys, in heavy boots that made it hard to climb the pillar. Robyn's hologram-self appeared untouchable. The people on the fairgrounds began to laugh and cheer.

From her place along the wall, Robyn saw Merryan and Tucker dart out of the woods, motioning for people to follow them to safety. Strangely, though, the people refused to follow. They looked up at Robyn, waving and clapping instead.

"We are Sherwood," Robyn's voice bellowed. "Join me. All breath, all blood, all bone: For Sherwood, unite. For Sherwood, we fight!"

Then the sound of singing filled the air. Robyn stumbled over her feet. That was her own voice—singing! Had she sung into the recording? The memory of speaking into the hologram felt hazy. As if the words—and the song?—had risen out of her from some place beyond.

The tune was a lullaby her parents used to sing to her, mixed with Laurel's lyrics:

*Gather the Elements as you will:*
*Earth to ground you, Water to fill,*
*Air to sustain, a Fire to ignite;*
*Elements gather, all to fight.*

Scarlet had placed the last portion on a loop. "We are

Sherwood . . ." Robyn's voice boomed again. And when the song came around, this time her voice was not alone. The crowd joined in. Singing. Shouting. Struggling.

Robyn joined in the song, which rose from a place she had forgotten existed. Mom and Dad used to sing her to sleep at night. The music and rhythm of this song had been inside her all this while.

The people surged forward like a wave. No longer a passive, gathered mob, now they fought and struggled. The MPs were suddenly the ones surrounded. Some were armed, but the weapon they had been relying on most was intimidation. The fierce pressing anger of the crowd surprised and engulfed them.

The MPs had guns, but the people had numbers. And nothing to lose by fighting—if they stayed quiet, capture or death was certain.

Key stood alone in the pickup bed now. The MPs who had been holding him jumped into the fray to help their colleagues.

There was never going to be a better chance. Robyn rolled over the wall and ran full tilt toward the truck where Key was bound.

She understood that he had left her, left their small courageous team to strike out on his own. Yet it never occurred to her not to try to save him. What was the meaning of a team if you could walk away so easily?

Robyn leaped into the bed of the truck and used her pocketknife to cut the ropes that bound his ankles together and pinned his arms to his sides. There was nothing she could do about his handcuffs, but freeing his legs was enough. They rolled over the side of the truck.

Key yanked down the cloth gag. "Thanks," he said, but his voice was more angry than grateful. "What are you doing here?"

Robyn felt a surge of anger, too. "Uh, saving you?" She grabbed his arm and they ran from the pickup, ducking for shelter beneath one of the larger canvas trucks.

Key shook his head. "Haven't you figured it out yet?" he said. "Everyone in T.C. would willingly go to jail for you. They were all lined up to do it. Why would you come here?"

"I don't want anyone to go to jail. Certainly not for me," Robyn said, as they crouched behind the truck tires. Running feet stormed past. She concentrated on planning the next dash. Into the tents, then make for the woods? Or race toward the wall, heading back to Sherwood? Many obstacles stood in either direction.

"We have to get out of here." Key sighed. "What now?"

"No idea. I came here to fake my surrender, remember?" Robyn admitted. "Saving your butt wasn't part of the plan." She gave him a pointed look.

"Sometimes you just have to seize an opportunity," Key answered, only slightly grudgingly.

Robyn grinned. "Is that your way of saying I was right?"

Key didn't smile in return. "It's my way of saying you weren't totally wrong."

"I'll take it," Robyn said. She tugged him out from under the truck and they ran toward the next truck. From here it would be a short jog to the cardboard, and then they could get to the woods beyond. Robyn started out, but Key held her back.

MP legs raced past. Close call.

Robyn's pendants dangled from her chest. She took Dad's crescent moon pendant in one hand, and mom's orb necklace in the other. The two fit together, like puzzle pieces! They formed one smooth round circle, part Shadows, part Light. Like Robyn herself. Pieces of the curtain verse started to make more sense.

"It's chaos," Key whispered. "We'll never get out of here."

"No, you won't," said a deep voice behind them. They spun around, and an MP bore down on them, gun drawn.

The MP grabbed hold of Robyn's arm and tucked his gun away. Key struggled to free Robyn, to no avail. The MP shoved him off, focused on Robyn as the prize.

"Run," Robyn advised him. "It's me they want."

Key disappeared into the crowd. The MP yanked her arms and half carried her to the truck where the Sheriff waited. "Here!" He called out. "I have her!"

"Now we've got her." Mallet smiled with satisfaction. "Let's get out of here." Over her shoulder she nodded to a senior MP. "Burn it."

The MP held Robyn's wrists and dragged her up into the pickup bed. She stood and faced the sheriff, looking straight into her eyes.

"At long last," Mallet said. "The real Robyn."

# ≪CHAPTER SEVENTY≫

## *Robyn, Hoodlum*

"That's right," the hoodlum declared, hitching her chin up a notch. "I'm the real Robyn."

"At last we meet," Sheriff Mallet answered. She surveyed the defiant girl. Tall for her age, thin, skin the pale brown color of Mallet's own, and complete with the intricate braid.

Papers poked out of a pocket in her stretch pants. Mallet delighted in the fear that flashed across Robyn's face as she reached over and plucked the pages free. Green sticky notes, some kind of rhyme dashed upon them. A folded canvas.

Harmless trinkets, Mallet figured. But the pendant that hung at the girl's neck was a different story. *The crescent of Shadows, the orb of Light.* There was something in the moon lore, she seemed to remember . . .

Mallet reached toward the pendant. It would be hers now.

A small figure, limbs sprawling, came flying off the truck cab.

"Laurel!" Robyn gasped.

The blond child dove full force on top of the MP holding Robyn. She knocked him off his feet, freeing Robyn. Without hesitation, Robyn dove past Mallet's outstretched arm, off the tailgate and into the crowd of T.C. residents.

They caught her.

Now they knew who Robyn was—and the people of Sherwood were determined to protect her. She crowd surfed above a swelling chant of her name.

Mallet stood in the pickup bed, eyes narrowed. "No," she muttered. "I had you!"

Her lip curled in disgust. The MPs appeared cowed by the lunging people; her men were showing all manner of weakness not in keeping with their training. That would have to change.

A red glow rose from the cardboard city. Much like the fire rising behind them, the crowd hissed and surged. The hoodlum Robyn floated atop their raised hands like a ship rocking at sea. Mallet surveyed the chaos and made the call.

"Let's go," she ordered the MPs. "Leave it to burn."

They would all learn their lesson soon enough.

The people delivered Robyn to the far edge of the crowd, away from the MPs, close to the edge of the tents. Something was wrong. The crowd fought on and the MPs began to retreat, but something was terribly wrong.

Robyn came to her feet. She could smell the campfire burning—but no, it wasn't that. This smoke carried the stench of things that should not be burning. T.C. itself was on fire.

Coughing and choking, the people in the crowd stumbled away from the edge of the shelters. Robyn gazed at the flaming cardboard. *Burn it*, Mallet had said.

No!

A flap of cardboard rustled and Chazz staggered out of the burning rubble. His eyes were closed, lungs wheezing. He was barely on his feet. Robyn reached out automatically to catch him as he lurched toward her. "Chazz!" she exclaimed. "You were in there the whole time?" How had the MPs not found him in their search?

"Heh." He wheezed. "Been on the run a long time, girlie. I know all the tricks." He leaned against her awkwardly as he worked to catch his breath. "Heck, they don't even know what I'm up to now. They still after me for the last round."

Tongues of flame licked higher and higher. Soon all of T.C. would be consumed. How do you put out a fire? Robyn thought frantically.

*With water*, said Key.

*With air*, said Laurel.

*With earth*, said Tucker.

*We* are *the earth*, Nessa Croft had said. *I am inspired by air.*

Breath.

Blood.

Bone.

*Your friends will help you*, Eveline had said.

The Elements mentioned in the curtain's prophecy, and the cryptic verse written on the map . . . what if they weren't the actual substances out of the earth? What if they were people?

Maybe she needed her friends' help to put out the fire. Maybe she needed their help to solve Dad's clues and decipher the message in the moon lore curtain!

Together they had saved the day already—driven Mallet and the MPs from the fairgrounds with the power of numbers. Without Laurel, Scarlet, Key, Merryan, or Tucker—without any one of them—the distraction and the escape would have utterly failed.

"Quick," Robyn cried, pushing Chazz away. "I have to find my friends. We can put this fire out."

"Let it burn." Chazz caught her. "We can rebuild."

"But—" Robyn protested, struggling against his grip. She had finally found the answer to the riddle of the Elements. She couldn't stop now. "My friends are the Elements! We can do it. We have to try."

"Let it burn," Chazz repeated. His gruff voice turned quietly insistent. His hands on her shoulders were firm but surprisingly gentle. "I promise you, we will come back stronger."

Robyn's eyes filled with tears. The flames lapped and hissed as the corners of the cardboard city curled into themselves. "Everything will be destroyed," she whispered. "What will happen to all the people?"

Chazz did not answer. Alongside them, residents of T.C. stood or crouched or knelt in a loose circle around the fire. They wept, choking and clinging to one another as billows of smoke from the burning tents wafted over them. Robyn's eyes and mouth stung.

Laurel scampered up beside her. "I tried to get the hologram back," she said.

Robyn was relieved to see her safe after the flying rescue attempt. She held out her hand to retrieve the device. "You got it?"

The smaller girl shook her head sadly. "It's not there. I climbed all the way up both pillars to be sure."

Robyn deflated. Her shoulders sank and her spine curved. Dad's hologram. Gone. This time, forever. Lost to the hands of the MPs, or worse, Sheriff Mallet herself?

Robyn tried to breathe, but drawing in the smoke made her chest hurt even more. She tried to think about it being okay. She had given up the hologram to save Key. To bring hope and to inspire the people. To protect T.C.—and for what? The fire still blazed. It radiated a painful heat. Soon the lot would be covered in ashes. Nothing to show for her loss but greater loss.

"We have to put it out," she whispered. It was the tiniest, most desperate of breaths.

"We will come back stronger," Chazz wheezed from behind her. "It's when we think we have nothing that we learn who we truly are."

# CHAPTER SEVENTY-ONE

# The Elements

Nothing.

No parents. No hologram. No map. No curtain verse. Nothing.

But Robyn had more than nothing. She had her friends. They gathered around, one by one. Laurel stood beside her. Key moving out of the crowd to get closer. Merryan and Tucker emerged from the woods looking horrified at the wreckage that was once T.C. Scarlet was long gone to somewhere, but Robyn knew their paths would cross again.

"We should get out of here," Key said, rubbing his chafed wrists as Laurel picked his cuffs.

"We can't," Tucker said. "There are people who need our help."

Merryan nodded. One glance around told Robyn there were plenty of people wounded from the fire, or from the struggle. Clinic vans had begun to arrive. It was too late to save the structures, but not the people.

Robyn felt helpless to do anything. Tucker and Merryan

knew about helping people that way. She didn't. "There's somewhere I have to go," she told them. "Meet us back at the cathedral, okay?"

Tucker, Merryan, and Key began to tend to the people who had been injured.

Robyn hurried back toward Sherwood, with Laurel alongside. "You could have stayed, if you wanted," Robyn told her.

"You left me behind. AGAIN," Laurel said. "After you promised."

"Yeah." Robyn suddenly felt bad about that. "Well, you're supposed to be sick." The girl's skin still appeared slightly ashen. Her breath a bit shallower than Robyn would prefer. "That's not the same thing as before."

"Felt the same," Laurel grumbled.

"Well, you came anyway," Robyn said, putting an arm around the girl. "And it's a good thing, too."

Laurel smiled. "Where are we going now?"

"To get some answers," Robyn said. The TexTer at her waist vibrated. The small screen said: You alive?

Robyn glanced at Laurel. Her hands were empty "What—?" She held up the TexTer.

Laurel blushed, looking guilty. "Oh. I gave it to the other girl."

"Scarlet?"

Laurel nodded. So Robyn keyed in: I'm alive.

She felt a twinge of annoyance. Great. First the modem, now the TexTer. That girl was going to appropriate all of Robyn's coolest stuff.

As if Scarlet could read her mind, the next text read: You have cool old stuff.

Robyn answered: I want it back.

Yeah, yeah.

Okay, where?

Nottingham Cathedral.

When?

Now.

Fine.

Robyn turned to Laurel. "I wanted you to have the TexTer. So you keep it next time, okay? Don't let her trick you."

"She didn't trick me." The smaller girl turned even redder. "I-I don't know how to use it," she admitted.

Robyn was confused for a second. Then it dawned on her. Laurel didn't spend much time in school. Robyn put her arm around the smaller girl. "Well, okay. I can teach you to read better, and you can teach me how to pick locks," she said. "That seems like a fair trade."

Laurel beamed. "And pick pockets," she said. "I'm a really good pickpocket." She held up a pad of green sticky notes and Robyn's folded canvas map.

# ≪CHAPTER SEVENTY-TWO≫

## *Moon Child*

Eveline was sitting on the low bench in front of the braid shop when Robyn and Laurel arrived. Almost as though she was waiting for them. The old woman leaned her back against the glass window, eyes closed, tail of her braid clutched in one fist, tapping the palm of the other.

She opened her eyes as the girls approached. "Miss Robyn," she said. "What questions have you come with today?"

Robyn started, "I read the moon lore book, and then a bunch of things happened—"

"Feels like rain," Eveline commented, interrupting her.

The sky was only barely overcast, though the air had a humid feel about it. If it rained now, what good would it do? Why could the sky not have opened an hour ago, to put out the fire?

"Let us go indoors, shall we?" Eveline led the way to her room. She sat in the same chair, with Robyn across from her. Like before, except Laurel perched on the arm of Robyn's chair, quiet and holding herself unusually still.

Eveline softened with satisfaction as Robyn related the story of the moon shrine and the curtain. "I hope you will take me to this moon shrine someday," Eveline said. "I should like to kneel there for a while and pray."

Robyn and Laurel recited the curtain's message for her.

"The old spinners of the moon lore wove their verses into the moon cloth," Eveline said, adding wistfully, "So many of the verses have been lost."

"But what does it mean?" Robyn asked, feeling impatient.

"You don't need me to tell you," Eveline said. "Listen to your heart."

Robyn's heart was stubbornly silent on the subject. Dad's message was still incomplete. The Elements were only one part of the puzzle.

"For such a smart girl, you are slow to put pieces together," Eveline said, when Robyn remained quiet.

Robyn was offended. "I'm not a detective," she blurted. "Or a minister, or . . . or . . . a hairstylist. How am supposed to know?"

"The moon lore is not a mystery. It is truth, unfolding."

Ancient, cryptic verses woven into cloth in a secret court-yard? Hidden power pendants? It sounded like the stuff of mystery to Robyn.

"The verses are about you, my dear," Eveline informed her. "They have been waiting in that courtyard, for you."

"If the verses are so old," Robyn puzzled, "How can they be about me?"

"You are not the first moon child nor will you be the last," Eveline said. "The verses have come true before, and they will come true again."

"It's a prophecy?" Robyn asked.

"I don't know that it is," Eveline mused. "The moon lore does not seek to predict, but to explain."

*Explain what?* Robyn wondered.

"Our world turns in circles. The earth itself is a circle. The moon. The sun. All things are woven, like the braid. They recur. Each strand at times, on the surface; at times woven deep." She moved her hands gracefully as if to braid the air.

Robyn fought the urge to pound her foot. The old woman's slow rhythmic words did not answer her questions. "But it mentions my parents," she said. "And what about the power of the moon pendant?"

"It is not the pendant that has power," Eveline said. "It is the one who carries it."

"That doesn't make any sense," Robyn said. "I don't have any power."

Eveline looked at the skylight. "You are wrong." A strange light began to glow in the old woman's eyes. A trick of shadows, maybe, or something mystical. Robyn shifted in her seat.

"On the contrary, my dear. You are the blessed child. The first in many decades."

"Blessed how?" Robyn asked.

"You are a child of Shadows and Light."

Robyn resisted the urge to roll her eyes. She needed a fortune teller for this? Anyone who saw her skin color could see that she fell somewhere between dark skinned and light skinned. How hard was it to guess she came from one dark parent and one light? "Well, duh," she said.

The old woman gripped Robyn's hand, gazing at her like a treasure. "Do you realize what this means?"

Robyn pulled her hand free. "Uh—I'm not exactly the first kid of this color to come along. There are plenty of us."

"Those who trust the moon lore believe that the first humans who walked the earth were blessed by either Shadows, or Light. Their lineages continue," she said. The old woman reached into a drawer and brought out a stack of fine parchment pages. "Occasionally they meet. Occasionally, they fall in love, as Shadows and Light were always supposed to."

"What are these symbols?"

"The arrow represents the unity of the Elements," Eveline explained. "We are all human, but we are also of the earth. The Elements drive us each. Our character. Our skills. The passions of our hearts."

"This one," Eveline commented, indicating Laurel. "My dear, you are driven by air and blessed by Light."

Laurel beamed.

"The Elements are not things, they are people," Robyn confirmed.

Eveline nodded. "Separately, we flounder. Together, we strike." She folded one wrinkled hand into a fist.

Robyn stared at the parchment until she found her own name. The two large family trees came together at her parents, creating her. Robyn touched the place where her mother's and father's names were written.

"A man like Crown fights for power," Eveline said. "A man like your father fights for justice."

"You know my father?" Robyn whispered.

But Eveline continued, heedless of the question. "There have always been men like these. They always clash, and the whole world clashes with them."

"Your existence quakes these tensions," the old woman said. "But it can also heal them."

# ≪CHAPTER SEVENTY-THREE≫

## *Bricks in the Bell Tower*

Robyn and Laurel returned to Nottingham Cathedral to join the others. They found Tucker exuberantly regaling Key and Merryan with the history of the old church.

Key appeared pleased with the new digs. "Like I said, I could stand to give up the risk of walking through the woods every night."

"We all could," Robyn agreed. "Come here, I want to show you what else we found."

Tucker and Laurel followed as Robyn led Key and Merryan into the moon courtyard for the first time. They stared at the shrine in awe. "Tonight, when the moon is up, it'll start to glow," she told them. She explained about the braided verse.

"There's another door," Robyn said. She pointed at the second staircase. "Up there. I think the sun pendant from my mom will open it."

"That's amazing!" Tucker exclaimed, jotting down notes. He chattered at Laurel and Merryan, explaining about his paper.

Key stared at the curtain, like he was trying to read the lines without the moonlight. The distant expression on his face was familiar and unpleasant. He looked as frustrated and annoyed as he had when he left a few nights ago.

"You don't have to stay," Robyn whispered. "I thought you were done with us."

"You don't need me," Key answered. "You would manage on your own." He smiled sadly. "You always do, right?"

*So far,* Robyn thought. *I've gotten lucky.* Today she'd needed a lot of help.

"I get it, okay? Why you only care about doing what your parents wanted."

"I care about other people, too," she said. "And they would want me to."

Key fingered the curtain. "My mother swore by the moon lore," he said softly. "She would have been overwhelmed to see something like this."

"Your mother?" Robyn was confused. "I thought you were an orphan." They—and Laurel—had bonded over the mutual lack of parents.

"I wasn't raised by wolves," Key said. "I have a family. They're just not my blood."

"Why are you living like a fugitive, then?" Robyn asked him.

Key glared at her. "You expect me to tell you my life story? You won't even tell me your last name."

Robyn could have pointed out that she didn't know his real name, either, but she recognized the anger and the sadness burning in his gaze. Something terrible had happened to his family, she imagined. They were still alike, after all.

Robyn turned away from Key, back to the curtain. "I'm sorry," she said. The silver strands seemed to speak the truth better than she could, even though their truth was currently hidden. "I guess we all have secrets."

Key nodded.

Robyn breathed deeply. "I think we can help each other anyway," she said.

"Yeah," Key agreed. "I think so."

Laurel bounced around the chamber, retelling the story, from her perspective, of Robyn's crazy escape. "And then she dove across the crowd! *Swoosh!*" Laurel pantomimed. "For Sherwood, unite. For Sherwood, we fight!" Clearly, she was feeling much better.

Robyn turned to Key and stuck out her hand. "Unite?" she said.

"Fight," he said. They shook hands, as Laurel's antics continued. Tucker and Merryan laughed at her tale.

Robyn's TexTer vibrated. Here. Where are you?

NW corner, Robyn answered. She raced up to the sanctuary and let Scarlet in through the plywood.

"Cool," Scarlet said, as she entered. She held the modem and the TexTer in her outstretched hand.

"Keep them," Robyn surprised herself by saying. "You know how to use the modem. I don't. Maybe it was meant for you."

"Wow. Thanks." Scarlet smiled and clipped the TexTer to her belt. "I guess we should keep in touch."

"You're looking for the prisoners, too, aren't you?" Robyn said. "Maybe we can help each other."

"Maybe," Scarlet murmured as they entered the moon shrine to rejoin the others. "But I'm used to working alone."

"Me, too," Robyn said. "But things are changing."

Robyn made proper introductions between Scarlet and the others. The six new friends stood in a loose half circle staring at the shrine. The curtain was blank, but Robyn recited its verse out loud.

"I think we are the Elements," Robyn told her friends. "I think we're supposed to work together."

"But there are six of us," Laurel said. "And only three Elements."

"Chazz told me I was looking for six," Robyn said. "And then Eveline said that you are driven by air, blessed by Light."

"That would fit with the moon lore," Tucker chimed in. "Maybe there are two sides of each Element, one from Shadows and one from Light."

"I think so," Robyn agreed. "It's easy enough to tell Shadows from Light, but how do you know your Element?"

"You just do," said Merryan quietly. "Once you know to ask yourself. I'm Earth."

"Water," Key said softly.

"Water," Scarlet echoed.

"Earth," said Tucker.

"Air," Laurel confirmed. "I felt it as soon as she told me."

They all looked at Robyn. But she could only shake her head. She searched her heart, for the answer she knew must be there. "I must be air, too," she said. "That's the only one that's missing." But it didn't feel right.

"No, it isn't," said Tucker. "What if you are more than just an Element? What if you are the one who is meant to lead us?"

"You brought us together," Merryan said. "You made us all want to help."

"You're both Shadows and Light," Key said. "Like the verse says."

"You are the fire they can't put out," Scarlet added. "It's obvious."

It wasn't obvious to Robyn, though the thought did make her chest glow warm. *How do you put out a flame?* Eveline had asked her. Everyone else's answer rose immediately from their element. Instead, Robyn had wondered: *Why would you want to put it out? Fire is useful in so many ways.*

Could it be?

Robyn lifted her pendant. Her parents had known it, long before she did. It must be why Dad had left her the moon pendant, and why Mom had risked trusting Merryan to pass her the sun pendant, too.

Robyn took a deep breath and headed up the second staircase. "Let's find out." With the sun pendant, she keyed in through the door. She stepped into a dim chamber. The slim, rickety ladder wasn't exactly fun to climb. The space grew narrower and narrower as she went up the throat of the tower, then it widened into a square surrounding the huge tower bell. She hoisted herself into a catwalk-like service space near the apex of the old church.

The brick walls of the bell tower had seen better days. Fresh air whispered through the cracks. Robyn breathed deeply. Her fingers played against the rusted shell of the old church bell as she eased onto a ledge of ragged bricks. The surface seemed rough but sturdy.

On the inner wall, a large painted arrow bore the familiar words above it: BREATH BLOOD BONE. And below it: AIR EARTH WATER. A few small stone carvings were scattered about the floor. Robyn nearly tripped over a full quiver of arrows, carved in the old style she had seen Nessa Croft carrying. Each was made of a feather, a stick, and a stone from the sea. They were beautiful.

Her friends crowded into the narrow space with her. Together they peered out over the buildings of Sherwood. Amazing, how this place had grown so close to her heart in such a short time. She knew now that she would never have survived if she had tried to stay near home. Sherwood had protected her and folded her in as if she belonged.

Robyn took in the familiar sights: the sagging, dilapidated roofs and colorful flapping stretches of clothesline; the dark tops of people's heads as they walked along the streets. Soul music beats drifted up to her from open apartment windows and parks where young people had gathered. Waves of laughter and chatter rose up from knots of old men at the street corners.

She had come here to hide, but now she had a chance to make a real difference, to bring a little bit of hope and justice and power to the community, just as her father had always tried to. His dream had become her dream. She was the one who remained to carry it through.

In the distance, beyond the deep stretch of woods, stood the towering bulk of the governor's mansion. Its gold, glittery dome evoked nothing but anger in Robyn, in contrast to the beauty and sorrow that characterized Sherwood. Mom was in there, somewhere.

Robyn imagined Crown lurking somewhere in those endless marble halls, cushioned by the resources he was slowly draining from the people. Along with the food and the money, he sucked away their opportunities, their livelihoods, their independence, and even their dreams.

When you had nothing, as Robyn did now, it was easy to see through the promises Crown was making to the people. It was easy to see how much they lacked. Especially since Robyn had once had everything.

She clutched her parents' pendant—literally the key to it all. When hunger threatened to get the best of her, she would think of Mom and Dad. When the creeping doubts threatened to let her forget what she was fighting for, she would think of them.

Robyn would never stop looking for them. But she had a bigger job now, too. It was what they would have wanted.

Soon, she and her friends would start planning the next supply run. It was all going to be more dangerous, now that Mallet had a clear picture of her face. Robyn was sure that new Wanted posters were up already. She breathed the thought away.

As long as Crown sat on his throne of power, as long as her parents remained trapped in his prisons, as long as the people of Sherwood continued to suffer, Robyn would fight. And she was no longer alone.

The people of Sherwood were counting on her. She couldn't let them down.

# ≪CHAPTER SEVENTY-FOUR≫

## *Cracking the Code*

The forensics lab hummed with activity. Sheriff Mallet stood just inside the doorway perusing the many posters, charts, and images plastered along the gray-green walls. Anything to avoid staring at the shouting hologram of the hoodlum Robyn. The techs had placed the sphere inside a sound-muffling glass container, but they could not shut it off entirely. The looped image danced above the glass, projecting that confident rallying cry from behind a grin so lifelike that Mallet itched to step up and slap cuffs on the insolent creature.

The lead forensic tech stood in front of her, babbling about the procedures they would use to crack the recovered hologram sphere. Mallet glossed over the technical mumbo jumbo. She understood enough. Robyn's identity would not be a secret for long. When the techs discovered what Mallet already knew, she'd have no choice but to report the truth to Crown.

"How long will it take?" she asked, interrupting his rambling.

The lead technician shrugged. "It's DNA coded in three ways: by touch, breath, and blood. Could be a few days or a few weeks."

Mallet presided over the operation for a minute. She stared into the projected face of her enemy. A teasing, taunting child: "For Sherwood, unite. For Sherwood, we fight!" It was enough to drive anyone mad.

"But don't worry," the tech added. "We'll crack it. And if she's anywhere in the system, we'll have her pegged. Once and for all, we'll know who this hoodlum Robyn really is. And how to bring her down."

# ≪CHAPTER SEVENTY-FIVE≫

## *Necessary Mischief*

### One Week Later

Robyn listened for guards as she, Laurel, and Key raced away from the supply depot on the Cannonway hefting two burlap sacks each, full of the last of their night's haul. Robyn set down her own sacks long enough to grab her TexTer and pull the pad of green sticky notes out of her back pocket.

We're clear, she told Scarlet, and the InstaScan doors eased shut as if nothing had happened. One glance down the alley told her Tucker and Merryan's distraction must be working. The two were out of sight around the corner, but so were the depot guards. Robyn could hear Merryan's pitiful wailing as she lay in the street pretending to have sprained her ankle. Not only could the girl talk your ear off, she could raise a ruckus like nothing Robyn had ever heard.

She grinned. Teamwork. It definitely had potential.

Robyn peeled off the top sticky note, with her prewritten message. She turned around and smacked the bright-green page in the middle of the glass. Right where they wouldn't miss it.

But the note didn't feel complete, somehow. Robyn hesitated, shifting the other heavy sack of apples in her hand, even though Key and Laurel were long gone and running. Robyn pulled the marker from her pocket, spun back, and tacked on one final word after her signature. There, that looked better.

Governor Crown and Sheriff Mallet and all the MPs knew who they were dealing with now. And it served them right. They had destroyed her family, threatened her friends, chased her, and labeled her. They had made her.

Robyn smiled with satisfaction. She wasn't afraid any more. Her parents' pendant rested secure against her chest, as secure as their memory rested within her heart. *But it isn't over*, she promised them. *We'll see each other again.* Standing here, she could feel their blood pumping in her veins.

*Offspring of Shadows, daughter of Light.* With the moon's mixed blessing upon her, Robyn was becoming everything she was supposed to be. She patted the sticky note in place for good measure, hefted the apple bags over her shoulder, then turned and ran after her friends.

*To whom it may concern:*

*You didn't really need so many bushels of fruit, did you? They were just lying around, so I have returned them to the hungry people of Sherwood.*

*With best wishes,*
*Robyn Hoodlum*

# *Acknowledgments*

Many people helped in the process of taking this story from idea to reality. Thanks as always to my family for their constant support. My writers' groups pored over many a draft and version of this concept, and I'm grateful for their input. I'm sure they're as happy as I am to see Robyn finally making her way into the world: Josanne, Laurie, Wiley, Kitsy, Susan, Holly, Diana, and Vicki. Many friends took me in during the writing process and/or lent ideas to the story that still survive: special thanks to Kerry, Sarah, Kristina, Kiara, Zu, Allison, Grace, Eric, Shawn, Jane, Nicole, and Peter. Thanks to my colleagues at Vermont College of Fine Arts and my agent, Michelle Humphrey, for creating new opportunities for me. Most of all, thanks to my editor, Mary Kate Castellani, and everyone at Bloomsbury who has worked hard to transform my manuscript into a book!

**≪Robyn's story continues in . . .≫**

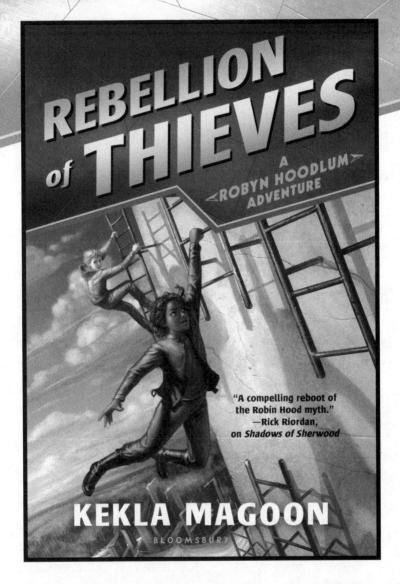

**Read on for a sneak peek at Robyn Hoodlum's next high-stakes adventure: infiltrating Governor Crown's mansion to rescue her parents.**

Robyn stayed curled in the claw of the backhoe for what felt like an eternity. It must have been an hour, at least. She waited until the sirens came, and receded. Until the footsteps prowling the lot ceased their crunching and the voices that accompanied them no longer swirled around her. Her butt fell asleep. Her knees ached from being drawn in tight. Her arms ached from holding them. Her mind drifted back and forth, from the present to the past to the future. She could see two of the three very clearly.

Her father's smile, her mother's arms, a feeling of home. The past.

The anonymous urgent message, her aching body, her aching heart. The present.

Nott City without Governor Crown. That was the future Robyn envisioned. Crown was evil. Not everyone could see it yet, but she could. She had. He had tipped his hand too hard and she had seen the cards. Two months ago, when Crown marched into power without regard for pesky little formalities like an election. Late one night, he quietly destroyed his opposition. He sent men to bust into their homes and take them out, one by one. And just like that, it was over.

At first, people were upset. But Crown was good on TV. He had a nice smile and people thought it was all going to be okay. The people who mattered, anyway. The ones with money and nice houses, who lived happy, carefree lives, going to work and going to school and coming home and always having enough of everything. Robyn remembered what that felt like. To be safe within the bubble of Castle District, with everything you ever wanted right at your fingertips. But she had a new life now. A life without, a life of longing. Her new people, the struggling people of neighborhoods like Sherwood, knew better than to trust Crown's tactics. They were the ones who paid when things got rough. The ones who, like her, knew it was time to take action.

Robyn waited until the commotion in the yard had ceased entirely. The floodlights dimmed and went off. The construction guys rolled out in some vehicle or another, off to start their night-shift work. She heard it all happen, then the air stilled, the way it does when you're alone.

Robyn held out as long as she could, for insurance, but the ache in her legs spurred her to shift position.

She unfolded her body and twisted out of the claw, lowering herself to the ground as quietly as possible. Then she looked around. It felt like no one was there, but Robyn wasn't taking any chances. She retrieved the cones from their hiding place and slung her backpack over her shoulders again. She crept through the maze of machines toward the fence, away from the main entrance.

It was not pitch-black. The ambient light from the rest of the city cast a gray wash over everything. The buildings loomed as great distant shadows. Two tiny lights were on over by the entry gate, possibly to light the way home for the workers when they returned.

Robyn slunk along the fence, headed back toward the slit she had used to climb in. No better way to get out, she figured. That had been her plan all along. She moved slowly, hoping she blended with the shadows. She pressed along the fence until she reached the spot where it bowed open.

She paused. In the middle of her quick escape, she'd forgotten the fun part. Robyn reached into her inner jacket pocket and extracted a small folded note. She unfolded the page and smoothed it. It was a half sheet of luscious cream-colored stationery lifted from the governor's personal office supply stash. Little added extras like that made her work all the more meaningful.

She couldn't go back to the warehouse. Instead she punched the note onto one of the clipped fence links.

The message read:

*Dear Nott City Dept. of Construction,*

*I visited your warehouse this evening and helped myself to a few useful things. Please don't think of these items as "stolen." They have simply been borrowed by a concerned citizen.*

*Robyn Hoodlum*

Robyn pushed the bag of cones through the fence, followed by the stuffed backpack. She squeezed through after it and tugged the straps over her shoulders again. She righted the stack of cones, then turned at the sound of something moving.

The floodlights flicked on, blinding her. Robyn grabbed up the cones and started to run but found herself face-to-face with a Nott City Military Police officer. She spun around, but there was another MP.

She was surrounded.

KERRY LAND

**KEKLA MAGOON** is the author of *Shadows of Sherwood* and *Rebellion of Thieves*, as well as several young adult novels, including the Coretta Scott King Honor Book *How It Went Down* and *The Rock and the River*, for which she received the Coretta Scott King/John Steptoe New Talent Award and an NAACP Image Award nomination. She also coauthored *X: A Novel* (with Ilyasah Shabazz), which was longlisted for the National Book Award and received an NAACP Image Award and a Coretta Scott King Honor. In addition to writing fiction, Kekla visits schools and libraries nationwide and teaches writing at Vermont College of Fine Arts.

www.keklamagoon.com
@KeklaMagoon